This book
(such as it is)
belongs to the delightful Mrs
....
(insert surname of preferred footballer)
What the hell is this, Donna?
Chardonnay Lane loves Kyle Pascoe
22032
4235
658
1113
224
46%
It's a bear, Tanya. I like bears
Chardonnay, you've ruined it now!
1000%
Sorry Tan
D1091382

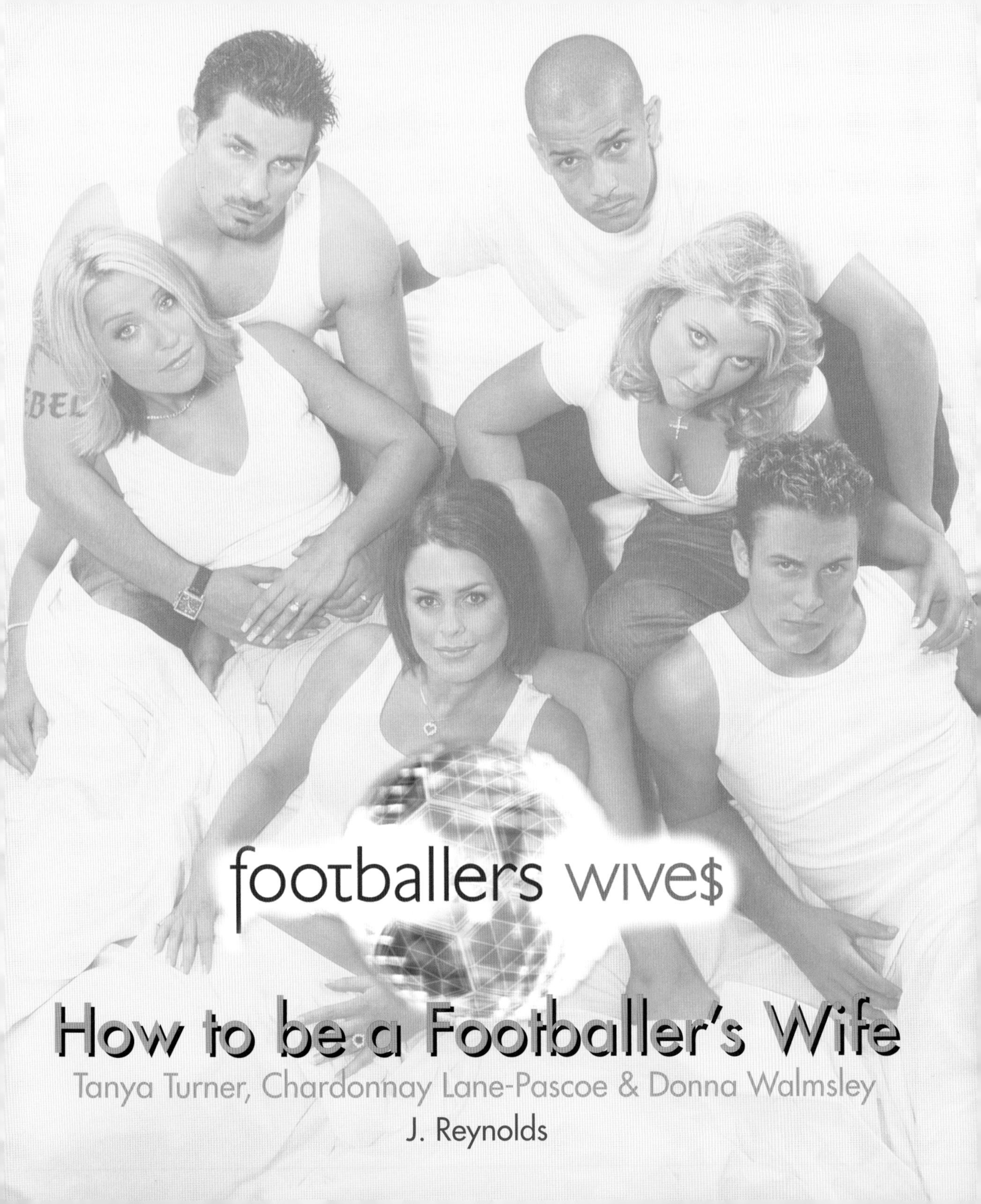

How to be a Footballer's Wife

Tanya Turner, Chardonnay Lane-Pascoe & Donna Walmsley

J. Reynolds

TVR
4 TAN

2 BGO

content$

In every issue

Fashion & beauty

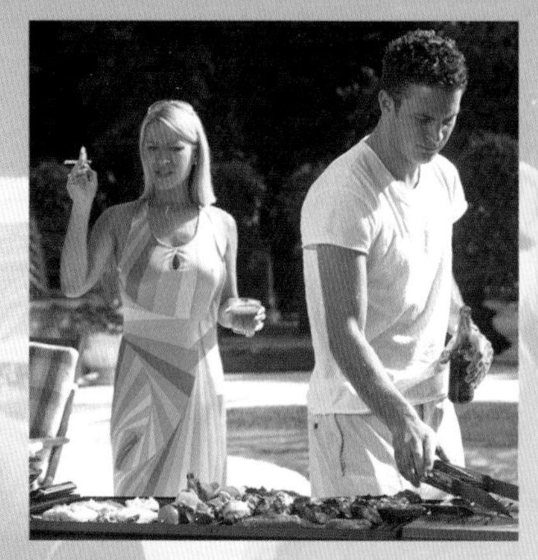

Features

Entertainment

Style & living

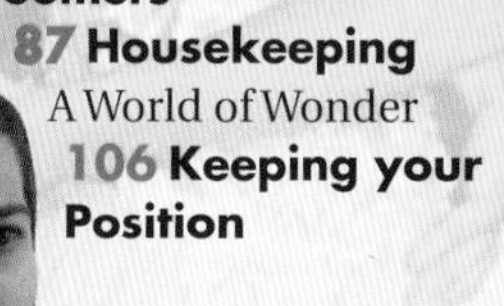

First published 2003 by Boxtree
an imprint of Pan Macmillan Ltd
Pan Macmillan, 20 New Wharf Road,
London N1 9RR
Basingstoke and Oxford
Associated companies throughout the world
www.panmacmillan.com

ISBN 0 7522 2500 6

9 8 7 6 5 4 3 2 1

A CIP catalogue record for this book is available from the British Library.

Designed by Dan Newman/Perfect Bound Ltd
Printed and bound in Great Britain by Bath Press

Illustrations: Gavin Reece/Digital Vision and Jodi Reynolds.
Photos: Ken McKay, Jon Hall, Rachel Joseph, Mike Vaughan and Nicky Johnston.

Acknowledgments:
I don't remember when I agreed to take a break from my almost proper job in television to write this book. Possibly I was momentarily distracted and thought I was agreeing to a coffee. Regardless, despite undertaking a work of comparable penetrating social commentary to Boney M's incisive 'Belfast' and the responsibility therein, it's been a thoroughly enjoyable experience thanks in the main to the delightful people who I've had the continuing pleasure to work with.

Thanks must first go to Ann McManus and Maureen Chadwick who created the show from Paul Marquis' 'so good – you wonder why you didn't think of it' idea. They continue to provide the engine for the programme, never failing to come up with storylines that entertain, surprise and amaze. In addition, Eileen Gallagher, Shed's MD and Brian Park who set the style and feel of the show as producer. Ann, 'Chad', Eileen and Brian as the powerhouses behind Shed prove definitively that being jolly nice is not a prohibition to success and I can also emphatically recommend their company for an evening out.

I must also give swathes of appreciation to Stuart Porter for his patience in the Shed Office, Jacqui Butler for her patience at Boxtree and my own loved ones for their patience and subsequent forgiveness for me maintaining radio silence for over a month whilst I alternated between laughing, crying and thinking about what sofas I wanted whilst writing this book.

Lastly credit must be given to the cast and crew for their dedication to the show and of course to all footballers' wives, real, fictional or aspiring whose inspiration leaves me enveloped in a pink and fluffy Ready Brek-style glow.

As lifestyles go
I can thoroughly
recommend it

a lovely foreword

from the Lovely Zoë Lucker who is Lovely . . .

You may notice my uncanny resemblance to Tanya Turner. I'm happy to report this is **not** coincidental because for the last two years I've had the pleasure to play that Grande Madame of Football. This has put me in the enviable position of experiencing attempted murder, a drugs bust and a fairytale wedding replete with seven dwarves without the threat of arrest. Even for the dwarves. And all this with one of the best dressing-up boxes in television.

Yes, dedicated as I am to my craft, I've had to immerse myself into a champagne lifestyle of celebrity parties, glamorous haute couture and then even more champagne to breathe life into my character. As lifestyles go I can thoroughly recommend it. Which brings me to why this book is so important. This book provides a once in a lifetime opportunity to learn how to be a Footballer's Wife so you too can have a champagne lifestyle of celebrity parties, glamorous haute couture and then even more champagne.

Finally, you will notice how every effort has been made for you to enjoy this book. The publishers have used paper, pictures and even translated the author's scrawl from the back of a council tax envelope into typeface. As such there is little I can do but resoundingly endorse it and suggest you buy it for every friend and relative. I believe there is a footballer's wife in all of us – so it's up to each of us to find it.

You know what you must do. Just don't forget us when you make it!

Zoë x

introduction

So You Want to be a Footballer's Wife …

So you want to be a Footballer's Wife! Congratulations. Despite your Comprehensive education, you worked out the bus timetable, used language skills to ask directions to a bookshop and are now the proud owner of your very own ticket out of your tenement. As you recover from your adventure with an own-brand cider – know you've made your first step from the high street to the high life.

Snagging, shagging, nagging

We (the not-at-all-smug Wives who have already made it) are committed to helping you snag, shag and nag your very own soccer cash point into shape. There's mock Tudor money out there and why shouldn't you have a piece of it – we know we have.

Being a Footballer's Wife is a lifestyle and a vocation and one that involves considerably more waxing and grooming than, for example, nursing. Think – before you step up to the mark can you endure being sprayed orange on a regular basis? In our exhaustive research we found that you will need to find a footballer who either hasn't already got a wife or is willing to be persuaded out of his present one (but not any of us because that would just be ungrateful). Your footballer will need to be injury free so make sure he gets a regular service. And he will need to have premiership potential – you don't want to end up spending your Sundays avoiding the attentions of a Labrador and cheering local park league FC.

Can you endure being sprayed orange on a regular basis?

But the potential rewards are great in this folly that is football. Gracious living rooms, cash that swipes rather than folds – and for ten glorious years the opportunity to nuzzle up to some of the finest thighs in the country. How you will laugh as you scatter the begging letters from former friends like rose petals before you as you tiptoe to your Jacuzzi. Tanya's still laughing as we write this. Laughing and scattering.

No darts skill required

You may find your soccer spouse husband cheats, beats or bleats. You may be thinking, 'Have I got what it takes to beat the opposition and not only find my own footballer but impress him enough to take me on full time?' Well, keep the faith! It's surprising how the promise of that Gucci handbag will put power to your elbow. Not since the tragic demise of *Bullseye* has the proletariat had a chance to own such outrageous fortune. You don't even need a skill such as darts. You just need to put out.

Now if you are already a fellow Footballer's Wife we obviously don't mean you in anything we say in this book – we mean someone you know and don't like. Donna for instance is nothing like any stereotyped image. She is a good mother, friend and wife and therefore incredibly dull so we will be keeping her contribution to a minimum and her tea making to a maximum. If you are a man and bought this expecting Readers' Wives, you will probably be disappointed, but you may learn a little something about the sort of totty you could have attracted if you'd paid a little less attention in school and a little more attention to ball kicking.

A little bit damp

By way of introduction – here's the fast facts YOU need to know about us whilst dispelling all of the hideous lies you'll have already read about us in the papers. We have written this while chilling out in Tanya's Jacuzzi so apologies in advance if the pages are a little damp. fw

meet the wive$...

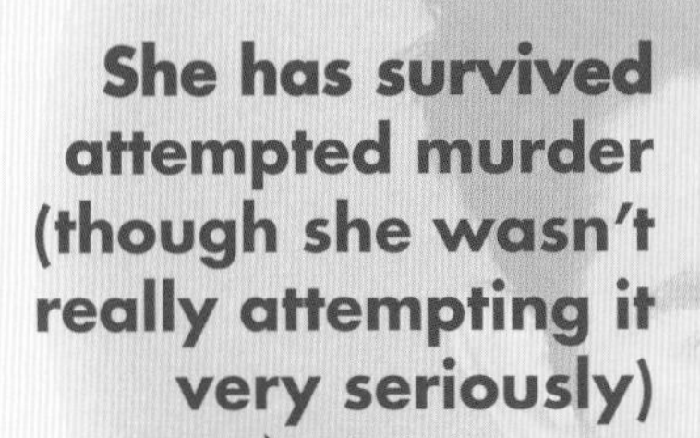

Tanya Turner

Tanya is a blonde vixen who claims her hobbies are community service and abstinence. In reality she is a blonde vixen with a platinum card she doesn't just use for shopping. Her CV includes spending the last ten years nursing, cajoling and motivating her hot-headed, but talented, husband Jason. Able to play the game better than anyone in recorded history, she gives off the impression that she's just a flashy shopaholic. She is – in truth – the power, drive and intelligence behind her husband's throne. She's saved Jason from more scrapes than even she can remember (or certainly that he chooses to remember, the ungrateful bastard). As Jason approaches the end of his playing career – a state of affairs he seems committed to prematurely bringing about with his hedonistic and brutish behaviour – Tanya always has to keep her eyes on the next prize although in quieter moments she confesses that Jason is truly the love of her life.

Her savvy, style and ruthlessness mask a vulnerable person who seems destined by Lady Bad Luck to live her life constantly in an ambience of Greek Tragedy and master plate spinning. In the last two years she has survived attempted murder (though she wasn't really attempting it very seriously), drugs, blackmail, her husband's indefatigable philandering and much, much more. She has dished out more forgiveness to Jason than a priest (though the analogy stops there). She is ambitious and her crutch is power. Power and a recreational drug habit that is spiralling out of control. She can wear hair extensions like nobody else and is the undisputed leader of the wifely pack.

Chardonnay Lane-Pascoe

Chardonnay loves life – and she attacks it with a vengeance – all without chipping a perfectly manicured nail. She's been a glamour model for three years and had gained a modicum of celebrity in her own right. The crowning glory was, however, her marriage to soccer superstar Kyle Pascoe. The pair became the Crown Prince and Princess of Soccer with media hounds baying for any copy about them, their lives and any shopping trips to get in milk.

Chardonnay sensibly opted to be a brunette and states that she loves nothing better than to wear navel revealing dresses as long as they are artfully done. We would scoff at most if they revealed that they wanted to see world peace and an end to poverty but Chardonnay, in Chardonnay land, is sincere. It would be wrong to think that Chardonnay is marrying Kyle for his fame or his money because she already has that in abundance. This is a love job. It would also be wrong to think that Chardonnay's a bimbo (wrong, but not overwhelmingly so).

It would be wrong to think that Chardonnay is a bimbo

She's a highly motivated, confident young woman, well aware that she's attractive and unafraid to exploit this fact for her own ends. Her Page Three career was a sensation before it – or rather they – were sadly put on ice (with a pack of frozen peas) when she received bosom burnage at the hands of some idiot fans.

She loves the photographers, the parties, the autographs. It's all her dreams come true – and we love her for it. She won't compromise herself, however – no matter how great the reward. Along with pink fluffy bits there are some serious principles in that delightful brown head. When Kyle tried to encourage her to give up glamour modelling she stood up for all women and said no.

Life at the Happy Valley hasn't been without its little problems however. Her assets being sent up in flames sent Chardonnay in a downward spiral of eating disorders and hair cutting. She recovered enough to adopt her mother-in-law Jackie's intersex baby Paddy, and with a plan complex enough to create cold fusion, they fooled the press into thinking it was hers and Kyle's. However – and isn't this typical – in the middle of a photo shoot, a floater turned up in her familial pool. It turned out to be a stalker that was pestering Kyle. Kyle was exonerated but not before he admitted he had looked upon Sheena the swimming stalker with something approaching lust.

Finally one cannot stress enough that Chardonnay is pretty.

She loves the photographers, the parties, the autographs. It's all her dreams come true – and we love her for it

Her sordid secret is that she'd
prefer to do the washing up
than anything else at all

Donna Walmsley

Donna's an ordinary woman – attractive, warm and loving – who was catapulted into an extraordinary world with her husband Ian's momentous promotion from a Third Division club to the Premier League.

Donna married Ian when she was sixteen – much against her parents' wishes – and they have a five-year-old daughter Holly and a seven year old son, Daniel who they were forced to give up for adoption (but have since been able to gift with a savings fund and a replica shirt).

Donna was genuinely proud of Ian's new-found success but was never able to abide the side effects of stardom with only marginally more tolerance for even the good bits. All in all, whilst she is a lovely girl, she's taking up room on the wife pedestal that would be better appreciated by just about anybody else. Of all the wives, her knowledge and appreciation of the beautiful game is lacking. She would prefer to do the washing up than go to a game though her sordid secret is that she'd prefer to do the washing up than anything else at all. She imported her younger, wilder sister Marie with the nominal title of 'mother's help' which was only to the further chagrin of the other wives who realised their husbands would have to be put on a very short leash in her presence.

Donna rather naively, was unprepared for how money and fame would change Ian, who just didn't seem as committed to washing up as once he was. In his esteemed opinion, he sweated blood to get to the top and wants all the trimmings. His betrayal of her in favour of two lap dancers and more often his home gym sent Donna spiralling into most uncharacteristic behaviour and into the arms of the resident Italian Stallion, Salvatore Biaggi. Sal was able to provide love, support and a hand in the kitchen but Donna was consumed by shame as well as Mediterranean loving.

Just to cap off a real annus horribilis, her daughter Holly was kidnapped by the pool cleaner who seemed to buy magazines to scratch out the capitalist pigs faces more than pick up fashion tips. Donna has never really got used to having money and regularly buys own-brand items and in so doing flouts every unwritten (until now) code of being a Footballer's Wife.

Donna is also blonde but she doesn't wear much make up so that's another thing wasted on her.

Three separate women, parachuted into a whirlwind life of paparazzi and shopping. We bare open our lives, loves, dreams and nightmares for you to pick over like buzzards. Tanya bares her private journal, Donna briefly divests her housekeeping tips and Chardonnay thankfully was persuaded to keep her top on but talks in detail about how hairspray changed her life.

Alone, we are just fabulously wealthy and gorgeous women who managed to get a husband. Together, we are…**The Footballers' Wives.**

Now play up, play up and play the game… fw

She's taking up room on the wife pedestal that would be better appreciated by just about anybody else

captain's wife's log

Wednesday

Jason home in foul mood, just to ring the changes. Of course only a wife would know. A wife picks up the little signs – like him smashing up the place again. Next mood swing: six minutes ding, ding.

He's got a bee in his bonnet about rumours of a new signing at Earl's Park – who just happens to play in his position and who just happens to be almost young enough to call Jason 'Da da'. In fairness I'm worried too. It would help of course if he'd act just a little bit keen. I did more exercise this morning with a fifty pound note and my nose than he did at training. Back to me to sort it all out again I suppose. He wants me to work on Frank. Sounds a little like asking Mr Greek tragedy round for tea – but as always, his wish...

To do: book manicure for Weds. File insurance claim, our insurers are going to give us a direct line soon like the bat phone. I'm almost tempted to stop spending his money on nice things if he's just going to keep bashing them up. No ... I take that back. I'll go and hug the pool room by way of apology – I love all our nice things really.

Thursday

Got something slutty out of the wardrobe and visited Frank. He assured me that the whole thing was newspaper copy. Surprised he even heard the question he had his eyes so far down my top his ears would have been muffled. I don't think Jason knows what I do for him. Frank said Jason was a pain in the neck. For Jason that's a compliment. Most people have an even lower opinion of him.

Friday

Had manicure. Nails now resemble shears. Am having to write this by holding the pen in my mouth – which is at least something that life with Jason has prepared me for. Tried to spice up the marital bed by buying some lingerie. Thanks Char for that tip – it had all the success of Accrington Stanley. I think the only thing that turns Jason on is an 18 year old with her knees behind her ears.

You know Jase seems to think I married him for his footballer's money and so can treat me like dirt. I've earnt every penny a thousand times over. Anyway – it's not strictly true. I don't care how he earns it.

Saturday

Jason out for dinner again. Surprised he made it back for breakfast actually.

He might have struck out of course. No. Most likely a non-inclusive motel again. Shame he wasn't as tight with his manhood as he is with his cash. Anyway – I played dead by some artful arrangement of a few pills. I know it's a cheap shot but short of taking Stefan on the front lawn it's the only way I can get his attention. I'm no fool. It wasn't concern flashing in his eyes – it was headlines.

Sunday

This has officially been the worst night of my life, which is saying something after being married to Jason all these years. Will have to write more tomorrow. My hands are still shaking.

Monday

OK – my hand's still shaking but I need to get this off my chest. There was a party at somewhere with a manicured lawn. Might have been a golf course. Jason had been baiting me the whole time and it was as much as I could do to keep smiling and mildly tolerating most of the other guests.

I spent most of the evening trading banalities with Donna 'Day' Walmsley. What do you say to someone who obviously cooks their own food anyway? After ditching her with the promise that we must swap recipes I tried to pump Stefan for information on Jason's contract. He was resolute about not getting pumped. That man is stitched up tighter than a pair of nun's knickers.

Anyway Jason got back from God knows where just in time to see the traitorous bastard Frank introduce the new Italian signing who was wearing some royal blue monstrosity that might be called fashion somewhere in Italy.

We confronted Frank after the party when he pulled over on a deserted road. Big argument ensued and I gave him the tiniest little shove. Anyway to cut a long story short – I killed him. So we had to stick him back in his car and push it into a ditch.

I'm going to hell.

Tuesday

10:05 Frank is alive. I'm not a murderess. I'm an attempted murderess. He was found unconscious and is in a coma.

10:10 I'm so dead.

10:15 Jason is in full panic mode; thank goodness one of us is trying to stay calm.

10:20 Frank could wake up at any minute. Jason's alright but I'm too pretty to go to jail.

I can't even sleep without four pillows and a bottle of gin – how could I survive on bunk beds?

To top it all off – its Chardonnay's hen night tonight – so I've got to keep it together. The only saving grace is that there's a midweek fixture tomorrow so Stefan's put a two drink embargo on the boy's stag do.

Wednesday

Was too exhausted to write last night. In fact I'm still too exhausted. Suffice to say Chardonnay was set alight by two yobs wandering around with a candle like Wee Willie Winkie, and remains in bed with what's left of her charred tits. I got home early to find Jason having his weapon inspected by a power puff girl in the hot tub.

Suffice also to say I didn't buy his explanation that he'd jumped in to save her from drowning and in fact they were in the recovery position. Suffice again to say that by virtue of being a hot tub it's highly unlikely he was naked to share his body heat to prevent her going into shock.

Hell, knowing Jason as I do – even I'm not in shock.

As for tonight ... we lost. In fact we lost so badly the less said the better. Stefan looked shifty when I complimented Jason's performance. I wasn't particularly surprised. Jason had all the grace of a weeble and lolled about the pitch about 6 months behind the ball.

The only cheery part of the day was when Lara said she'd put on 2 lbs this week. A conservative estimate in my opinion. No challenger yet on the fairest of them all stakes despite a stark lack of appreciation from Jason.

trouble and $trife

find out which wife!

Despite the tabloid stereotypes there are many types of Footballer's Wife. For example you could be a blonde, brunette or redhead. With all of this confusion – use this handy quiz to help you decide.

1 You've been told that Jason Turner is the last man on earth. Do you:

A Cancel your two o'clock with the sub?
B Get a gun? Not for much longer...
C Sigh . . . Put some chips in the oven for the kids' tea?
D Demand a recount?

2 You are quizzed about the offside trap. Do you:

A Give a full account. You've had to explain it to your husband enough times?
B Giggle charmingly and apply more lip gloss?
C Sigh . . . Cut out the high street labels from your clothes and pretend they're couture?
D Move on to Q3?

3 It's the first match of the season. Will you be:

A In the players' lounge from 9 a.m. wearing an evening dress?
B With Tanya in the players' lounge from 9 a.m. wearing an evening dress?
C Far, far too busy tracking down your first born?
D Scratching your head wondering why you bought this book?

4 There's a new Italian Stallion in town. Do you:

A Become an attempted murderer and spend the next year in a downward spiral of cause and effect?
B Concentrate on cutting your hair with nail scissors after the trauma of your hen night?
C Finally get mama some sugar?
D Conclude that you actually meant to pick up the latest John Grisham but the shop's air conditioning must have caused an oxygen deficiency in your brain?

5 A tabloid photographer is hiding in your bushes. Are you:

A Wondering what or *who* your husband's done now?
B Checking your swimming pool for floaters?
C Cutting the bushes at the time to save money on a gardener?
D Taking him out a cup of tea and asking him who he's looking for?

6 You have three grams of white powder in your Gucci handbag. Is it:

A Just for recreational use?
B Talcum powder for you/your mother-in-law's baby?
C Ajax, because three bathrooms don't clean themselves?
D You don't even have a handbag. You have a sensible briefcase to carry all of your paperwork and a packed lunch?

7 Your husband has reached retirement at the advanced age of thirty-five. Do you:

A Test drive a new model?
B Dye his temples grey and groom him as a TV sports pundit?
C Breathe a sigh of relief and put the kettle on?
D Declare your suspicions, because computer programmers usually have a longer career expectancy?

8 It's your hen night. Do you:

A Inform the Press Association, pour yourself a large G and T and wait for the bidding war?
B Get third degree burns?
C Put the kettle on?
D Wear an L-plate and stay up past your bedtime at a chain restaurant?

9 You are expecting a child. Do you:

A Find a priest and pray it's not a jackal?
B Stuff a cushion up your jumper?
C Butter another round of sandwiches?
D Paint the box room?

10 Your style is:

A Styled
B Wild
C Child
D Mild

You are...

Mainly A's: You are Tanya. Either that or you are Lady Macbeth. You are strong, some would say ruthless and you can think on your Jimmy Choos. If the Wives had their own league you'd be 10 points clear with a vast goal difference. You'd also make it as a gardener you've spent so much time digging your way out of muck. Over the last year you've had to contend with comagate, carry-on-nurse dunkleygate and community servicegate, as well as your husband's continued away games. You deserve a medal or a lobotomy. You are an excellent mother to your husband.

Mainly B's: You are Chardonnay. Either that or you are Diana Dors. You are sweet, genuine and as ambitious as Cain. You are glamorous though your hair gets noticeably smaller with age and you wear pyjama bottoms more often than is advisable even for those in trauma. You love your husband and he loves you – so you're a bit sickening really. You know your assets and they aren't just a nice house in the country. You probably smell of daisies. You are an excellent mother to your brother-in-law.

Mainly C's: You are Donna. Either that or you are Pauline Fowler. You are sweet, kind and quite frankly the lifestyle is thoroughly wasted on you so you should give someone else a go who would really appreciate it. You are an ordinary lady in an extraordinary world with a swimming pool that you don't actually swim in but do have cleaned. You are a poor judge of pool cleaners. Your pool cleaners transpire to be pool cleaners with a casual interest in kidnapping your child for bank-breaking ransoms. Occasionally you'll do something naughty like an Italian – but even then racy for you is wearing a V-neck instead of a cowl. Long may you reign, you flower among Venus flytraps. You are an excellent mother to all of your children wherever they are.

Mainly D's: You are an ordinary member of the public who picked up this book by mistake. If you haven't creased the spine you might still be able to return it for a refund. Either way you should not be a Footballer's Wife and should continue wearing sensible shoes and listening to Radio 2. You may well be an excellent mother, we just don't know.

playing the field

Or 'There's a reason Mounties always get their man'.

The take him, break him and re-make him of premiership football…

Take him.

Consider yourself like a little squirrel foraging for nuts. There's rich pickins' for a floozy who's not choosy. Don't expect any married wives to give you advice – they pull the ladder up after them and non married wives will be of little real use to you. But with a bit of persistence and necklines that start and indeed stop at your kneecaps you stand as good a chance of nabbing him as anyone else.

But who to take?

Obviously unlike in show business you can't guarantee that celebrity footballers won't look like a Dali nightmare. But this is for the good. When big game hunting pick out the weak ones in the herd, ones with faces like scrambled up Rubik's cubes who are generally stampeding in the opposite direction with far less conviction. You can always upgrade later (see our upgrade tips further on).

How to take (Fields of Play)

There are several ways of harpooning the mighty sperm whale.

1 School sweethearts This is undoubtedly high risk with about the same odds as the lottery. You could be putting your money on the wrong horse – though if he really is a horse then stick with him footballer or no. Look for the signs. Is he inept around the girls? Does he hang out behind the bike sheds just to kick a ball against it? Does he have all the verbal dexterity of a feral ape-boy? Does he have bad hair and trample mud everywhere? These are all good signs.

If all else is failing... Try the desperate fan route. Inundate him with fan letters (see example below) extolling your ample virtues whilst always including a copy of your birth certificate to remove any legality issues and obviously a pair of knickers (the true stalker fan's calling card). Or if you're fast approaching your sell-by date (current indicators point to the stately age of 26 as being time to move in with your spinster sister) try cold calling, mailshots or parading up and down in a bloody sandwich board if you think it will help. You've got to be in it to win it so come on you girl scout!

2 Try placing a **personal ad** in the match programme. Personal ads – or at least the ones that Chardonnay did before she was famous – usually start with something like 'if you're single, or even if you're not…'. Then you might say something like 'Busty blonde seeks footballer for hurried sex or something more. Ring size – M, one previous owner + full service history. Buyer collects'. For the bigger gesture you could try hiring the score board.

3 **Nightclubs** Come on. It's Friday night Cinders and it's a buoyant market. These are excellent and well tried and tested venues. You also have alchohol on your side which may be useful if he's Peter Beardsley. Show keen and dress mean. It's no good looking demure. In the world of professional sports that's equivalent to putting out a lesbian forcefield. Look available and possibly horizontal.

4 **Training Ground** Also excellent though more for your brief encounters. The advantage clearly is that you have high density footballerage penned off in one area and regardless of how fast their sports car is – they'll have to approach it on foot rendering them vulnerable to attack. The disadvantages are that you may be seen as fan rather than potential life partner. That's if you can be seen at all over the top of the gaggle of teenage girls in hormonal hyperdrive and replica shirts.

5 **Celebrity schmoozing** If you become a celebrity (and there is a stark and significant difference between fame and celebrity, need we remind you) then congratulations, head down to Ratners and start choosing diamond clusters. Try TV Chef, TV interior designer, TV exterior designer, local radio – hell – hospital radio. D-List status is positive, you don't want to price yourself out of the market. All celebrities emit a high frequency mating call audible only to other celebrities. So you can sit back and relax. Your tabloid-friendly siren's call will lead him to you like a Bisto Kid. Ahhhh, celebrity to the power of two.

Dear Premiership footballer

Having recently turned the age of consent, I feel ready to begin marital relations. I'm a 36FF. My hobbies include anything you want them to be and I am currently low maintenance, expecting only a pat on the back and my bus fare home for my troubles. I have several willing friends of similar dimensions and even lower expectations so I feel a definite party coming on. I feel I would be as asset to your life and would fit in well with your requirements. I enclose a pair of tanga briefs for your consideration. I have 2 GCSE's and would suit similar. Please apply within.

Yours faithfully, A Nutter Fan

A Sample Fan Letter

Remember, fan letters are a little like resumes – everyone expects you to exaggerate a little bit. But keep it within the realms of what mascara and an uplift bra can achieve lest he take you up on it.

Nightclubs are well tried and tested venues. Show keen and dress mean...

Untried methods that in all conscience we cannot recommend:

1. Become internationally famous as a Nobel Prize Winner
2. Irony and/or good humour
3. Being a moose

Moving in for the kill:

Being dressed up like an extremely provocative bauble means you might get attention from a footballer. But attention is not the same thing as love and is certainly some distance away from being a kept woman. To keep them keen there should be no such thing as 'Try before you buy'. Treat footballers like wild animals, with caution, something approaching respect and if possible, a tranquiliser gun. Other lessons from the animal kingdom include killing almost

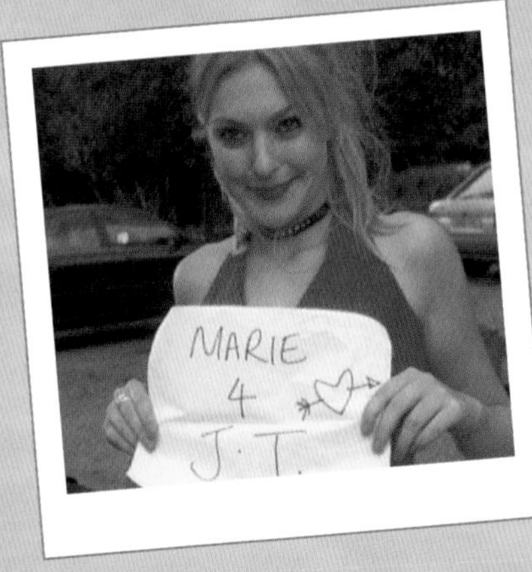

immediately after breeding but that is a lesson for a later day. Try not to seek his heart – odds are you already have a perfectly good one of your own. Seek his wallet.

What to say:

There are many ways to be alluring and it's not all about wearing chicken wire and a nicotine patch. Sometimes there are unusual ways to get a man with your mouth – and these are commonly referred to as 'talking' and 'chatting'. A common misnomer is that you bear some responsibility for this 'talking'. You don't. You bear the equally grave responsibility of giggling at the ends of his sentences. Suffice to say he may not be very good at chat up lines and may resort to just playing with your breasts but then at least everyone knows where they stand.

With regards to putting your stall out, you could just sashay up to a footballer and say 'Give Mama some sugar…' In fact – do that. It's as good a bet as any.

So many footballers, so little time:

One issue is that you will only be able to marry a finite number of footballers in any one lifetime. We think about three as a maximum, though this figure obviously excludes affairs, liaisons and 'discreet cubicle couplings at club dinners'. So pick your 'I do's' carefully and with extreme prejudice. You may have to practise saying the word 'no'. To form this word, make a slight 'o' with your lips (see, you're a natural), raise your tongue to the roof of your mouth and project.

If in doubt and if you are in the fortunate position of having options, calculating how much he 'loves' you using basic numerology is an excellent method. Chardonnay has provided an example at the start of this book – though if you are reading this you've probably already used the margins to figure out your possibilities anyway.

Naked ambition:

Getting your bits out for the lads has the added advantage of being a good earner and will get you noticed. This is the one instance where being a brunette is an advantage. Chestnut locks will make you look slightly more posh and thereby elevate you above the rest of the bleached bosom wranglers. As a cautionary note once they're out they're out, so it's vital that you give your money making mammaries bi-annual enhancements in line with inflation.

Pregnancy for profit:

A no brainer. This one's as old as the hills. All it needs is one night in a club, with the electric hand dryer providing a useful timing device and you're looking at least at a kiss and tell and some CSA readies. There is however little precedent to confirm that this will lead to matrimony. A three day serialisation of you and football junior and your palimony problems is all in a 20%'s work for your modern football agent.

Alternatively, you could in a bold move, tell him before the newspapers. The simple words 'We need to talk.' should explain the situation thoroughly. He might appreciate your discretion and marry you. If he doesn't revert to plan A and take the philandering cad for all you can.

Break Him:

It's surprisingly easy to break a man. The phrase 'no sex before marriage' is a beauty. The allure of a chastity vow is as overpowering as Novacaine for a footballer. Besides, men respond remarkably well to reverse psychology. Tell him something is too heavy to lift and he is genetically programmed to kill himself trying. So play hard to get – wear a belt!

What to wear:

Use this handy guide by checking your age (real, imagined or what in artificial light you could get away with)

18–25 year olds = artfully arranged chicken wire, nicotine patches and a come hither smile

26–40 year olds = clothes and a hopeful expression

50–the big Subbuteo in the sky = Gold, ad infinitum

A note on Upgrading:

It is generally considered common courtesy to dump one footballer before upgrading to another. Thanks to modern technology this can be done for convenience by text message.

Dr (rejectee's name here),
Soz 2 tell u but ive upgraded. As u r prob aware competition tough + woz 100s of entriez with ++£'s so u aint made final cut. Wl keep u in fone bk in case openin comes up. Ttfn. xxx

A useful tactic to keep him in shape is to be photographed without your engagement ring. This can then be blown up and illuminated in a giant bubble in all celebrity tattle rags. And it will be. Covering pages 9–35 incl. That'll keep football boy on his toes.

Re-make him:

Like Pavlov's dog, it's a series of rewards and punishments.

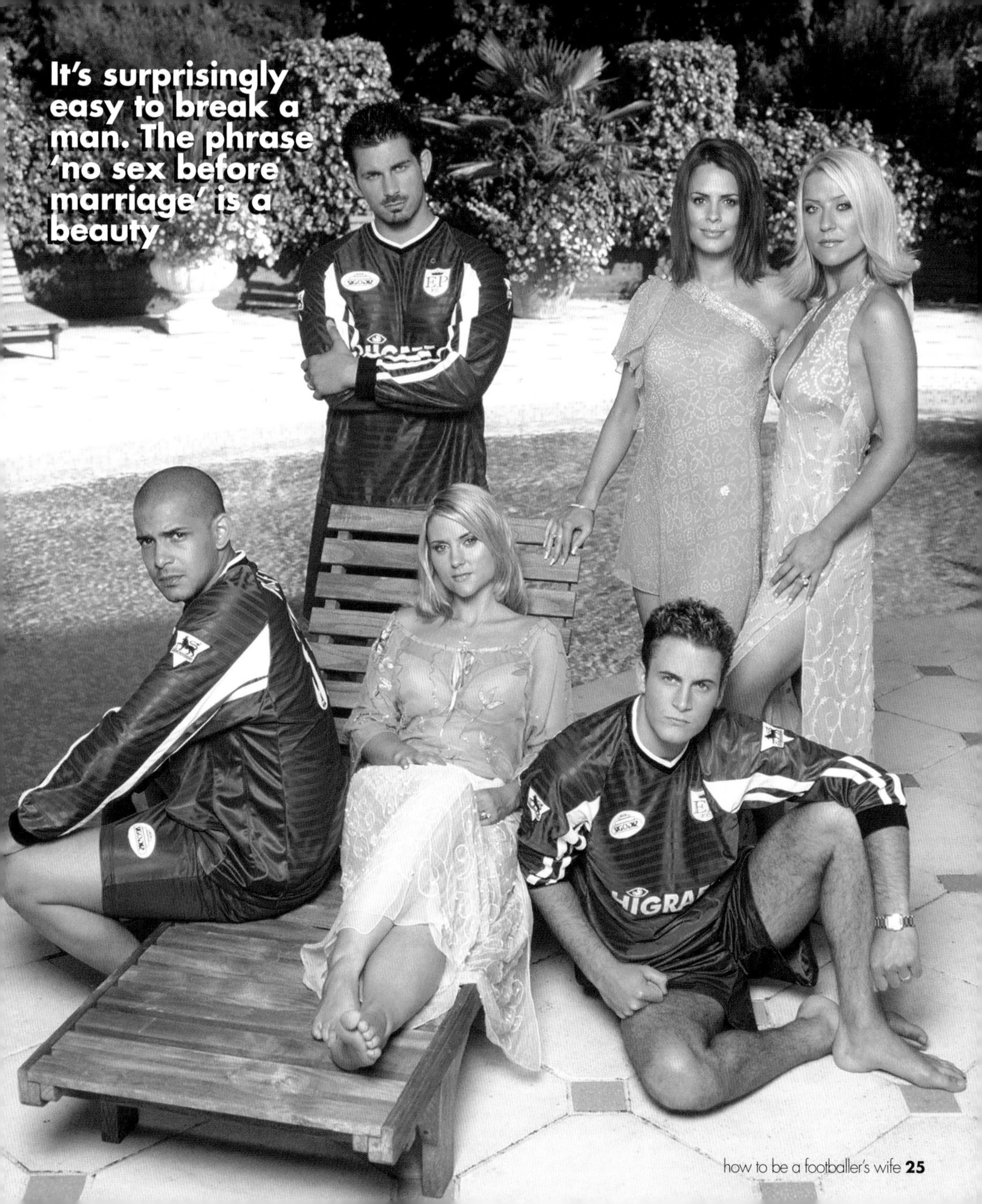

It's surprisingly easy to break a man. The phrase 'no sex before marriage' is a beauty

Men reacted most favourably to the names Bambi, Britney and Montana Mounds

Née Council...

How to Get a Footballer's Wife's Name

You may well have a distasteful name. Perhaps your mother had so many children she'd either run out of good options or simply stopped caring by the time you tipped up. Perhaps she was just a bit common. Perhaps for whatever reason that's worth forgetting your name sounds like an old fish wife. If you are going to be a sophisticated footballing wife you need to have the sort of name that sounds like it's never endured the rough side of a scouring brush.

Now it is important to note that men on the whole are immune to the subtleties of naming conventions. In psychological experiments that register increases in heart rates when exposed to a variety of stimuli – men reacted most favourably to the names Bambi, Britney and Montana Mounds so it's safe to assume your efforts will be wasted on them. Shakespeare proposed that a 'rose by any other name would smell as sweet.' This was not long after the Bard had changed his own moniker from Mr Ben Dover and so we can resolve that he knows not of what he speaks either. What women know is that catering to the social mores of the day is to impress other women or more specifically to engender their respect and mild envy. For instance, Donna – much as we love her – will never achieve her glamorous potential on account of sharing her name with a hunk of meat in a pita that would make even a buzzard fake fullness.

Remember the most heinous crime is to be ordinary. You should be an object of mystery and enigma so go a bit off piste and get unique with a name so sharp it will make your footballer's ears bleed.

Here's a handy reckoner to decide upon your new name. Remember once you have made the leap – refuse to answer if someone calls you by your birth name. Just ignore them. They're probably from your past and a bit mucky so you aren't missing anything. Also remember you might get divorced and have to change your surname again so make sure whatever you change will work with husband number five. Or – just pick an initial – then you can adapt with seasonal trends. fw

Christian name (the first name on your dole application form)	*Surname (as it appears on the back of his shirt – and this is important – minus the number)*
Your favourite alcoholic drink	Your favourite footballer's surname
Your favourite Alco pop drink	Your second favourite footballer's name
A breed of yappy dog	The full back in your favourite footballer's team's surname
A Disney princess	The brother's cousin twice removed of your favourite footballer's surname
Your own name just spelt funny (e.g. Tanya could be Xiamph)	Your favourite footballer's manager's surname
An anagram of another name that you like (e.g. Vicki could become Vikci)	Your favourite footballer's gardener's surname
Something hyphenated (as long as you don't have a double-barrelled surname because they won't be able to fit your name on your cheque book)	The surname of your friend who quite likes football
Something that Anita Roddick would make a hand cream out of	Clough. There seems to be a vast footballing dynasty with that name

love and fairytale marriage$

Or 'It's a Nice Day for a White Wedding'

Your Definitive One Stop Nuptial Checklist for the 'Happy' Day

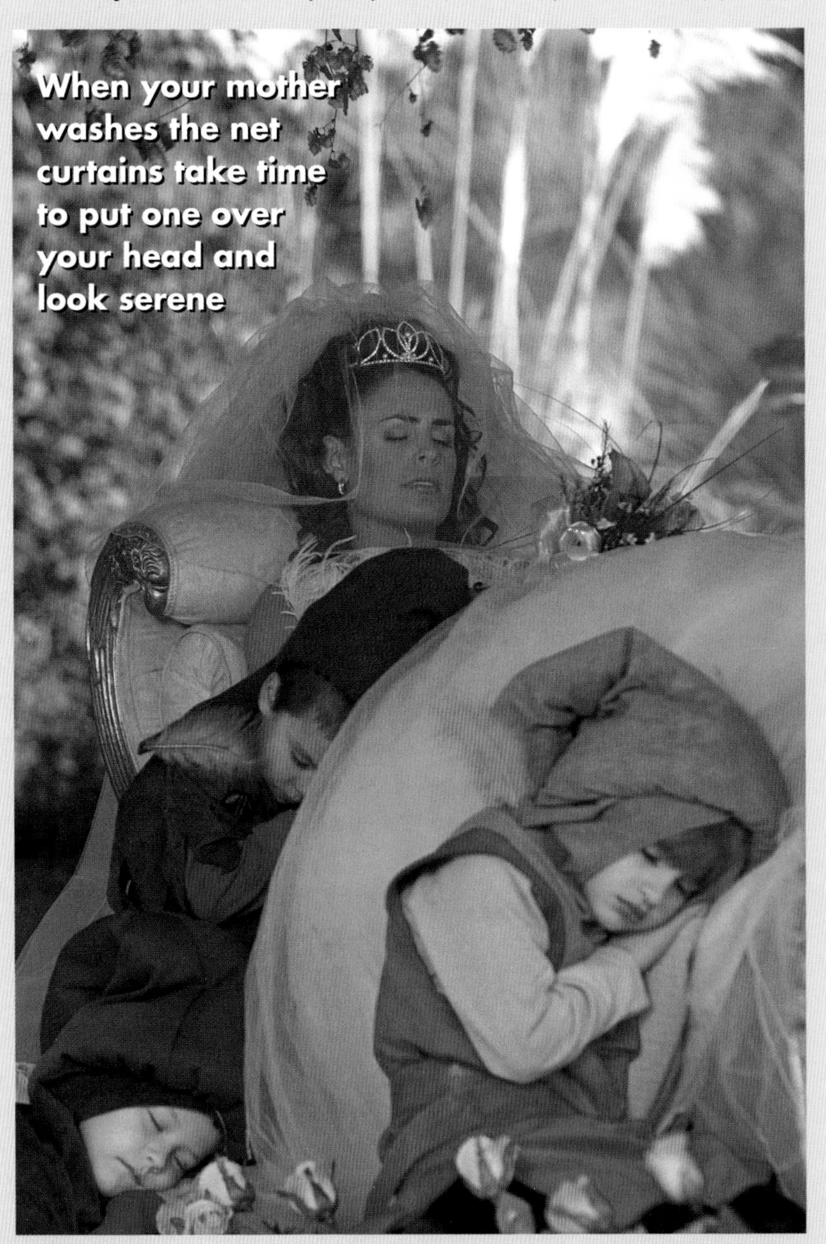

Ten years ahead (on a bi-weekly basis)

- ❍ Decide what sort of wedding you want and preferred style of dress.
- ❍ Watch lots of Hollywood films about weddings. Try to concentrate on ones that make you cry and in an unrelated respect, have Steve Martin in.
- ❍ When your mother washes the net curtains take time to put one over your head and look serene.

One year ahead

- ❍ Decide upon which husband you will take.
- ❍ Arrange for that husband to offer to be that husband.
- ❍ Threaten to leave him when he's not quick enough to agree.
- ❍ Tell him you are with child.

Eleven months, three weeks, six days, twenty hours ahead

- ❍ Confirm that 'yes – it is his child you are with and that you are devastated that he should have to ask'.
- ❍ Pretend to run off weeping.
- ❍ Find diary to check your dates. Confirm that 'yes – it is his child you are with and that you are devastated that he should have to ask'.

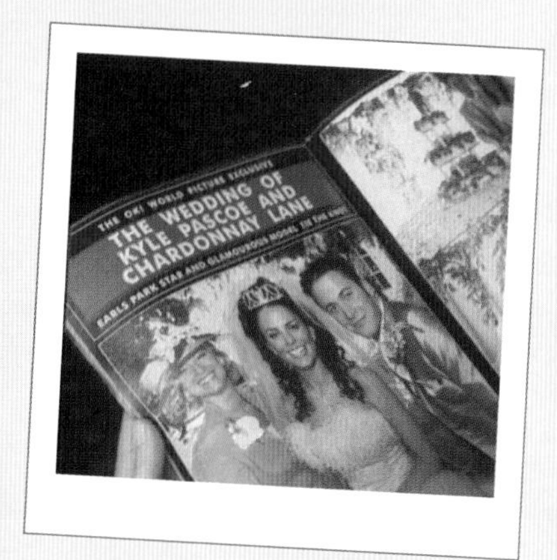

Six months ahead

- ❍ Decide which publication you will grant exclusive publishing contract to.
- ❍ Oh and set date, draw up guest list, book ceremony, choose reception venue and caterers, order your stationery, choose ushers and bridesmaids, choose dresses (including accessories), order bespoke rings, book a honeymoon (check on season fixtures and contractual obligations of exclusive publishing deal), book cars, photographer and videographer, arrange suits for groom and best man.
- ❍ Remember to choose best man for your fiancé.

Five months, three weeks, twenty minutes ahead

- ❍ Read through exclusive publishing contract.

Five months, three weeks ahead

- ❍ Realize exclusive publishing contract is dependent upon you having a theme to your wedding.
- ❍ Realize guest list will need to be supplemented by several B and C list celebrities you haven't actually met and may have to pay.

Five months, two weeks ahead

- ❍ Brief panic about whether bump will show.
- ❍ Remember that pregnancy was just a little incentive to move things along a bit. Remove cushion and dismiss the initial weight gain as water retention.
- ❍ After several frenzied phone calls decide upon a woodland creatures meets Busby Berkley theme. *Note:* your idea must be original – if you are going to pick an historical theme ensure it is proper history – i.e. BH (Before *Hello!*)
- ❍ Break news to eight-year-old sister that she is to be replaced as bridesmaid by Anthea Turner.
- ❍ Cancel videographer. Channel 5 have offered to film a docusoap of the event.

Five months, one week ahead

- ❍ Delay wedding by four months. Magazine has advised a winter wedding so as to avoid the log jam of nuptials occurring in July when they cannot guarantee the cover.

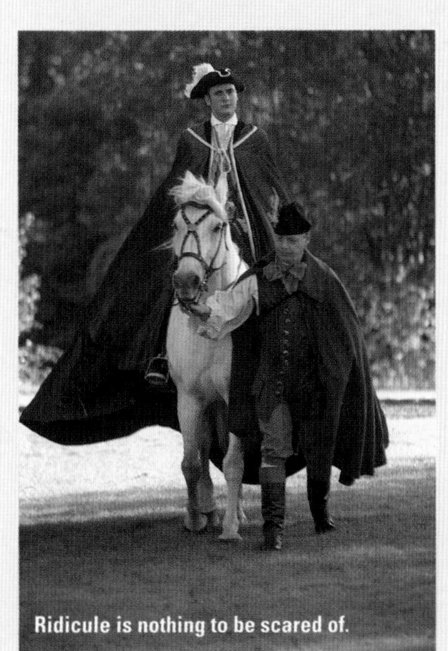

Ridicule is nothing to be scared of.

Four months ahead

- ❍ Change dresses and flowers again. Apparently the daffodils you were going to use as an ironic statement only grow in spring and don't hold their lustre if packed in between peas in the freezer.

Three months ahead

- ❍ Cancel wedding. Your fiancé has been caught by paparazzi wedged between three gogo girls and a fruit basket.

Two months, three weeks, six days, twenty-four hours, forty-three minutes ahead

- ❍ Have bijou nervous breakdown, hack off hair with nail scissors.

Two months, three weeks and one hour ahead

- ❍ Magazine have dispatched guidance counsellor and twig diviner who have advised you to forgive your husband who only cheated because he was experiencing normal pre-wedding jitters and expressing his Id.
- ❍ Agree with guidance counsellor and twig diviner when they remind you of how much you would be set to lose if you break the contract when any judge worth his salt reviewed said exclusive watertight publishing contract.

Two months, two weeks ahead

❍ Anthea walks out thanks to errant fiancé et fruit basket debacle. Apparently she doesn't need any more bad publicity. Magazine advises at short notice they can only arrange for Jade Goody or a Nolan Sister to step in.

❍ Opt for Nolan Sister as the dress has already been made.

Two months, one week ahead

❍ Jamie Oliver apparently busy giving alms of rocket and vine tomatoes to the great unwashed. Magazine offers *Ready Steady Cook* as replacement caterers.

❍ Catering crisis talks ensue. Your threat to pull out is for once accepted as reasonable and legally defensible.

Two months, five days ahead

❍ Magazine accepts your Aunt Ivy's offer to butter some baps instead. Pub Grub is de rigeur right now as long as you don't actually get it from a pub.

Two months, four days ahead

❍ Magazine suggests politely that your outfit is a little pedestrian and would benefit from an unusual headdress as is the vogue.

❍ A designer from *Changing Rooms* is drafted in to create something new and exotic.

Two months, two days ahead

❍ You have your first fitting for your crash helmet/art installation with water feature headdress made out of mdf and some twigs donated at the last moment by the twig diviner who perhaps more than any other is keeping this wedding party afloat.

Two months, one day ahead

❍ Magazine assistant sub-editor to the sub-editor lets slip that a wedding train is traditionally made of netting.

❍ Cancel Thomas the Tank Engine.

❍ Don't issue gift list. That would be as passé as asking the price of something. Naturally you have everything and you don't need anything. Hint at jewellery. It's OK to need jewellery. You will always need jewellery. Jewellery is good.

Two months ahead

❍ Remove two-storey extension on wedding dress when it is discovered that it won't actually fit down the aisle without you having to shunt your way down sideways.

❍ Ask mother-in-law to replace the marquee.

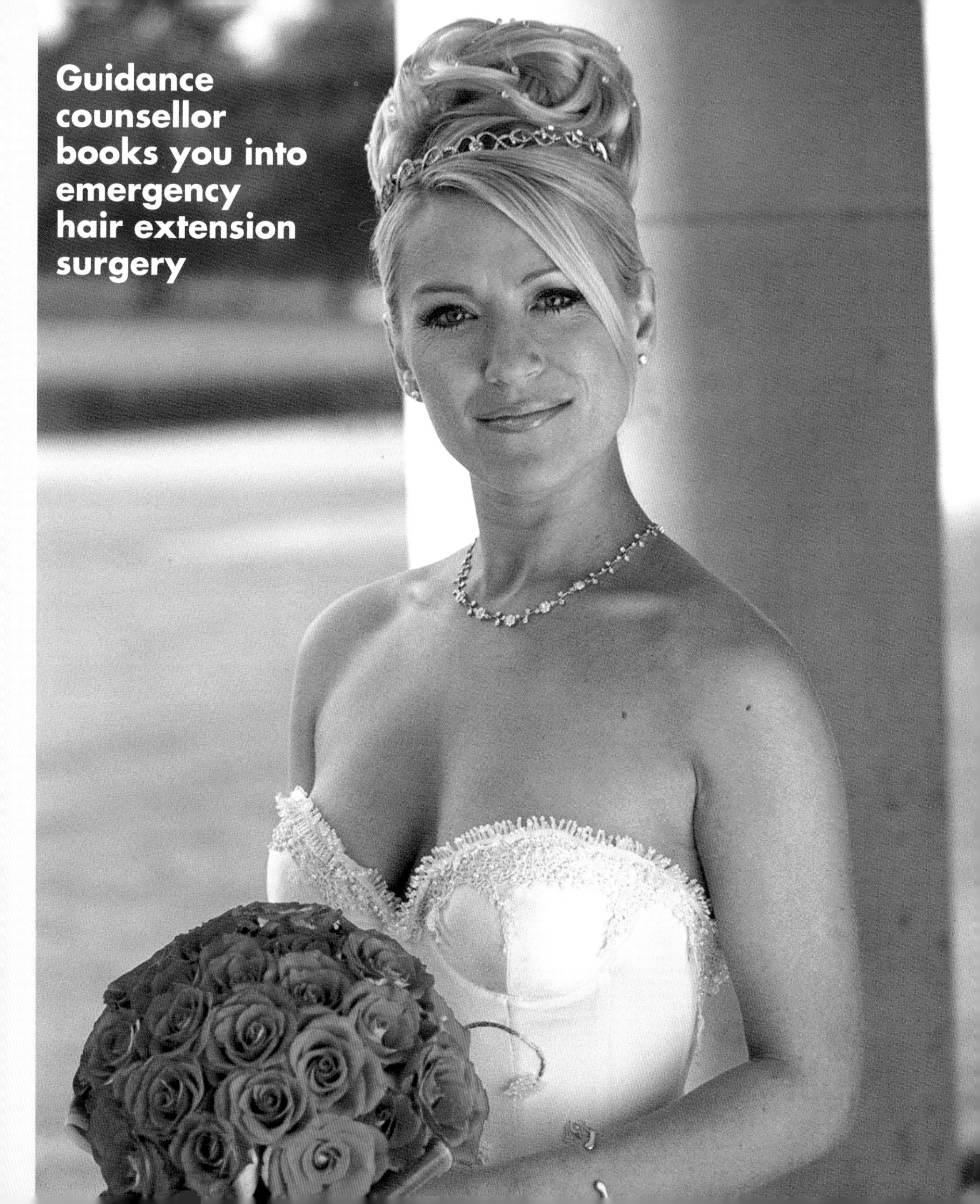
Guidance counsellor books you into emergency hair extension surgery

One month, three weeks ahead

❍ Hire Poet Laureate to write your personalized wedding vows.

❍ Hire Pam Ayres to rewrite personalized wedding vows as first lot didn't rhyme.

❍ Check with fiancé to see whether he has written his. You remind him to keep the beer mat safe as he won't want to rewrite them.

One month, two weeks ahead

❍ Magazine suggests that they choose the photographer instead. Apparently photographers who do pictures of Labradors on rugs and babies in supermarkets are a little last year. They hire in a seventeen-year-old boy called simply 'The Padre' who's been causing waves with his gritty heroin smack bitch signature look.

One month, one week ahead

❍ Magazine insists that you issue a strict dress code to guests. They may elect from gold lamé, whimsical fairy or frisky beaver. Keep these plans closely guarded then you'll easily be able to ferret out the gatecrashing paparazzi. If someone turns up in a tux you'll know they're either a tabloid journalist or a cat burglar. Or of course the man from Milk Tray.

❍ Magazine calls back with an addendum. Old and/or ugly guests are to be subtly given directions to a different church as they would only disrupt the aesthetics and symmetry of the day.

❍ Magazine calls back again to suggest you withdraw your invitation to Claudia Schiffer if you want someone actually to notice you. They suggest you invite a few comedians to pull delightfully funny faces in the candid photo section.

One month ahead

❍ You've realized this event has got rather out of control and what was meant to be the most special day of your life is fast becoming more organizationally complex than the Normandy landings.

❍ You put your foot down and insist to your agent that she mustn't book any more interviews on the day itself without your express permission.

❍ Swedish *Vogue* calls. Well, just one more…

Three weeks ahead

❍ Slight panic. Apparently there is a reason most weddings take place in the summer. The football season is specifically arranged to give a few months off to encourage footballers to settle down. As it is, your fiancé is scheduled to be on a coach travelling to Newcastle.

❍ Magazine has refused to stump up for helicopter. Agent thankfully secures last-minute air ambulance promotion deal. *Changing Rooms* designer called back in to incorporate gauzes and neckbrace into headdress design. Result actually an improvement.

Two weeks, forty-seven minutes ahead

❍ Cancel wedding again. The blushing groom it transpires has 'hired' – yes 'hired' – his outfit!

Two weeks, forty minutes ahead

❍ Wedding back on. *Changing Rooms* designer commissioned to create matching headdress for groom avec medical equipment.

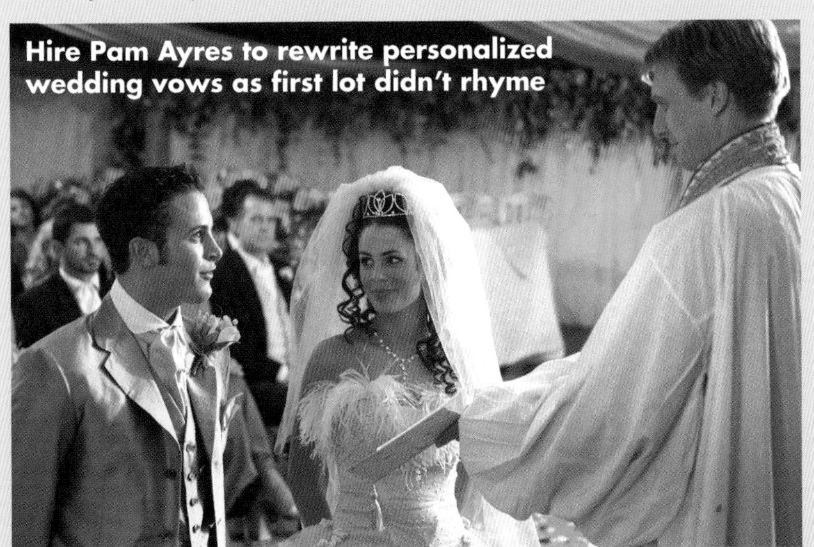

Hire Pam Ayres to rewrite personalized wedding vows as first lot didn't rhyme

Two weeks thirty-seven minutes ahead

- ❍ Told to breathe into a paper bag to regulate airflow when you realise you have no minister to perform service or indeed any musical entertainment.
- ❍ Cliff Richard booked to officiate at ceremony.
- ❍ Stairlifts – the Steps tribute band – booked to provide the musical 'entertainment'.
- ❍ Remind mother-in-law to issue the choreography to the guests in time for them to learn it.

Two weeks ahead

- ❍ As it is a non-traditional wedding you decide to forgo the wedding march in favour of the 'That's Martini' theme from the Seventies.
- ❍ GMTV offer to do a morning makeover slot to do your wedding hair and make-up. They're going to pull in the Shampoo and Setter of the Year.
- ❍ Decide to drop the seating plan convention of his and hers in favour of splitting up divorced partners. Bitter harridans to the left and cheating bastards to the right.

One week, six days ahead

- ❍ Bastard politicians are apparently in seizure or something and the Houses of Parliament, despite their misleading churchlike appearance, are apparently almost never hired out for private functions.
- ❍ Stonehenge resolutely refuses to allow Bedouin tenting to be lashed over the stone bits as rain cover.
- ❍ Police also insist that they cannot possibly redirect traffic away from Eros and that the RSPCA would also have a thing or two to say about the dangers inherent in setting eight badgers and an otter free to frolic on a weekday in Piccadilly Circus.
- ❍ Emergency talks with magazine results in settling on the New Forest. Forestry Commission pleased with the business are happy to accede to any demands with the exception of the panthers. Apparently they are not an indigenous species and the risk to the local water vole population is too great.
- ❍ Forestry Commission won't budge on helipad either. Magazine suggests getting in Boutros Boutros Galli to mediate.

One week, five days ahead

- ❍ Forestry Commission agree to forest clearing for air ambulance if you agree to turn some of your own land over to pasture and adopt a squirrel.
- ❍ Apparently you don't even get to keep the squirrel – it'll just send you an anniversary card once a year.

One week, four days ahead

- ❍ Cake arrives. Only after you take out the patio doors and Charlie Dimmock lends a hand with a forklift.
- ❍ Replace father with Gary Lineker. The silver fox will look far more dignified steadying your passage down the aisle and your dress being what it is – the more help with the inbuilt scaffolding system the better.

Wedding service rehearsal. All well apart from a truculent badger who doesn't know his markers.

Five days ahead

- ❍ Badgers pull out in a show of solidarity. Hurried phone calls to drag in four ferrets and a weasel.

Three days ahead

- Last-ditch affair with the best man who proves that titles can be misleading. Fiancé decides to wait until the day itself for his indiscretion.
- Provide portaloos for journalists camped outside. You don't want your special day smelling like a football terrace.

Two days ahead

- Flowers delivered to New Forest. Visitors to Kew Gardens are subsequently baffled by the new barren desert feature look but are assured all foliage will be returned in three days.
- Damn Nolan's pulled out. Sister to step back up to the mark after she promises to enter *Pop Idol* this year and up her celebrity rating.
- Diaries consulted with a general agreement on honeymoon in late May next year. Venue tbc – depending on where's in at the time.

One day ahead

- Hen night passes without incident apart from two hospitalizations and a police caution regarding inappropriate use of a learner sign and a 737. Air traffic control have no sense of humour. Three hundred Edinburgh to London commuters incensed and a lifetime ban from Economy Airlines. Like you'd want to travel on the sort of plane you have to pedal yourself with the rest of the pleb galley slaves.
- Stag night not so lucky. Air and Sea Rescue eventually locate fiancé somewhere off the coast of Southend and it takes several hours of intrusive surgery to remove the high tide sign.

The Big Day

- Hand-designed wedding rings apparently lost with best man who was last seen floating in the general direction of Denmark.
- End up resorting to buying them on the 'high street'. They look like a hula hoop dipped in cubic zirconia and possibly are.
- Don't worry – you will always get to the day and realize you've forgotten something. A few phone calls should organize a few supporting artistes/non-speaking actors to be determined rival photographers. Can't have anyone thinking that no one wants to snap happy now do we?
- Fiancé arrives from Newcastle with air ambulance and some squatter who fell walks in November.
- You and your 'father' Gary to arrive at the forest clearing in a rustic coach pulled by Shetland ponies.
- Ensure the fairy people (from Sylvia Young) know when to do their musical montage sequence from *Cats* (sometime after the I do's and before the toast).
- Wedding goes well despite some confusion with regards to the Steps choreography and the sanctity of marriage with husband's teammates.
- Ferrets hit markers putting the badgers to shame.
- Party favours of Stairlifts albums receive cool reception.
- Husband should try to sleep with the bridesmaid/s before rather than

after or especially during the ceremony.

❍ The best man staggers back just in time to act as northern club comic anchorman to the festivities. In his speech he will uncover and reveal more nasty little secrets about the bride than a phalanx of rabid reporters ever could.

❍ When you are pronounced man and wife set off headdress fountain.

The Reception

❍ Do try to take time out from your round robin of interviews to attend.

❍ Well, of course you can throw money at a reception but at the end of the day – it's safe to say several things are a given. The DJ will play 'Rock the Boat' and 'Lady in Red'. It goes without saying – don't wear red or you'll have fifty pissed up letches pointing at you in the choruses. One of the men will drink too much and try to start a fight. All the men who are marginally less drunk will tell him to calm down, body block and hug him. In an unrelated incident one of the women will get emotional, hog the one toilet cubicle that isn't flooded and weep into the last of the bog roll. Managers will dance badly (dad dancing) and their wives will wear dresses that show off their crinkly cleavages. If you wish to avail yourself of the facilities do it early in the evening because it will become a shag station later. Maybe have a buddy system to take care of each other. Ensure the free bar doesn't run out or the whole place will descend into a melee of violence and trampled wild flowers.

❍ The groom will spill Advocaat on his cummerbund.

I now pronounce you footballer and wife! Congratulations! fw

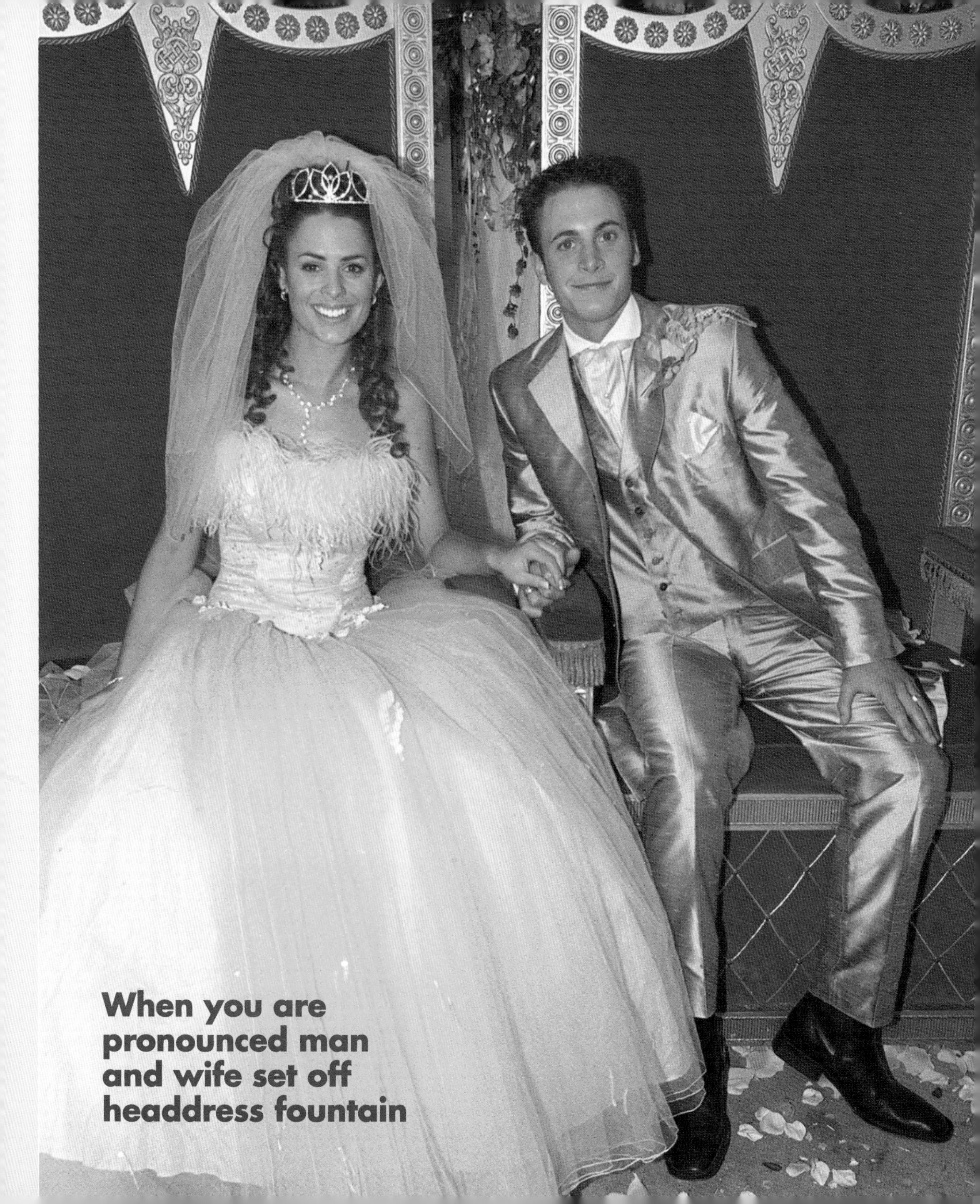

When you are pronounced man and wife set off headdress fountain

captain's wife's log

Friday
Don't get me wrong but I've seen it all now. Turned up to Chardonnay and Kyle's wedding to find I'd got misdirected to a panto with Jason as Widow Twanky. I should have known when I read the invite which directed all guests to wear hot pink. The whole affair was reminiscent of what might happen if you stuck 20 lbs of TNT under a marshmallow depository.

First we watched Kyle aka Prince Charming arrive on a white steed to awaken the Princess Chardonnay from her golden slumbers surrounded by seven rug rats in dwarf costumes. Then I got saddled with sitting next to Donna Day and Simone who was charged with letting off the doves. It was like Dresden. The little pigeon bastards blanket bombed the marquee in seconds.

I tell you if Chardonnay needed awakening with a kiss – I needed a stiff drink after all that. Still she looked lovely and seemed happy enough so mustn't let the squalid sordidness of my life make me cynical eh?

To do: find out which way to London Dick.

Saturday
Thought about my wedding day today. I'll never forget it though I won't stop trying.

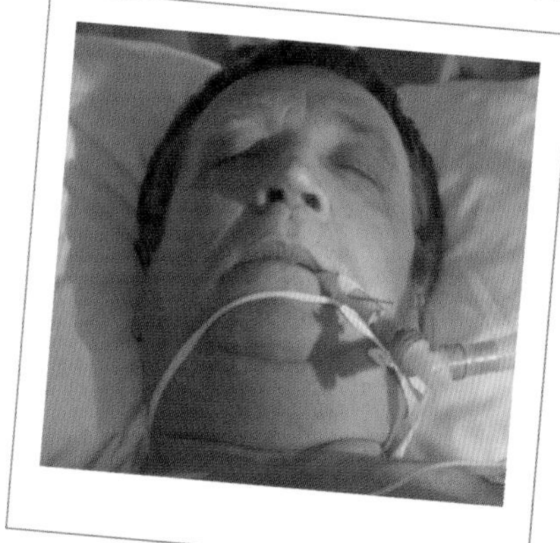

Sunday
Nightmares start.

Monday
Had to convince Nurse Drab that my interest in Frank was purely devotional and almost a little righteous. Good God but I know now how Jason gets the birds. It's so easy: flattery gets you everywhere – it's the second most powerful tool next to money. I've got a horrible sinking feeling I might regret saying that. Friends come and go, but the money grasping tends to accumulate.

To do: Buy something semi-expensive for Nurse Insipid – I may need her yet...

Saturday
Nightmare's continue. Am having to get through week in cocaine blur. Had to go to the hospital on my own again. I've given up asking Jason to at least pretend to be a nice guy. He's not Rory Bremner.

Sunday
Chardonnay is by all accounts still suffering from depression. Apparently she hasn't actually got out of bed since the wedding apart from to chop off her hair. Neither has Frank, but you don't see him getting busy with nail scissors.

I'll rot in hell for that one. I wonder what hell is like. Still, comforting to know Jason will be right by my side. That should stem any after life boredom in the bud. After life. There's a joke. Like this one qualifies as something worthy of an encore. Don't suppose I'll have to waste my time cosseting Nurse Dunkley from the fiery pits of eternity though. The woman is practically a saint fussing around Frank. I think she actually lives at the hospital with some sort of umbilical cord attaching her to his bedside.

Monday
More lies – this time about Chardonnay's hairstyle. The woman is depressed enough without hearing what her barnet looks like.

Tuesday
I've practically snorted Columbia up my nose over the last week and still the nightmares don't abate. The only cheery news was seeing Donna Day's husband Ian gracing the front pages with his three in a bed romps and not Jason for once.

Wednesday
Chardonnay's had her hair lopped off even shorter. She now no longer looks like a lesbian, she looks like a lesbian mechanic. Kyle is

walking round rubbing his temples in a state of shock. Knowing men – it's probably not all he's rubbing.

Thursday
Caught Donna Day's sister Marie bent double over Jason in his car. I don't think she was panning for gold. Jason is like a frigging toilet door – either he's vacant in the extreme or otherwise engaged in something mucky. I freaked out which I think was perfectly understandable. He promised he'd never see her again. I've reconciled myself to the fact that there'll probably never be a time in my life when I don't want to take him out with a cosh.
How could he do it with her? She was screeching away like a banshee when I grabbed her slut hair out of the car. I accept that love can be blind – but can it be deaf as well?

Friday
Spent some quality time bunkered up with my duvet and only a bottle of firewater for company.

Saturday
Intercepted a call from Marie. It wasn't all over at all. And why should I have believed it was. God, The Stepford Wives was just a

cruel, cruel lie. Our marriage is such a sham. All we need now is the Vicar to come round for tea and we can all exchange pleasantries on the joys of marital bliss over a chocolate hobnob.

Anyway – Jason lost it big time when I confronted him. Apparently the fact that he keeps finding himself playing ball boy with the international association of bed warmers is in some way my fault. He told me the marriage was over and stormed out.

He said he didn't love me which hurt like hell. On reflection I don't think that's true. In our own insubstantial and immature way we do love each other. Or at least are co-dependent and that's much more pure.

When he got home I threatened to go to the police and turn myself – and by association him – in over the Frank debacle. He realized I meant it. Which was odd – because so did I.

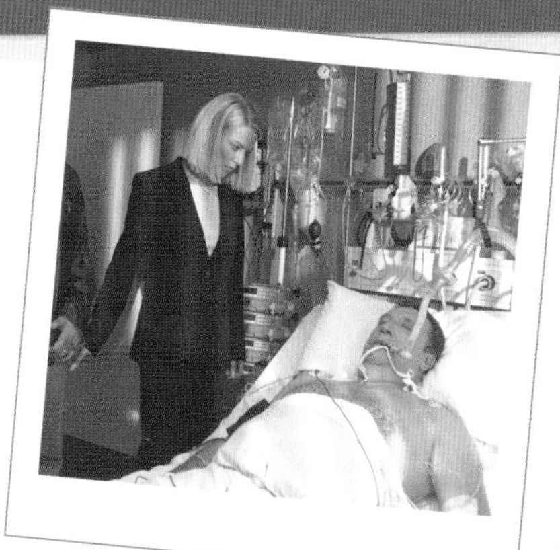

Friday

Asked Janette round for tea. Jason stomached her company until just after the fish course which was more than my money would have been on. I tried to gauge Frank's chances. The bugger looks like he might pull through.

Saturday

Scratch that entry about Nurse Attentive Bedside Manner and her 'don't wait in line, jump to the front of the queue' ticket to Heaven. Walked in on her giving Frank some mouth-to-mouth that I'm pretty certain isn't in the Nurses' Guide to Being a Nice Nurse Handbook.

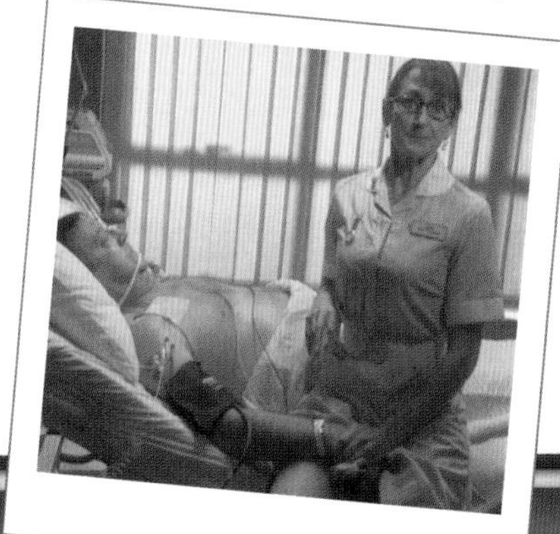

God knows what Frank would say if he knew he was being forced to have a Bunkley with Dunkley. The involuntary bodily muscle spasms may be willing but…

Just finished emergency abluting session. Still – I know something that Nurse Frankenstein doesn't want me to know. This may have been the most crucial discovery of a game of doctors and nurses ever.

To do: cancel the flowers I'd been planning to send to the Dunkster. She's getting enough plant life without my contribution.

Monday

Told Janette to use all of her albeit limited social skills of persuasion to get Marguerite, Frank's ex to switch off the life support and do us all – I mean Frank – a favour. Obviously, from a humanitarian angle of course. Apparently it's not strictly down to her as ex-wives – despite their years of servitude – haven't earnt themselves the right to decide whether their husband lives or dies. Sometimes the laws of the land just dazzle me.

Anyway, we have a chain reaction. I told Janette, who told Marguerite who told their son – who does have the privilege. Of course Nurse Nightmare wasn't overly keen but then with Frank gone she'll be saying au revoir to her only sure thing. Then again – the threat of the world knowing her sordid little secret was enough to convince her to stand straight, look smart and get with the programme.

Monday

The deed done, no sooner am I home celebrating with a short glass of long liquid when I find out Jason's been done for speeding. I'd been trying to get in touch with him all day but he kept cancelling my calls. Jees – even ET phoned home once in a while. I'll probably never know the full details but I suspect it has something to do with that vendetta he has with the new bit of mafia muscle on the team. My only regret is that he didn't drive so fast he careered off the cliffs of Dover. As far as I'm concerned right now he could keep on speeding till he hits China.

To do: buy something appropriate for the plug pulling ceremony.

Tuesday

What is appropriate for a plug pulling ceremony? Black seems a bit presumptuous.

Life is one non-stop search for answers, isn't it.

Wednesday

The eighteen-year-old worm has turned. Jason's managed to turn even his strumpet against him – and she doesn't even have to live with him – so quite an achievement. Shame we can't hook Jason up to Frank and do a two in one special.

I was on my way to the ceremony (I chose navy – respectful with just the most modest twinkling of hope against the odds) when I got a call from Marie telling me that Jason was waiting for her in a fancy restaurant with bubbly chilling gently at his side. Her main purpose seemed to be letting me know the earth-shattering news that Jason is a giant knob – and would I be so good as to retrieve my property.

So on this, the day when I finally manage to upgrade from attempted to full premeditated, sociopathic homicide to save Jason's flagging career, he chooses to forgo the pleasantries of pretending to be grateful in favour of boinking some little scrubber with tits the size of satsumas.

Decide not to retrieve him. Instead I just embellished his appearance with the champagne. It seemed like a waste of good liquor but my only real regret was not following through with the bottle.

Oh my God. Just got back from the hospital. We'd said prayers, looked sombre for an hour and my choice of navy was vindicated. Then just as they reach for the socket Frank opened his eyes and stared at me.

It's alive, alive I tell you!

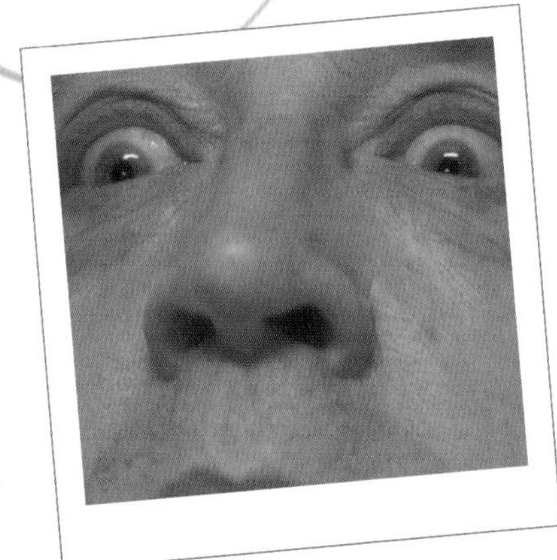

Thursday

Janette confirmed that while Frank is still officially vegetative – there are rules about doctors killing live people in hospitals. Honestly – they're alright unless you actually want them to do it, aren't they! My life has become a waking nightmare. At any minute he could start tapping out his accusations against me in Morse code or something.

God – I don't even know if they still have the death penalty.

Friday
After some frantic persuasion – well, blackmail really – Janette has agreed with me that it would still be the kindest thing to put Frank down. I've left her to figure out the details but she assures me she can do it without getting caught. Her track record does nothing to reassure me.

To do: take back the navy suit. Try and swap it for a black one, fingers crossed.

Saturday
Dunkley is going to give Frank a fatal injection of potassium. I stay for a while just to make sure it's really happening – but at the last minute my stomach churns up and I leave her to it. I head back to base control awaiting confirmation that the 'eagle has landed'.

Of course I can't do anything apart from pace. I think Frank's coma has had a detrimental effect on my health as his. For all his slowed heart rate – I think he gave the missing beats to me because my heart was yammering like an express train.

Right, I've just received the call. My life is officially over. Nurse Nasty was poised to administer the nice needle to la la land when Frank – becoming of Lazarus himself – practically rose from the dead. He's awake. All I can do now is drink so much I'm not.

Friday
Day 2 of Frank watch. All quiet so far. Only event was Jason beating the crap out of Sal the Italian Stallion's car. Nice work. It's at this point that every gin and tonic counts.

To do: Take back the black suit – it could all be used as evidence.

Saturday
Jason on the bench again in favour of Sal. It would seem Stefan takes a dim view of inter-team brutality. Jason the stupid git said he wanted to be put on the transfer list. Permission granted. We're now firmly down the creek of crap without the proverbial.

After all we've (no – I've) been through to keep him on that team as well ... Jason lost it and I thought he was going to belt me for a moment. The little tyke just didn't have it in him though and he begged me to forgive him – or more specifically save his backside again.

Day 3 – Frank Watch – all's quiet on the western front – though I'm assured his memory loss is only short term. There's a relief eh?

Sunday
The police are taking statements from everything down to the pot plant in Frank's room. Nurse Nightshade has offered to disappear to avoid any awkward questions in return for an incredibly generous cash gift from the ever emptying wallet of Mrs Turner. She can go and molest another patient in another town. God help the NHS.

I arrived for my standard bedside vigil to find out that Janette had left a parting gift for me too. She'd told Frank all about my constant devotion and 'reminded' him of the affair we'd been having. If he looked shocked you can imagine how I felt. I wish I'd disappeared at the same time Dunkley did.

cut out and keep

Something to do with those nail scissors apart from hacking off your hair in nervous breakdown-related pique

Jase Tan

Cut out and enlarge this template to put in the windscreen of your GTI posh car and look posh Footballers' Wives' style!

Keep this sign handy for those impromptu romantic moments

THIS CUBICLE IS RESERVED FOR

....

AND

....

DO NOT DISTURB FOR A GOOD TEN MINUTES BECAUSE I'M MAKING A NIGHT OF IT!

ADVERTISEMENT

Marie: Saves 20p a week with Piggybank Plus

Marie, a 19 year old from a dirty Northern town says:

'I wanted to save for laser surgery to get rid of an offensive tattoo. Actually the tattoo itself wasn't offensive but it was of Jason Turner who is offensive in anyone's money. My 20p a week won't cover it but the fee I got paid for doing this advert will so I wholeheartedly endorse Piggybank Plus!'

Lara: Saves £50,000 a week

Lara (What do you mean how old am I, I'm not old at all – do I look it? Oh God, hold on a minute while I get some slap on) is from the much cleaner South:

'I'm a really nice person who smiles ever such a lot so when they asked me to say how marvellous Piggybank Plus is I found my head bobbing up and down like one of those nodding dogs in a car. Actually I can't stop because the removal men have arrived. Since I've started saving with Piggybank Plus we've had to sell the house and move in with my in-laws which I'm sure will be nice for the kids especially with Ron maybe having to go to jail because of the debts. Though I'm sure it's got nothing to do with Piggybank Plus and my Teasmade is so useful!'

Ron: Saved £50,000 apparently

Ron is currently feeling about twenty years older than he really is and hails from HMP Surrey:

'I need to endorse Piggybank Plus because apparently I don't qualify for legal aid and my counsellor thinks as part of my healing process I should learn to forgive!'

START SAVING NOW

INSTEAD OF SPENDING IT ALL ON EXPENSIVE DRESSES BECAUSE IT'S JUST SILLY TO PAY SO MUCH FOR A BIT OF CLOTH, ISN'T IT.

SAYS D-LIST CELEBRITY DONNA WALMSLEY

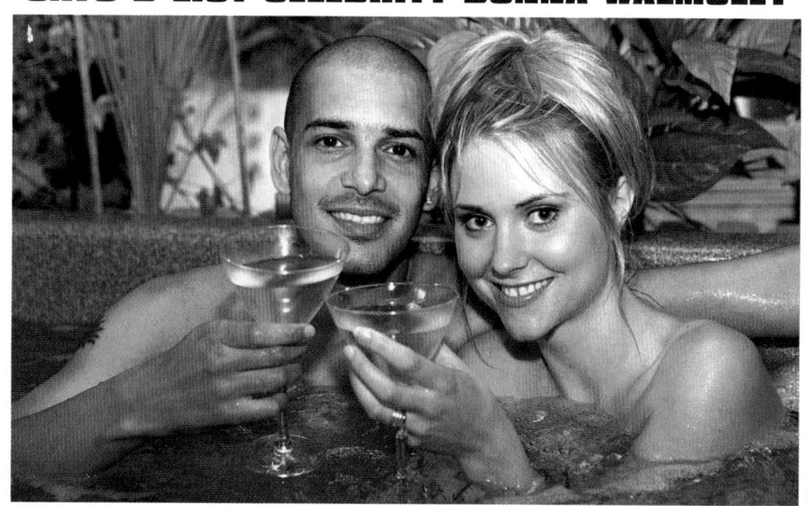

As a Footballer's Wife I'm often called upon to have money. When Piggybank Plus asked me to endorse their marvellous product I wanted to ensure I was totally confident with putting my name to it. Unfortunately I couldn't really understand all the words in the file they gave me but I do know I believe in saving so I unreservedly say to you this is the best investment you could make for your family's future.

MONEY IF YOU DIE but not if you don't (because you should be happy enough about just not being dead. Actually you don't even need it if you do die because you'll be dead, so how about we give you £50 when you get retired or made redundant).

Notice how we have put into bold – tempting words which are meant to draw your eye away from the detail safe in the knowledge you probably won't even notice. We could blah blah blah blah **BIG CASH REWARDS** blah blah. Itsy Bitsy teeny weeny yellow **YOU'LL BE BLOODY LOADED YOU WILL** polka dot bikini. You are **GUARANTEED** to give us **MONEY**. Now you're probably very clever indeed with your cash so we've included a picture of a 'bouncy' child to provide you with the reassurance you should and can expect.

Small Print If you invest in this scheme there is a high likelihood you will lose everything. On the plus side, if you invest in this scheme you'll be securing the future of a man with a very obviously fake beard who operates (according to several Metropolitan Police Authorities) under several pseudonyms but is commonly known to officers as Slippery Steve. No really – don't take our word for it. Watchdog alone have one whole room at BBC television centre in White City given over to the mailbags of complaints. Despite Anne Robinson's best efforts in her tenure on the show – only one letter was ever found to be complimentary to the scheme and that was later discovered to be an application for a Blue Peter badge from 1982 that had been buried by Goldie which to the best of our memory was a Labrador but might have been a retriever. Either way the important thing is that he was not a border collie because only John Noakes could handle a working dog like that.

EXTRA BONUS GIFT THAT YOU DON'T WANT, WOULD NEVER ACTUALLY BUY – BUT ADMIT IT – THE FACT IT'S FREE IS TEMPTING YOU ISN'T IT!

!!! L@@K!!! Brown and cream 1970's Teasmade!!! L@@K!!! (also available – towel bale!!!!!)

FREE FREE FREE FREE FREE

Money, Money, Monet

Retail therapy – burn it as they earn it on classy things

While Einstein laboured over the Theory of Relativity, it took pioneer wives to calculate the real deal.

They discovered an economic formula that has continued to inspire and guide their successors to this day. Using applied algebra they reasoned that one simple rule could not only be applied to all purchases but also would provide answers to the questions that have haunted humanity for all eternity – in essence – the meaning of life.

Namely, money should talk, and when it does it should talk loudly. This can be presented mathematically through the following equation:

£ x £^{2} = joy and poshness

Please note: if you're not going to go crazy with cash you have no right to be a Footballer's Wife. There are people who win the lottery and then stay in their council ashtrays and say money won't change them. We say if you're in it to win it (and frankly you're not in it to ensure some interpretative dance charity group gets to work with pensioners in crisis), then you should bloody well appreciate it. That said – you can take the girl out of her own brand, but can you take that working-class cheap nastiness out of the girl? The answer is YES because we are trying to encourage you – even though it is really no.

Remember that while there's no more unsightly 'buy now, pay laters' for you, there are costs in marital endurance you'll be paying so add these up in the total reckonings you demand from husband. Of course money does not equate love even in the premiership.

For some it is a painful transition. You may have come from a slum or a tenement where you had to step over tramps to get in your front door. At leaner Christmases you might have had to eat one of them. And now here you are with enough spare change in your BMW's ashtray to keep that tramp in meths for a lifetime. You'll have to make lots of changes – gold hoop earrings are out and that must be an end to the matter. You can still show your legs but do it 'classy' – have a split in your skirt rather than a skirt in your split. You should not show egads – knickers – because celebrities of your calibre don't wear them on account of VPLs necessitating immediate emigration to a trailer park. This said, it's always a compliment if someone says you look like a bit of a Kipling. Remember 'Tart' says it's worth charging for. You should at least look like a gifted amateur. The other option is that you'd have to give it away for free.

As a style icon you will be gifted a lot of gratis. For the new wife it's easy to get carried away with this but beware the magic words 'Product placement'. What might sound like sense under the influence of a seven-figure contract might be less appealing in the cold light of having to wear

orthopaedic slippers. Beware anything that comes with the promise 'not available in the shops'.

Now what should you spend all that lovely dough, bread and folding specialness on? Unfortunately as long as minimalism is in you can't have everything – at least on display – so you should contain your aspirations to some well chosen and outrageously priced items. These are an investment. Designer labels facilitate even the most strained of social relations and credit limits are so Sunday league.

Money should talk,
and when it does it
should talk loudly

If you're not going to go crazy with cash you have no right to be a Footballer's Wife

Some classy things to spend his hard earned money on

£ **Why not get some books?** Every house should have at least one book. Books are normally about six inches long and most do not have a month or issue number on the front. We recommend ones with blue spines as this will tie in well with Earl's Park's colours. If you want all of your books to match – try turning them around!

£ **Try to incorporate cream and gold into your colour scheme.** Bold and dark walls are for Satanists and Laurence Llewellyn-Bowen.

£ **A handbag?** Yes, clasp, shoulder or micro-backpack. Bags will never go out of style for six weeks.

£ **It is imperative that you buy the sort of shoes that will be bad for your feet.** Please try to make an effort and snap a heel. It is an excellent flirting technique that requires men to become heroes with glue.

£ **Car.** Your wifemobile should have a full leather interior, a sound system to rival Knebworth and blackened windows to enable you to drive with your heated rollers in. To avoid embarrassment, when choosing your car opt for an MG, BMW or similar… They are much easier to spell on your road tax than a Maserati.

£ **Use your husband's money to hire a personal trainer.** These are not footwear. These are men that will shout at you in a way that you would divorce your husband for if he did it. For the full effect – try to get ex-paramilitary. It must of course be a man otherwise they'd be no subsequent juicy rumour mill. Plus the alternative is that you'd spend a lot of time staring through your legs at a bottom more pert than your own.

£ **House.** The largest one you can find on the largest plot of land. Possibly buy Hertfordshire.

more classy stuff you really need now

£ **Plasma screens.** If your home entertainment system is not inducing premature deafness you should upgrade. The screen should be roughly the size of a barn and you should have to sit in Wales to see it.

£ **Family portrait.** Please ensure this is not in abstract. Pictures should look like what they're meant to.

£ You may eat the same **diet** as you once did but just make sure you only ever eat it in French. Who wouldn't pay more for petit pois than peas?

£ **Lush carpet.** On the floors, walls, ceilings and possibly kitchenware. The deepest recorded shag pile in a footballer's house was registered at over 15 foot deep. In fact the owners had to commando crawl on top of it to avoid banging their head on the ceiling.

£ **Staff.** They are God's way of telling you your washing needs airing.

£ **Recreational drugs.** They are God's way of telling you your bank account needs airing.

£ **Public school.** With education it is imperative that your child has the best or at least the most expensive education money can buy. If your child isn't experiencing fagging, cold showers, apple pie beds and unrequited lustful interludes involving matron, then we want to know why! fw

£ **Your husband** Don't spend money on them. It will only eat up future alimony and they are easily impressed with a soap on a rope and a universal remote control.

As long as minimalism is in, you can't have everything – at least on display

changing tomb$

If you're not a victim of taste – you may well be a criminal of it

1. Start at Gracelands.

2. Work up.

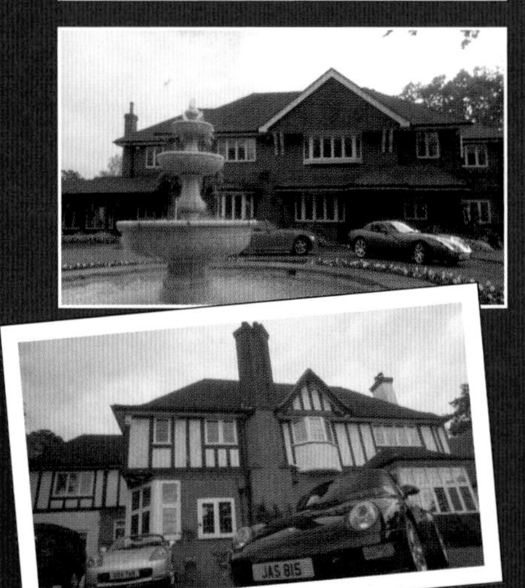

There are only so many porcelain pumas one living room can take (we think about five is reasonable)

It's hard work spending this much cash, but no-one said being a Footballer's Wife was going to be easy

Footballers' past wives: The Renaissance

A continuing series where we look at history's lessons

Did you know?

1. *Renaissance* means 'rebirth' in foreign but is not to be confused with real 'rebirth' as provided by alternative therapy.
2. Lots of art made in *Renaissance* times concerned The Madonna. This referred neither to the Material Girl nor pint-sized soccer superstar Maradona.
3. The title *Renaissance* is often given to three-piece suites and wallpaper ranges. These are only transcendentally linked.
4. The *Renaissance* covered almost all of Europe and is expected to reach Essex any day now.

The Instructive Yesteryear Bit

(*Please consult your doctor before starting any academic study)*

During the Renaissance, artistic endeavour flourished and the feudal system was eroded by economic migrants to the developing cities. Perhaps most significantly Henry VIII had legalized divorce, signalling the start of serial football marriages and generally a more open market for the matrimonially jaded.

Much of Europe was decimated by the Plague which vied with the cruciate ligament in benching vast numbers of promising footballers. Numerous wives were left with a husband no longer able to play premiership football and with disfiguring boils that precluded a media career. Let us never forget these women…

As the epidemic ravaged the towns and cities, those wealthy enough fled to the country. Unfortunately being under thirty and rural was not then a serious style option as pox-ridden medieval cities (i.e. Manchester City and Leicester City) found to their cost. Earl's Park, by virtue of its eponymous countryside location, won the double every year for a decade simply by being the only team to have 11 players with their full requisite of limbs.

Exploration and maritime advancements allowed travel to new continents and holiday destinations. A little known fact was that telescopes were invented around this time to allow journalists to hide in bushes and sketch topless wives in the skimpiest of jerkins. International trade emerged which really opened up the transfer market and spices were imported from the east including nutmeg, cinnamon and Sporty. Now would-be wives were able to get cheap designer knock offs from the Orient and a premier wife of the day 'Donnatella De Walmsley' documented her delight in finally getting her hands on a real bit of Italian leather.

When Gutenberg invented the printing press in 1445, he forever changed the media, allowing a greater circulation for Page Three and kisseths and telleths. Hitherto, it had taken so long for shocking exposés to be disseminated that key characters had either died of old age or had let time be a marvellous healer before everyone had a chance to be scandalized. Previously, bookmaking entailed copying lots of words by hand onto parchment made from animal skin. This exempted many wives from the displeasure of buying books because of their active support of animal skin rights' groups such as 'Skin Ain't In so Make Mead Don't Read'. Indeed the later proliferation of books prompted protests from men who missed the group's various promotional stunts which always seemed to include the wives getting out their jugs as a positive reinforcement of their pro-ale policy.

Da Vinci was one of the forefathers of the celebrity lifestyle inventing, among other necessities, helicopters and exercise bikes. Many new cathedrals were erected to accommodate larger celebrity footballers' weddings and guilds were created to unify masons, builders and football writers. The Renaissance was a particularly good time for despots. The rule of law had not yet been conceived which meant soccer stars could speed in their carriages with impunity. No sorry, that's still the case.

Pioneers in natural sciences discovered that the earth and ergo footballs could in fact be round. This greatly reduced the popular fear that it was possible to simply plip off the planet if one fell asleep till the last stop of a Sedan ride and also reduced the stark number of stubbed toes for footballers. Of course it was not all positive: Rubens and his cronies popularized bulk in women which meant for the first (and last) time, intellectual thought was considered more alluring than having the dimensions of a reed.

A fashionable pursuit for wives at the time was thinking about philosophy. Sadly – many so called 'philosophies' were too primitive to encompass exercise techniques and as such didn't endure beyond 'fad' status. Rhetorical argument was highly valued, creating a whole new breed of soccer pundits and thereby an elephants' graveyard for ex footballers. It is arguably no coincidence that the murder rate of retired footballers by their wives decreased dramatically with this trend as they were no longer getting under the broom, cluttering the house sobbing sonnets about their lost youth.

Suppers (before all daylight grazing was invented) were a lively affair of a boar and a few tarts, kicked off by some whore d'oeuvres. A wife would start many festivities by leading guests in a stroll around her swimming pool engaged in contented philosophical debate followed by music and song and a bit of recitation. Some of these were good and rhymed, others concentrated heavily on topical subjects such as why someone's goose wasn't laying. All were bawdy and therefore retain some interest.

Some authentic Renaissance recitations for you to try:

Marie Marie quite contrary
how does your garden grow?
A nail would I break
If I picked up a rake
So how the f&%k would I know!

When Tanya got her soccer Mr
Kyle's mother said as he kissed her,
That fellow you've won,
Won't be much fun,
He's done me and that other
tart's sister.

Jackie was feeling quite blue
and said as Jason withdrew
No one could be thicker
And they couldn't be quicker
But they'd be two inches longer
than you.

Why doth my liege he say
That while doth my goose not lay
the monies on, my sister may?

I will sing thee one, lo
that green grow the pitches, oh!
and ever more shall it be so
that you shall be a soccer ho.

looking nice with

Hi, Chardonnay here! **Sometimes I used to wonder why I wasn't born blonde. Then I realized you shouldn't let society's prejudice against your handicap hold you back. So turn that frown at being brown upside down and think positive. Being a brunette is not all about looking undesirable and dull – but looking classy and intelligent. Now it's my chance to share all those beauty tips that got me a man and a celebrity lifestyle. So set your hairdryer to stun (as in stunning) and your sunbed to chemotherapy and prepare to *look nice!***

Tint Hints

If you are living in shame as a peroxide deficient don't feel you have to be flat and matt. There are so many wildly different tint options for a brunette – so why not try one of these...

Mocha-choca-glory

Antique teak chic

Sweet as a Sepia Chestnut

Autumnal coffee toffee Montelimar

Chardonnay

Tan

You no longer have to spit roast out in the sun to get that leather look. Just get sandblasted with something developed at Porton Down and banned in most Nato countries as a chemical weapon.

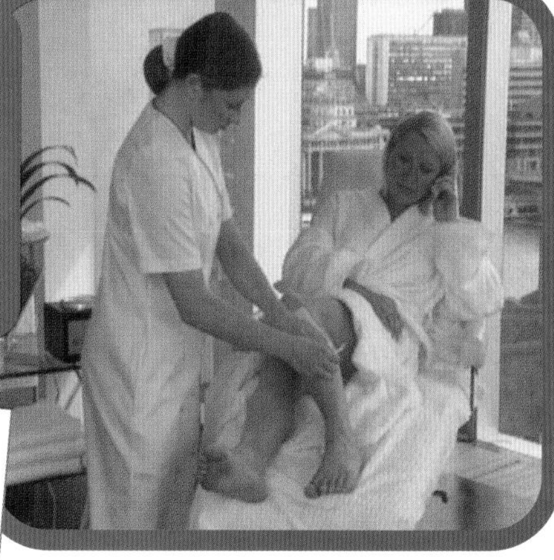

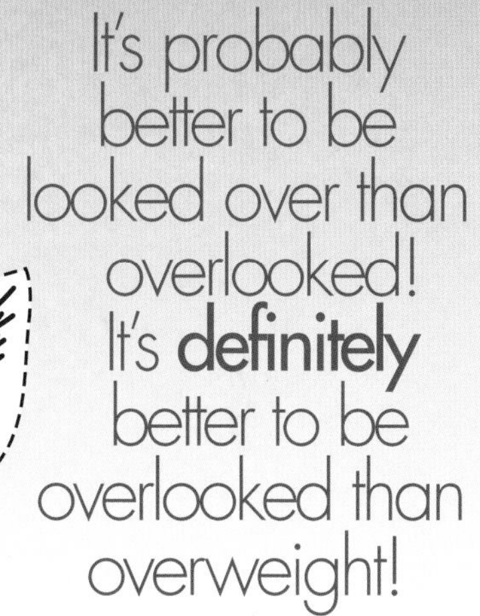

Shutter Flutters!

Cut Out and Keep eyelashes for those special occasions when you need to look like a startled cow.

It's probably better to be looked over than overlooked! It's **definitely** better to be overlooked than overweight!

Top of the Crops...for men

Football has not been traditionally associated with happy hair. Of course we can forgive foreign transfers who don't know any better but any man who has his own woman should be coached and trained not to embarrass himself. Here's a style guide that any soccer legend should be very happy to chose from!

The 'Microphone'

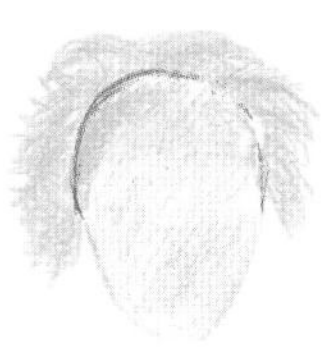

The 'Alice in Sunderland'

The Escaped Convict / The Bachelor

The Brazilian

Like aeroplanes, sometimes I get mental fatigue. There are lots of ways to combat this. I did try childhood regression therapy but it was over in minutes so I stand by *looking nice* as a sure fire way to ensure you're tressed for success!

Tit bits!

I think on principle that every woman should be happy with her breasts, though obviously that's not always possible if they are small or floppy. Use this handy reference chart to show your cosmetic surgeon which model you'd like to sport this season. Note – these are not to scale.

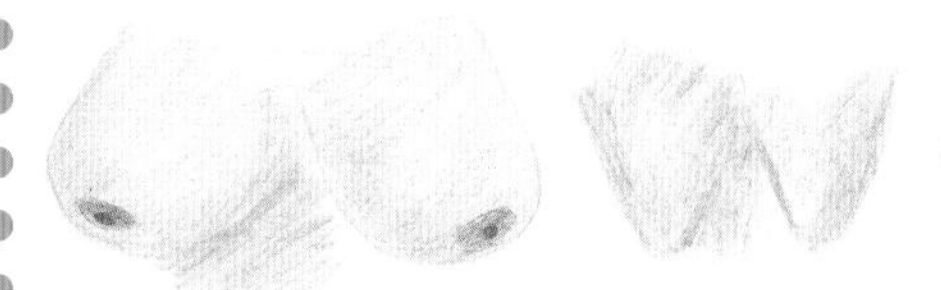

The Airbags

The Barbie

The Zeppelins

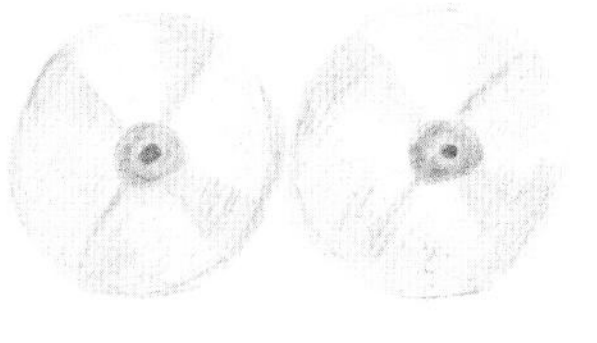

The Hot Cross Buns

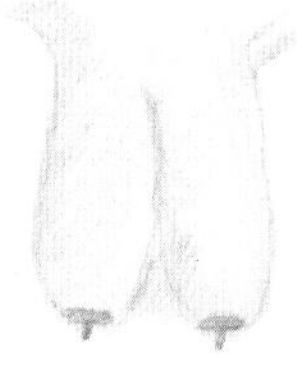

The Udders

The Alps

BEAUTY IS SKIN DEEP, WHICH IS YET ANOTHER GOOD ARGUMENT FOR EXFOLIATION.

Nail Grail!

Ask yourself! Can you can dial a phone without using your Mascara wand? Can you visit the littlest room without giving yourself a DIY smear? If the answer to these probing questions is yes then you need to stop nibbling those nails you little squirrel. Just say no to finger food and have some nail nouse!

A few suggestions:
The Ziggy Stardust
The Scythe
The Aide-Memoire
The Mystical Religious text
The Traffic Sign

A cautionary tale!

A word on product endorsements

Please do not endorse products that relate to any of the following social diseases: dandruff, haemorrhoids, skin disease, constipation., diarrhoea. Even if we all know better we will still assume you have those ailments and will think you are dirty.

You can't win them all...
If you're not smiling
you could be talking.
If you're not talking
– you could be
thinking of saying
something really
intelligent any
minute.
Keep your
mystique!
Don't worry
about treatments
that burn through
your delicate skin
like acid. That's
how you know
it's working.

HOW TO HAVE A CELEBRITY
PHOTOSHOOT

WHAT'S THE POINT IN HAVING A GRACIOUS LIVING ROOM IF NO ONE WHO DISSED YOU AT SCHOOL GETS TO SEE IT?

The time has come. Every moment of your life belongs to Kodak. You have enough marble in your downstairs powder room to shame Elgin. You have a husband with pneumatic thighs and your whole being appears to have been generously coated in lipgloss. What's more someone is willing to pay ten year's worth of school fees to confirm it. Take the money and add another guest wing.

Some Do's and Don'ts – a handy guide

DO Recline on your bed and throw back your head in mirth. Laughter is a constant companion at chez soccer. Show teeth.

DON'T Crease the bed linen. Show fillings.

DO Clasp a child in a maternal pose. Possibly in a conservatory. Go for informal and candid – consider being barefoot.

Above: Don't display food apart from fruit and bottled water. This would set a bad example.
Below: Show marble.

Below: Clasp a child in a maternal pose. Go for informal and candid.

Don't forget to tell your husband he has to be there.

DON'T Rule out leasing a neater child model from Sylvia Young.

DO Scatter a toy or two haphazardly on the floor of their bedroom. That's how much of a modern parent you are.

DON'T Be swayed by tantrums. Your child will get back the bear with one eye when the nice photographer's gone. You don't want people to think you bought your stuff at a jumble.

DO Flush your house of dirt with nuclear efficiency. A happy home is a sterilized one. The happiest home is one you only visit occasionally to take the cellophane off.

DON'T Display food apart from fruit and bottled water. This would set a bad example.

DO Show marble.

DON'T Show toiletries. The banned list includes Tampax, contraceptives, antiperspirant and anything bought from a store. Exceptions – if labels are posh and in foreign.

DO It is permissible to mention staff that've become part of the family.

DON'T Show them unless they are happily employed in the background and are out of focus.

DO Bring the outside in – have fresh flowers. For example the outside of Holland.

DON'T Forget to buy vases. You can't just bung them in a bucket.

DO If you are having a bad hair day compensate by doing something hilarious. Sing into your showerhead. Frolic under a sprinkler.

DON'T Have a bad hair day.

DO Take down children's scribblings from fridge. They are probably not very good. Alternatively – hang in lounge and mention you collect abstract art.

DON'T Display your collection of novelty erasers, porcelain pigs or Steps' albums.

DO Have a family portrait with two golden retrievers at your feet if you have children or something yappy and sporting a bow on its forehead if not.

DON'T Forget to tell your husband he has to be there.

DO Remember to say motherhood is heaven and that since having a child, they have become the sole and most rewarding focus of your life.

DON'T Forget to be there.

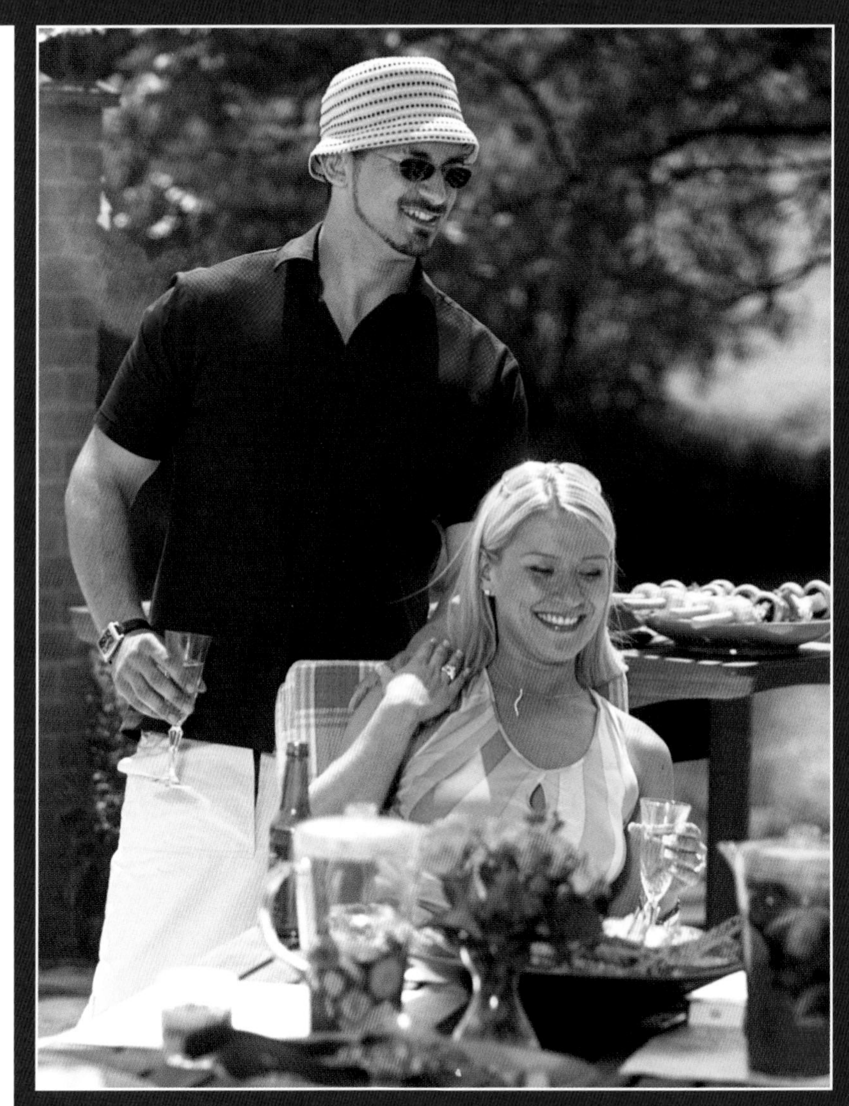

Above: Laughter is a constant companion at chez soccer. Show teeth.

puzzle$

Oh dear! Nurse Dunkley has got herself in a right tizzy and scrambled up these quite important words. Can you help her out?

M E D C I A L   E T H I S C

_ _ _ _ _ _ _ _   _ _ _ _ _ _ _

Can you help Chardonnay complete her crossword? If you get stuck she's provided a handy hint at the bottom of the page.

1 Across: What my name means.

1 Down: Oh. The same as above but the first bit of it. So do this bit first.

Spot the Ball gown for Donna. Please, because she can't find it and the post match party starts in ten minutes...

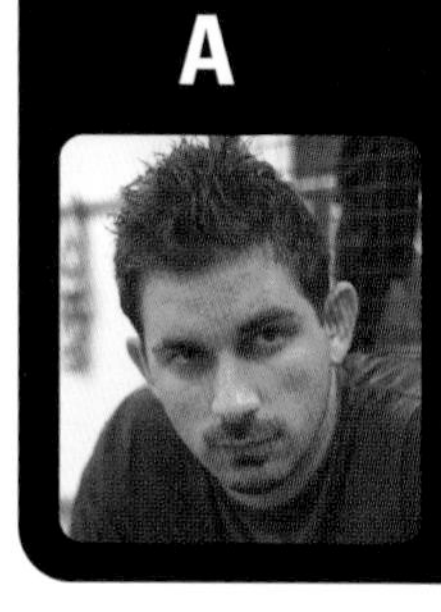

Answers on a postcard for this brainteaser! Tanya can't spot the difference. Of course, she's married to him – so how the hell you're meant to know...

A

B

Roll up a £5 note and follow the lines to help Freddie nab her dream date. To help we've given you a little clue...

Whatever's on Jason's mind? Join the dots to find out ... If you've got something more important to do – don't let us stop you – there's no real surprises here.

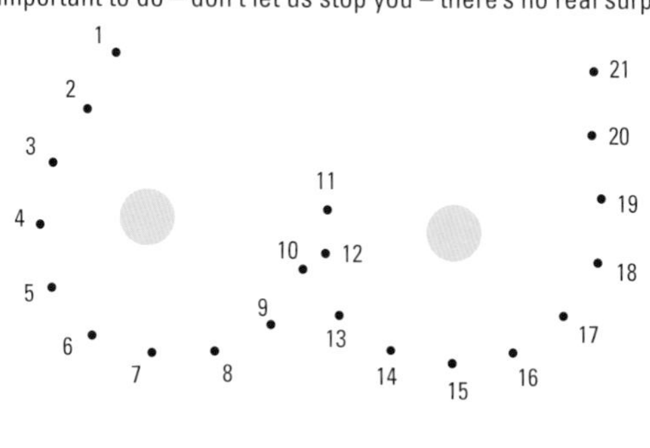

The answer is white wine. N.B. You don't have to write the answer upside down.

warming the bench: the reserve$

Tanya's Handy Guide to the Wind beneath Wings Reserves

Welcome to Football Town, population 20,000 hangers on. You've hit the big time so you can guarantee there'll be your nearest and dearest with their vice like grips on your coat tails. Obviously at the top of the food chain are the wives, followed by the footballers with slut sisters like Marie squirming amoeba-like at the bottom – that my friends is the Theory of Relativity!

These are the reserves on my bench – familiarize yourself with their habits and rituals. Learn from them and their mistakes. These people are like the press, you'll want to see them on your terms and never with your pants down.

Sunrise, sunset…

	Who?	Mating rituals
	This gentle creature loses whole seconds of sleep when forced to play the tough-talking, ball-breaking mogul. **Hazel** learnt everything she needed to know from watching Dynasty and has expressed her disappointment that for all her wealth and success she never got to have an erotic hay barn tussle with Krystal.	**When settling down for an evening of snuggling, the ever considerate Hazel likes to ensure her partner is so high only dogs can hear him/her…**
	All-round nice guy and general Fuhrer of Earl's Park. **Frank** believes in the sanctity of football and is keen to keep alive the old traditions. To this end, Frank is never seen at the training ground without a sheepskin coat and an ever-present threat that he might throw a medicine ball at an errant player's head.	**Frank tries to ensure he always has a pulse and involuntary muscle spasms when he's with a lucky lady.**
	While advised by the Earl's Park board not to wear lederhosen at club events **Stefan** continues to be steadfastly European in temperament. Rumours that Stefan was himself a world-class footballer in his day remain unconfirmed and there has been speculation that he was a tourist who got lucky.	**Rumours that Stefan has at one point had his own footballing wife persist despite his only ever being seen in the company of his right-hand man and a couple of balls.**
	A psychiatrist would point out that **Nurse Dunkley** suffers from low self-esteem and poor social skills. Most people would point out that she's mad, bad and dangerous to know when in a coma. In any language she is a strange and disturbed individual who takes the concept of total care to a new and somewhat intrusive territory.	**Nurse Dunkley likens her nursing methods to Nurse Gladys Emmanuel. This generally manifests itself as something 'intravenous'.**
	**Marie** Minshull is when all is said and done – a bit council. In fact for aspiring wives she is almost a blueprint in how not to do it. Wearing skirts so short they're almost Alice Bands, she commits the cardinal error of handing over the goods before closing the sale. She believes if you can't be good then don't fight it.	**Marie likes a bit of romance. She will always take her time to check for CCTV. And if it's a special someone has even been known to remove skirt first.**
	In theory the product of Chardonnay and Kyle's love. In practice the product of Nancy Needle and Tom Thread ably assisted by Midwife Maureen Media Misinformation.	**Candles, soft music and knit one, purl one.**

Natural habitat	Give them	Caution	Their price	Did you know?
Hazel doesn't have a home as she doesn't believe in sleep, and reckons if you snooze you lose. Occasionally she will take a power nap at The Ivy.	**A Bacchanal fest of wine, women and song.**	A woman in a man's world, Hazel has been called a bitch. This isn't strictly sexist as if she was a man she would be called a bitch and would probably spend her life picking glass out of her neck.	**20%, but Hazel is not only in it for the money. She also likes to feel important and –occasionally – her client's wife.**	In a recent study it was found that when asked who most scared them – apart from Ann Widdecombe – nine out of ten tinpot dictators cited Hazel Bailey.
Frank carries around a smoke machine to ensure that wherever he goes he can recreate that essence of cigar-laden, hard-talking men's club.	**Lucozade and grapes.**	Frank is a formidable enemy especially when conscious. He will stop at nothing to get what he wants and will talk very slowly to show how intimidating he is.	**Punitive damages and legal fees.**	Asking Frank if he wants one lump or two can send this latter-day Lazarus diving under a table with a cushion over his head. And me diving under it to hold the cushion tighter.
Keen to quell rumours that he had no legs Stefan finally got up from behind his very big, important desk to pace occasionally at the end of a very long boardroom table.	**Rumours are that what Stefan wants, what he really, really wants is something to actually put in the Earl's Park trophy room apart from a carpet.**	Stefan is rumoured to be the original Ice King, whose cool exterior ensures the press never see ruffled feathers, though he has compromised on them seeing his legs.	**Poland.**	Stefan began his career as an extra in The Sound of Music. Stefan was also the original goatherd Peter in the much beloved BBC children's import drama Heidi. The sound of a cuckoo clock will even now get him yodelling and herding. Stefan is the proud father of two children, Freddie and Doogie Hauser MD.
Nurse Dunkley lives, breathes and literally sleeps with her work. She feels most at home on the ward and favours floral patterns, particularly on privacy screens.	**A wide berth. If the ward's a rocking don't come a knocking for this medical minx!**	For a nurse, she is more likely to raise your blood pressure than lower it so you are probably better just not getting ill. It is also worth noting that bed jackets are extremely ageing on this Naughty Nurse.	**Your freedom may be at stake if you don't keep up payments.**	Janette Dunkley is currently considering changing her name by deed poll to the more informal Nurse Dunkley after a recent survey uncovered that no one really knew her first name – including her! Her debut single 'Anyone who Had a Heart (beat)' is scheduled for release early next spring apparently . . .
Marie is most likely to be found about a foot under Jason Turner, or trying to be.	**Five minutes and a toilet cubicle that locks.**	Wives!	**Bus fare home.**	Marie recommends Velcro instead of buttons and zippers though as she buys all of her clothes in the kids section of a common garden high street shop, there's no real loss if you tear them, the cheap tramp. And another thing . . . check her coat is shiny and her nose is wet – you don't know where the bitch has been.
Sofa.	**A wipe with a damp cloth and a quick spurt of Fabreze.**	Flammable.	**£350 a pair.**	The cushion has an envelope back which is really simple to make at home and makes it easily removable for washing. Did you also know that a tapestry inlay on the front is very classy?

Who?	Mating rituals	Natural habitat
Marguerite is a veteran wife. For her years of service as a wife to Frank, she has been awarded an OBE, MBE, PDQ, CSE, TBC and a knighthood.	**Historical.**	Marguerite is most often to be found in a manner to which she has become accustomed.
As a Scot **Archie** probably likes a good double malt and his own parliament. Unfortunately it isn't all caber tossing with this right-hand man. He's an extremely dodgy individual who deserves to have that caber dropped on his head. From altitude.	**Nothing that a blunt pair of scissors wouldn't fix, the dirty old cradle-snatching bastard.**	Archie likes to stand on the by-lines with his chin contemplatively cupped in his hand. Periodically he takes time out to blow his whistle.
Lara: wife, professional blonde, a giggle that could grate cheese.	**Dyes hair blonde and gets comfortable.**	Lara is blonde.
Ron is protector of the Earl's Park goal. His role is especially important considering the distractions of the other ten men he would otherwise rely on. Ron likes to be big, hence his nickname, Big Ron.	**Goes home.**	Ron is never more at home than when in a bar apart from when he is by a snooker table and apart from when he is actually at home.
Tel juggles two careers, part- time footballer and full-time laughing boy.	**Tel has a full and active sex life with international models and starlets in his head.**	Tel likes to be beside Ron and is never more at home than when in a bar apart from when he is by a snooker table and apart from when he is actually at home.
Darius is like an Oompa Loompa, only less creepy. He is only the size of a matchbox and can fit easily into the palm of the hand. He is Earl's Park's newest boy wonder and has recently mastered the art of potato printing at the club's crèche. For a newcomer to the game of love, I can confirm he's a quick learner.	**Eager. He once kissed me in a private place (behind the clubhouse).**	Trailing behind me like a wide eyed puppy. Bless him. Bless him particularly if Jason catches him.
Freddie is Stefan's Swiss finishing schooled daughter. She has a Tomb Raider-like quality and at weekends does Evel Kneivel-style bike jumps over buses. A girl with a troubled past, she's more tightly sprung than a very tightly strung coiled cobra though her collar line is usually more modest. Occasionally given to fits of self-marinating in a rock and roll alcoholic binge fest.	**Freddie is a pretty and intelligent girl. Unfortunately she does have a tendency to use knife play as a come on, which is not known for its aphrodisiacal qualities.**	**Freddie will pop up in the unlikeliest places so keep 'em peeled and don't turn your back on her, ever.**

Give them	Caution	Their price	Did you know?
Anything apart from the plug. Marguerite was startlingly keen to be energy-efficient with Frank's life support as she had to get to the post office before it closed.	Just when you think she'll stick around, she disappears leaving you in the unenviable position of having to sleep with Frank after all.	**Marguerite knew what price was right for her years of service. Unfortunately the IMF stepped in to cap the alimony.**	Marguerite is the sort of name that no matter how many times you write it you still have to think about the spelling. Marguerite confesses that for one brief moment she did consider coming back to Frank but blames this temporary insanity on the fact that a comatose Frank had about 300% more charm than the awake one, and that he always looked very nice in pyjamas.
Forementioned blunt scissors. A nice touch might be to add a little rust as well as a poor aim.	**Loch Nessie get out of the pool. There's a new monster in town.**	**Archie doesn't actually get paid by Earl's Park. He agreed to take the job on condition that he was given his own whistle.**	Archie likes nothing better than summoning a footballer from the showers to Stefan's office. Questioned on the subject he said, 'I like nothing better than summoning a footballer from the showers to Stefan's office.' He later admitted to wishing that just once he'd like to see Stefan use the two good legs God gave him and summon his own footballer.
Love and rainbows and trees made of candy.	Those suffering from hypoglycaemia should be aware that Lara is 100% saccharine to the extent that people sometimes stop in the street to lick her.	**Did I mention that Lara is blonde?**	**Lara once went to London Zoo to meet the Llama in the mistaken belief that she would find inner peace and Richard Gere.**
A pint, a slap on the back and first break.	Standing next to Big Ron will make most men feel like Ronnie Corbett. If Ronnie Corbett was shorter.	**A pint, a slap on the back and first break.**	Big Ron leads a clandestine double life. Unbeknownst even to his blonde wife Lara, he enjoys being sensitive and saving kittens from trees. He admits to having perpetuated rumours of his womanizing and boozing to deflect from his occasional excursions into town to watch the ballet. Ron has a signed photo of Wayne Sleep tucked in his shin pads for good luck.
Several more years of formal education shouldn't hurt.	There are not enough feet in the world for Tel to stuff in his mouth at inappropriate junctures.	**Tel prefers cash in £sterling but will accept a cheque with a guarantee card.**	Tel is so called because he is a huge fan of Terry Wogan. His birth name is in fact Prince Ludwig von Stradivarius but it wouldn't fit on the back of his shirt. Tel is most proud of his Blue Peter badge.
Love, respect for the boy he is and the man he'll become. And Baby Bio.	The little tyke will nip your ankles if you don't give respect to his woman. Luckily he will leave a bruise but has never broken the skin.	**Darius currently receives £10 a week for his paper round and frankly is glad of it.**	Darius was named after Darius Danesh of Pop Death Match Fame. His mother was a huge fan of the programme's presenters Ant and Dec and genetically combined the pair using advanced cloning techniques to produce Darius. Darius did not enjoy the spanking that Jason gave him, but unconfirmed rumours are that Tel did.
Your time. Preferably twenty-four hours a day of it. Freddie is a delicate flower beneath her bravado and needs tending and covering with fleece in winter.	Songs have been written about women like Freddie. Some of them quite good.	**Can't buy me love, it was once wisely spoken. However you can buy Freddie diamond engagement rings she has assured me.**	Freddie is pleased to report that anagrams of her name include 'a heifer udders', 'ar, defused heir' and the telling 'He desired Frau'. This excludes all of the possible anagrams that incorporated 'arse', though there's quite a few.

footballing pc for beginner$

Or 'long words to use at a dinner party but only when sitting down or your ears will bleed'

Football has had a lot of bad press with regards to being a bastion of sexism and archaic machismo piglike behaviour. Of course these were the bad old days when men wore sheepskin coats and ate pies in the presence of ladies. A new era has epoched and it's quite fashionable for men to be sensitive and in touch with their feminine (non-footballing) side. As long as they are married. If you get all girly when you are single you'll be given a very wide berth in the communal hot tub. Some purists still advocate electric shock treatment for single footballers who wear co-ordinated clothes. The same applies for girls. If you use this sort of language when not married to a man who spits as part of his living, then you will be dismissed as someone who should be wearing a boiler suit and growing vegetables in Hackney with the rest of your hirsute friends.

But if you are married – then here are some long words you can use to show how modern and enlightened you are. fw

Peter and the wolves

Footballers...
She is not skirt – she is a dromedarily attributed contributor.
She is not a crap cook – she is restaurant compatible.
She doesn't look like a graduate of Clown College – she is elegance intolerant.
She is not trying to replicate Fort Knox in Surrey – she is metallically inundated.
She's not a lard arse – she is a metabolic underachiever.
She doesn't nag you like an old woman – she is platitude restrained.
She's not a cheap slut – she's horizontally accessible.
She is not too skinny – she's skeletally distinguished.
She doesn't reek like a department store – she's fragrance dependent.
She does not have too much slap on – she has simply reached decorative saturation.
Wives...
He does not have a beer belly – he's invested in a portable grain storage facility.
He is not a Godawful dancer – he is chiropodistically otherwise engaged.
He's not a baldy – he's follically casual.
He is not a dirty old man – he venerates generationally differential mergers.
He's not a total dickhead – he's trouser-cranial inverted.
He's not an evolutionary throwback – he has ape empathy.
He's not perving – he's experiencing a meditative erotic resourcefulness.
He's not a dirty love cheat – he's carnally philanthropic.

$omething for the weekend

Match days and keeping up with the Pascoes

'We pay our money, we make our choices.' Someone wise once said that. Not wise enough to actually explain themselves properly but that's what you get with wise people … cleverness. What does this mean for wives? Well it may mean that every job has its shit side – and for the new wife on the block – it is being yelled at by 30,000 hooligans every Saturday afternoon who can make the word 'slag' last fourteen syllables.

Every queen has her court and yours is the Theatre of Dreams, the Stadium of Light and the Friends Provident St Mary's Stadium, Southampton. The plebs will fill the stands with their '*flasks*' and their godforsaken '*meat pies*' but you – you shall like a goddess be, shining in the glamorous carpet-tiled splendour of the executive box. So what do you need to know about your big day out? Well, first the shining goddess bit will partly be due to the amount of static generated between the EC carpet tile stock pile and all those manmade fibres you're sporting. The rest in all honesty you'll find out soon enough as you can kiss goodbye to your Saturdays for the next ten years.

What should I wear?

Well, try to include clothing in what you wear – but not too much of it. Try to take price tag as a guide if you are not sure and leave it dangling out of the back if it is one of the many designer dresses that looks like something Oxfam spat out. Please do make the effort to do your research and save everyone's blushes by not turning up to a game in the opposition's colours. This is particularly relevant if your husband is playing Blackburn. They of course have a perfectly serviceable kit but you would look like a jockey. The key elements are to wear little enough to make your husband's teammates jealous but enough to stop them encouraging you to meet them in the changing rooms post match and sans knickers. Your main role is to be decorative, like a bauble.

Your main role is to be decorative, like a bauble

What should I talk about?

Well, not football, obviously, as you are a girl and barely know what shaped bat they use. Try to incorporate talking about your children – that's always a safe, dull topic. When you've exhausted that topic try talking about other people's children. If conversation then dries up you may discuss handbags and the relative merits thereof.

It is almost never acceptable to talk about another teammate's flagging career unless you think you can be subtle enough to pull it off or if there is some currency to be had with any management who may be in earshot.

What is everyone else talking about?

The menfolk will gather to have a proverbial brandy and cigar to talk about menfolk things. Try not to hover. Your presence will be distracting and will bring shame to your mate. The management will be polite but will not wish to exchange more than pleasantries with you and will likely see through any desperate efforts on your part to gauge the status of your husband's new contract.

Don't stray too near the terraces. Aside from the inevitable lewd comments you'll receive, they smell of hotdogs and pee-pee

Don't show up
with a meat pie
and a flask of
Bovril. You will
be catered for.
Do however
bring lipstick.

Rather than getting drawn into any conversations that are too complicated for you, maybe ask the management about their children.

What is terrace talk?

Of course don't actually stray too near the terraces. Aside from the inevitable lewd comments you'll receive, they smell of hotdogs and pee-pee. In the old days, royalty used to parade among the unwashed. Thank God it's the twenty-first century and you don't have to do anything so silly. If you are interested in 'terrace talk' for anthropological reasons – it is characterized as bawdy, loud and expressed in its own language of primordial grunts and interpretative hand gestures. But mainly it smells of pee-pee.

Do I need to bring anything?

Don't show up with a meat pie and a flask of Bovril. You will be catered for. Do however bring lipstick. It will give you a distraction if someone asks you a difficult question such as 'did you enjoy the game?'

In case I hear that question should I watch the game?

Don't be silly.

Are there any other ways I could bring shame upon myself and my family that would result in an early transfer and social exclusion?

Do not laugh at, let alone make any of the following 'jokes'. They are wrong, evil and dirty and not for a polite lady's ears. You may hear them. Turn your head and apply some more lipstick.

Q: What is the difference between Earl's Park and the Bermuda triangle?
A: The Bermuda triangle has three points.

Q: What's the difference between Jason and Earl's Park?
A: None – they both have no point.

Q: What is the difference between Tanya with £50 and Jason?
A: Tanya can score.

Q: Why are men from Earl's Park the best lovers?
A: They are on top for ninety minutes and still come second!

When should I leave and how long will the experience take?

Each match lasts ninety minutes which is approximately an hour and a half. There is also the 'half-time' period that lasts another fifteen minutes and should give adequate time to reapply enough lipstick to guarantee your mouth entering a room before you do. At time of going to press there is little established precedent to change outfits at 'half time' as maybe one would if presenting Eurovision – but try to keep abreast of developments. There is also about three hours of post–match drinking and menfolk time but you should still get home in time for tea and *Millionaire*. So aim to arrive about four dolly steps behind your husband and leave in the same manner. He will let you know when he is ready to leave by telling you to get your coat. It is a further argument for having an original name (see the 'Your Footballer's Wife Name' chapter) as you all look alike and the only way he'll be able to distinguish you from the herd and find which one's his, is by calling your name and seeing who moves to get their coat.

captain's wife's log

Monday
Chardonnay's up the duff. Safe to say the baby will be beautiful with a great left foot and in no immediate danger of an A Level.

To do: book manicure for Thursday.

Tuesday
Met up with Frank to do a bit more for the 'Save Jason Turner's Career Campaign'. Like I haven't already given. I would find it practically implausible that I – Tanya Turner of sound mind and firm body – would have deigned to have an affair with Frank. It truly belies the arrogance of man that he has no such reservations. Still, you're always seeing beautiful young women with Attila the Huns these days aren't you. If I really had spent a year with Frank gasping for breath in my bed and calling my name it would only have meant that there was a pillow I hadn't held down long enough.

To do: Ensure that in my next life I come back as a man – it's the good life.

Wednesday
Frank has proved himself to be some use beyond being like a monster in a horror film that just won't die. He gave me the number to a new football agent called Hazel Bailey who he's promised will kick Jason into shape – so I don't have to.

Of course Jason had initial reservations based on rational concerns that Hazel by virtue of having breasts was a woman. Presumably breasts are inadequate ballast to sit at a board room table and hash out a contract on his behalf. Or perhaps it's because men work these things out by mud wrestling or something. His subsequent meeting with her seemed to convince him though. He's smiling a lot more but has jumped seven times at his own shadow. She sounds like a most formidable lady.

Thursday
Jason is eating only lettuce and rice cakes as per Hazel's instructions. He looks too in awe/terror of her to complain too loudly. It's about time he treated his body as a temple rather than as a whore and beer Hoover. His blood must have the consistency of tarmac.

Friday
I truly am amazed. Jason continues to get physical. Normally the only way to get Jason to do sit ups is to put a beer between his toes.

With him determined to stay at home and exercise – I too am held captive by his need for support. Time passes slowly here.

Saturday
It's a great day for undeserving bastards everywhere thanks to Jason – their poster boy. Hazel comes

round and we have an impromptu pool party to listen to Earl's Park's first game minus Jason. Ian delivers a stinker and promptly gets sent off in his first big game. Before we've barely had a snifter of the second bottle of bubbly Hazel has made a top notch deal with Frank to get Jason out from under my feet and back earning money with his.

The only compromise is that Jason has to play kiss and make up with Sal. Though even he has the sense to realize that much money is worth choking on some pride for.

Sunday
Start planning some serious spending now I know we're solvent again.

Monday
Start doing some serious spending now I know we're solvent again.

Tuesday
Continue doing some serious spending now I know we're solvent again.

Wednesday
There's almost nothing left for me to buy. I've never felt so alive.

Thursday
Nope. I was wrong. Can't stop, must shop...

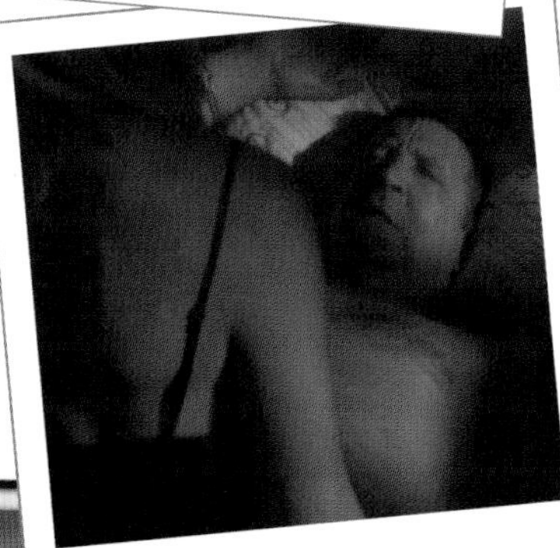

Friday
Well, the bubble had to burst some time. Now that he's got Jason back on the team, Frank feels that I owe him big. Now that his wretched wife has escaped back to eke out her days on his enormous alimony – the marital bed is free for me to fill it again for the first time.

Awful, gut-wrenching realization that I may have to get under Frank. I'll probably end up looking like one of those cartoon characters that's been flattened by a steamroller.

Saturday
I feel a little like prisoners must do when the bag has been put over their head and they've been backed up against a wall. My fate awaits me. I must have a chat with Chardonnay to see if there's any sort of that Eastern meditation bumf she's into that could help me faze it out.

Sunday
Well, Chardonnay didn't come up with the goods but it's fair to say it was an out of body experience. I'd run out of excuses, had my last meal and had to stand up and be counted, knowing full well that Jason must never find out about it and wouldn't appreciate my sacrifice if he did.

My precious Frank cherry. Gone. Gone I tell you...

Was concentrating on not hurling when suddenly I found myself literally being hurled about 20 feet off Frank, like I was a caber toss. Almost feel aggrieved that he could have an out-of-body experience and mistake my body for Nurse Numpty.

Jesus. That means his memory is coming back...

baby boomer$

Or 'Mommie Dearest – the new black?'

Perhaps one of the most enduring must-have accessories is a child or – if adequately spaced out to give your stomach muscles time to recover – children. Womb work is particularly au courant right now and is the one way you can get spherical and stay chic. Motherhood is one of the most important jobs in the world and

'Pregnancy might suit you, but I'd blow up like Vanessa Feltz!' ***Tanya Turner***

potentially the crappest paid, but look upon children as God's incentive to resist slaughtering your husband. Besides, being parental plays really well in the tabloids, particularly if you are losing your looks.

Of course it's important to remember a child is for life not just career dips. It's been scientifically proven that celebrity offspring will disappear off the media radar once they've outgrown the Prada Brats range and ceased to be cute. This is nature's way of saying you've probably ceased to be cute as well. In fact, you might consider leasing one and just upgrading it every 10,000 pram miles.

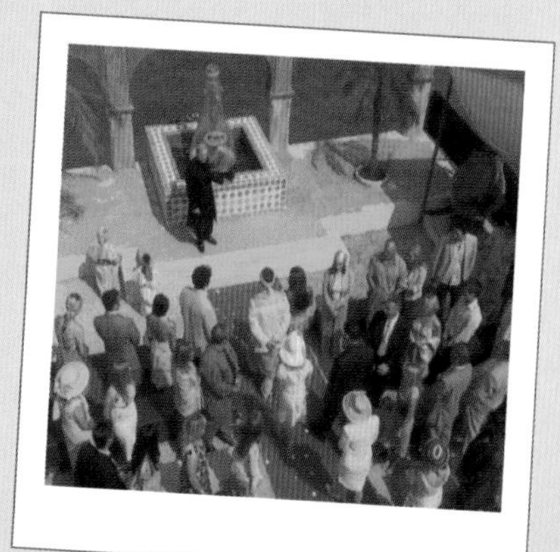

So you've decided to breed – Conception

Virgin birth. Not big on originality. Note: It doesn't strictly qualify just by employing Darius as the father.
Conception rituals. Tradition rituals such as belly dancing put too much emphasis on bellies and you'll be making more than enough sacrifices without that. Nowadays there are CD ROMs that talk you through your options but in reality just light some incense and do the dance from *Tales of the Unexpected* which looks pretty ethnic by anyone's standards.
The Whodunit. One fun way to get pregnant is to play 'Haven't got a Cluedo who the father is'. You and your husband could unilaterally decide that you will have a secret affair with one of his teammates to give your baby a chance of better ears than your husband could ever give. Roll the dice and see what happens. Could it be the Spanish striker in the dining room or the Uruguayan sweeper in the ballroom with his lead piping?

Please note – if you choose this route try to make the outcome plausible. If your husband is from Bolton suspicions may be raised if your baby pops out speaking Italian.
It's easier by tube. Science has brought undeniable benefits to modern living including running machines and Retinol A for the skin. But for the modern miss perhaps those speccy men have brought the world something else apart from sci-fi conventions – new ways to make babies. Certain developments with gene technology now allows you to select a baby that can wear boot cut, flare or twisted dirty denim and thus gift that child with the inestimable ability to match any fashion development.
Traditional methods. I suppose you could – but it's not really getting into the spirit of things.

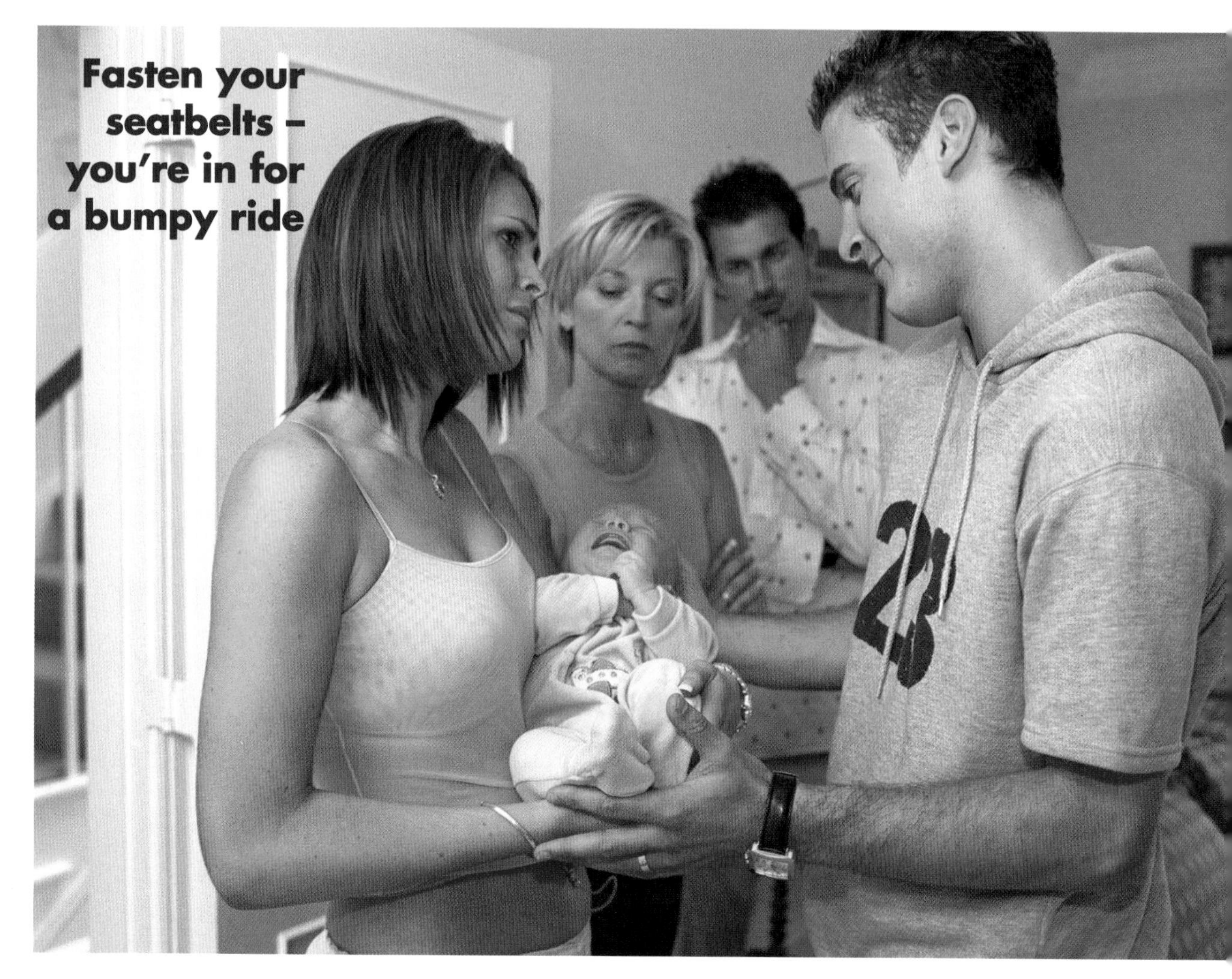

So you've decided to breed – Deception

Two key words really. *Cushion* and *jumper*. You also will need a mother-in-law, a pig teammate and a snooker table for the icky bit.

So you've decided not to breed

Good for you. Have a strong drink and make do with stroking your shiatsu.

So you've decided to breed – a note on with whom am I having the pleasure

Everybody out of the gene pool! You can't pick and mix your child-to-be's genes so contrary to popular opinion being intimate with multiple men will not provide you with a happy combination of each. If you are going to work your way round the team like a verruca your primary motivation must be fun. It's very stylish right now to have a child by your husband but in the time it has taken for this book to be published fashion might have changed so please consult the latest publications on the subject such as *Heat*.

So you've decided to breed – and can't be dissuaded despite every sane notion to the contrary and gross irresponsibility in bringing a child into this world of despair and apocalyptic awfulness

Fasten your seatbelts you're in for a bumpy ride.

The Pregnancy

You get fat.

The Delivery

The birth bit of having a baby can be a confusing affair. For the new mum it's perhaps disconcerting to enter a pre-

Children's parties are not only a way to spend a lot of money, but to spend a lot of money *in front of your friends.* Hire EuroDisney. Hell, why not hire Europe.

natal training regime more stringent than your husband has for a cup run. You may be thinking – gosh – nine months of squatting in a community centre every Wednesday evening – just to prepare for a few hours of breathing. Hell – you may say – I mastered breathing years ago, I could pant for Britain. Where's the training for a lifetime of childcare? Don't worry about this. No training could fully prepare you and none is offered. It's also worth pointing out that birth can smart a bit.

Obviously you will elect for a private, celebrity hospital for junior's debut. Not only will you not have to share the miracle of life with eight hacking pensioners but the nurses are less likely to sell the news of anything confidential you happen to have pierced. If they've previously had their Marigolds up Madonna there will be little you can do to surprise them. Remember natural birth is for people who're giving birth somewhere it's better to stay lucid enough to stop someone nicking off with your purse. You are not in that unhappy position so take whatever drugs are offered be it Agent Orange or Junior Aspro. Of course some celebrities with important commitments like a Smash Hits Tour are opting to pre-book a C-Section. If you decide upon this route, allow a few hours as this normally takes longer than a manicure.

Maternal Instinct Alert!
Don't worry. While cats can have litters of up to 300 kittens at any given birth you are statistically unlikely to top six so tell your sister she can keep her guest room!

Once in hospital/birthing asylum, various kind but buxom women will plump pillows and wear sensible shoes around you so you may be disorientated. Therefore we've given you a wife/medical dictionary of the key jargon you may hear as you slip in and out of consciousness.

- *Confinement:* The nurse will not let you go to any parties until the baby is fully out
- *Caesarean section*: A portion of salad with garlic vinaigrette and croutons
- *Delivery:* Harrods have tipped up with the birthing hamper
- *Labour:* We're not sure. We think it means work or something
- *Breech:* Jodhpurs
- *Gestation:* A dirty thing that makes you go blind
- *Trimester:* A sophisticated running machine

Don't allow your husband to attend the birth.

Facing your public

Congratulations, you're avec enfant and all without smudging your mascara. Please note that practically no hospitals operate a returns policy. If you are disappointed with the product of your labours try to remember that children are often born with no hair and that bonnets are freely available to avoid embarrassing explanations. Also please be assured you won't have to spend the rest of your life bound to your child like an astronaut to the mothership because the cord will be painlessly cut with a pair of nail scissors. Most private hospitals come equipped with underground escape routes for the recently surgically enhanced or pregnantly challenged. Stage your press call exit a couple of weeks after the actual birth, giving you ample time to shed those corpulent folds. If you do have to venture out in the meantime pop the tot in one of those marsupial papooses and hey presto – any convex is camouflaged.

Maternal Instinct Alert!
Breast feeding is akin to putting your nipples in a pencil sharpener.

Please be aware that if you have a boy you will be asked by everyone if you are growing your own football team. If you have a girl, you will be asked by everyone if you are disappointed about not growing your own football team. This will become tiresome. It's the enchantment of human interaction like this that forces some people to turn their backs on polite society and drink petrol from paper bags.

'Post-natal depression, boobs down to your knees... some blokes never go near you again once they see you giving birth, it freaks them out.'
Chardonnay Lane-Pascoe

You can't just call it Baldy

This more than any other is an opportunity to show once and for all just how classy you really are. There are many wonderful names to bequeath to your child. Perhaps the most important consideration should be given to girls. Their name will have to work with any future husband or until they change it for a glamour shoot at 18, so make it flexible and adaptable. Advice: Alliteration always achieves attractiveness (Tanya Turner, Marilyn Monroe, Daffy Duck).

Some suggestions include:

- Where baby was conceived. Please exercise discretion.

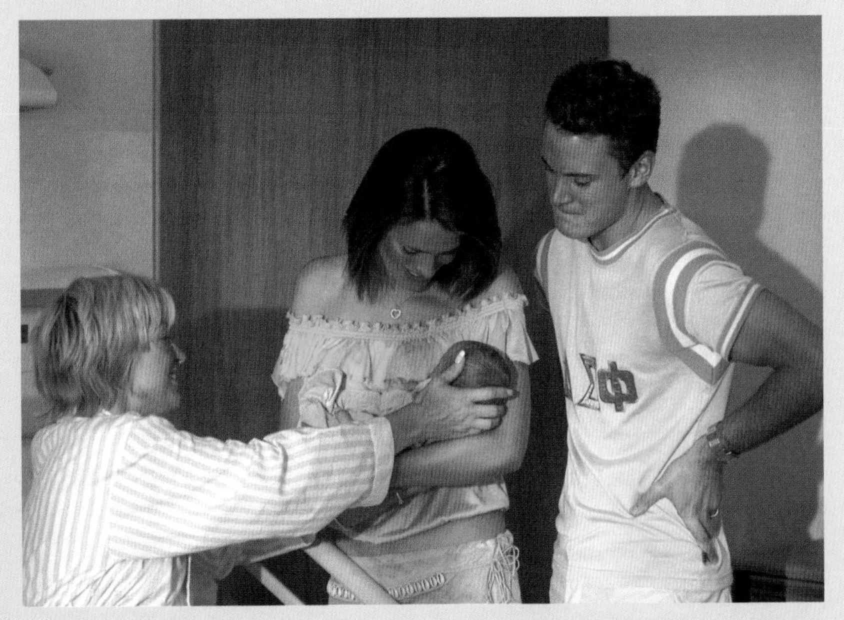

Please note that practically no hospitals operate a returns policy.

No child wants to be saddled with the forename Arsenal as happened tragically with Mr Wenger, thanks to a dyslexic registrar.

- The name of whoever won *Pop Idol* that year.
- Anything French. It doesn't matter what. Even Mange Tout or Bon Pantalon is sexy.
- If in doubt pick a name that is unquestionably classy like Oprah, Michelangelo or Clark Kent.

Afterbirth

Of course in the past, debutantes used to be introduced to polite society at eighteen. Now you're still wiping off the afterbirth. Introducing tiny tears to its press has to be executed with military precision and perfect timing. Is there a war or an election raging? Cross your legs. It's that or you'll be propping up page 27 underneath the satellite listings. One wife had – and you are not going to believe this – her child the day of the Oscars. Naturally the courts upheld *Hello!* Magazine's injunction and made her put it back in until a slow news day in August. Planning people, planning!

There's a lot of old hooey about the positive effects of breastfeeding. As it is, by the time your child is old enough to sue you for putting it on the bottle, you'll probably be a landlady at your husband's pub and on the bottle yourself. Getting out your mammaries gratis will severely limit your ability to charge for it later and anyway they'll end up limp and swinging around like a couple of hazelnuts in a pair of socks.

So you have your bundle of joy – where do you put it? Well, obviously your natural instincts would be to put it in a shoe box and bring it in when it rains but now you have money and the East Wing going spare so it's time to build a nursery. Think what little one needs. Obviously he won't want to share his toilette so plan for an en suite. Carol Smillie has introduced us to theming for a reason – and at great personal effort as she seems to be perennially pregnant. It doesn't matter what theme you use, Kurdish and Turkish Circus, Tiny, Little Creatures of the Enchanted Forest, just remember

The first thing you'll want to do is get your child a replica kit and an endorsement deal.

the golden rule. Check how much it would cost to buy a three-bedroom terrace in the town you grew up in, double it and spend that. Sometimes it's hard to find ways to spend that sort of cash but no one ever said being a Footballer's Wife was going to be easy.

The long haul

A few small notes on the bit after the postnatal stage and the bit before they move out...

- Send your children to private school so they don't ever have to associate with anyone like you. Then they can be the only children whose father's name is on the back of his shirt rather than in *Who's Who*. In fact the object is to educate your children in a manner that ensures they are so over-gentrified they will deny all knowledge of your existence and not notify you when they have a school sports day. Money well spent.
- Carrying photos of kids in your wallet is so last century. Tattoo them on your ankle instead.
- View them as potential clothes horses for your clothing ranges.
- Please remind your husband to say in any interview that the birth of his first child was more spectacular than winning the cup. If he hasn't won a cup yet ensure the father of your second child has.
- Children tend to be sticky little lunatics. Approach them with tweezers and wet wipes or that Versace will be gone for a Burton.
- Concentrating your affections and attention at a child is an excellent way to ignore your husband.
- Children's parties are not only a way to spend a lot of money but to spend a lot of money in front of your friends. Hire Euro Disney. Hell, hire Europe.

Maternal Instinct Alert!

Think! What would the Queen Mother, Victoria Beckham do in any given circumstance? And just do that.

Teddycam... menace?

Case Study – our kids

Paddy

Paddy had a curious start to the world and one that could possibly only be explained with the use of flipchart. Suffice to say our prayers are with him. His parents (all of them) decided to issue a press release concerning his medical condition: he was born with the sexual organs of both genders – i.e. a penis and a brain.

Jason, the birth father was ashamed of this, which is ironic when one accounts for the fact that Paddy is marvellously human, overcoming Jason's contribution to the genetic pot which was something approaching simian. His grandmother is his mother and his father is his brother, making Paddy something like his own grandpa. For all these issues perhaps young Paddy faces none greater than Teddy Cam, a twenty-four-hour surveillance device protruding from an otherwise innocent bear. Paddy has discovered this is a serious prohibition on the party lifestyle any wealthy toddler expects. On the plus side there seems no limit on the milk rations, thanks to Grandma lactating more than the Laughing Cow.

The tromp l'oeil baby

One of life's fighters. The cushion employed for nine months was cruelly dropped quicker than a fake hot bun from a fake hot oven. A spokesman from Courts has issued the following statement:

My client (whose identity has been protected) is currently filing a nuisance law suit citing emotional damage and a red wine stain. It wanted me to convey his regret at the turn of events and said 'When will you people learn. Fake pregnancy is not a game. Not a game I tell you!'

The Walmsleys' brood

Holly Walmsley at the grand age of eight was skipping along, content in the knowledge she was the one and only. As Chesney Hawkes had already so poignantly proved – this was not necessarily the sunniest of situations and, true to form, her parents introduced her to the older brother she never knew she had.

Daniel, the prodigal son, was reunited with his family, un-reunited, reunited and subsequently reunited again this time on a sort of amateur, part-time basis. Ian had originally resisted meeting up with the son they had given up for adoption – presumably because fighting a custody battle would interfere with his ability to make a public spectacle of himself in a pants-down, lap-dancers-up exposé. Being a tug-of-love child is never easy but never more so than

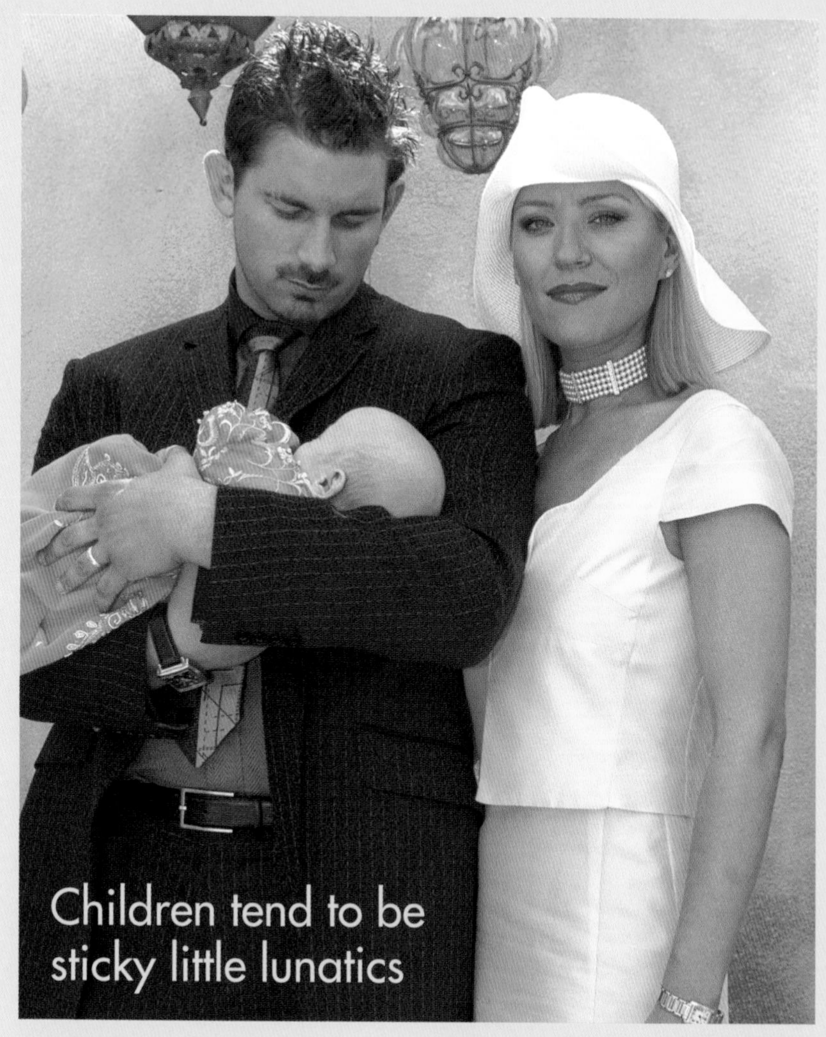

when your new family give you a magazine shoot when all you really wanted was a games console.

Holly was then kidnapped by the pool man who appeared to think that being rich and beautiful was adequate enough reason to make a family unhappy – unaware that intervention in such circumstances is not required. Holly was returned some time later, having been forced to subsist for several months watching daytime television in a caravan park only to find her mother was running off with 'Uncle' Sal the Italian stallion.

'He wants to have a kid? Not in my oven. . . anything he spawns will come out with four trotters!'
Tanya Turner

All of the above and more has ensured that if the Walmsley's children ever enter Repressed Memory therapy – they'll be the only clients encouraged to actually increase their repressing.

Chez Turner

Tanya when questioned on the subject perhaps unsurprisingly insisted she had no plans to have any more children besides her husband Jason.

Footballers' Past Wives: The Earl's Park Wife Trials

Thanks to the recent discovery of some crusty yellowing documents somewhere, we have learnt that in less modern times being a deficient Footballer's Wife was not just punishable by divorce but by other cruel and public tortures. What difference to today you may ask? Well, pull up a Phillip Stark chair and listen to the terrible tale of Goody Walmsley.

Perpetuity records the trial of the aforementioned wife who was accused of failing her duties as prescribed by popular stereotyping. Thank God those dark days are gone, we may say.

Here's the actual, real times-of-yore extract from the trial, tidied up a bit because they spelt stuff funny then and wrote S's like F's.

The honour'd Judge and Bench 'The famous referee with thee bald head that looks like Uncle Fester' sitting in Judicature in Earl's Park humbly sheweth the following petition:

Uncle Fester: *'What say you Mistress Walmsley? Are you guilty of perpetrating divers acts against Football Wifecraft, of wither you are suspected, on this our Lord's day in approximately puritanical times?'*

Mistress Walmsley: *'No Sire, I say before our Lord Goran Ericsson, before whom I stand, that these are wyked lies and, while I have not watched Sky Sports, I have been attendant at four home fixtures including one international.'*

Those Wenches being present remained standing as if strangely afflicted by a rare and tragik malady called sobriety. Mistress Lane, acting as if compelled by the Devil, started crying that she had been bound by Goody Walmsley to buy her knickers from British Home Stores on merit of no one being able to tell the difference and it being such good value. At this, Goody Turner proclaimed that Goody Walmsley had shamelessly not danced at a night fixture at Nottingham Forest and was chastely clothed throughout.

Uncle Fester: *'Prithee, did Goody Turner say not that you have no familiar? All righteous wives would have such a companion. What say you to this series of double negatives?'*

Mistress Walmsley: *'Beg pardon sire but for some time I have in fact been having a bit of extra-curricular with the foreign transfer with whom I am now moste familiar. Is there one among you who could claim this to be other than faithful to the expectations levelled at my footballing marriage?'*

Mr Ian Walmsley thereupon began to juggle a hog's bladder with his hands as though forgetful of how to kick or head it. The wenches descended into wracking sobs that did make their mascara run rendering their faces blotchy before their publyc. Another held aloft a George at Asda carrier bag and did spake that she was going upon adjournment to take to her home on a bus. Whereupon the courtroom gasped and several ladies were removed from the court exclaiming that Goody Walmsley was bidding them eat lard.

> **Goody Walmsley was bidding them eat lard**

Uncle Fester: *'As Goody Walmsley spake her defence when I asked for a testimonial instead of buying a new frock for a high profile charity game for a knackered footballer – I am inclined to question her commytment to Footballers' Wifecraft. I submit she be bade to take thee cruel and publyc tests to settle thee matter.'*

Goody Walmsley was then subjected to a series of cruel and unusual tests to ascertain the validity of her claims to a season ticket in the executive box.

Goody Turner proclaimed that Goody Walmsley had shamelessly not danced at a night fixture at Nottingham Forest and was chastely clothed throughout

Calls by purists to reinstate some of these traditions and purge the game of the undeserving have been cited as 'silly' but only by a slim majority.

Thee Olden Footballer's Wife Tests

The Dunking Stool: Goody Walmsley was tithed to a giant spoon and dunked in a barrel of water. If she could tell whether it was Evian she would be approved of her status. Sadly history records that Goody Walmsley could not even tell if it was sparkling or still.*

The Stocks: The second trial faced by Goody Walmsley was to be placed in the stocks before a battery of tabloid sketch artists. Again, alas she was to be found wanting. With a captive audience of parchment paparazzi not only did she not smile with an unrelentingly brave face but did not ask to reapply her lipstick before internment.

The Sink or Swim: In the most popular of the archaic rituals, she was thrown unceremoniously into the post-match communal bath. A true Footballers' Wife would obviously float for two reasons.

It is at this point that our study tragically concludes. Had Goody Walmsley survived she would have been vindicated by the fourth and final test which saw every female who Mr Walmsley said meant nothing to him being investigated to see if their maidenhood was intact. Not one passed. His indiscretions were proved to cover the entirety of his married life and were known about by his wife in their sordid entirety. Her weary acceptance demonstrated that she did indeed posthumously deserve not only her claim to the title of Footballer's Wife but possibly also a sainthood.

Her poignant last words were recorded and arguably remain just as relevant in their wisdom to contemporary wives. 'Make sure you pick the kids up from school and cancel my manicure appointment.' RIP Goody Walmsley… RIP.

** A curious addendum to this record attests to Goody Turner actually demanding to be given the Dunking Stool test herself on the condition of being dipped into champagne, thus reinforcing her lifetime tenure as not only a Footballer's but the Captain's Wife.*

Housekeeping is a much overlooked skill, for which I think I blame feminism.

hou$ekeeping a world of wonder

The other wives told me that I mutually agreed to keep my contribution to this guide modest and unobtrusive so as not to give the wrong impression to aspiring wives. It's just typical of them to be thoughtful, even though they have every other page in the book to worry about. Those girls, they just give and give!

We decided that I could have my very own page to talk about things that are important to me as a Footballer's Wife (as long as I didn't try to pretend I knew about fashion).

So I've decided to share some housekeeping tips. Housekeeping is a much overlooked skill, for which I think I blame feminism. Of course there are no hard and fast rules – you spell potato and I spell potatoe after all, but if you look after the pennies the hundreds of thousands look after themselves.

So here's some bright ideas to help keep your soccer ship in shape. (The exclamation marks were my idea – I think they add a certain enthusiasm – don't you?!)

If the strap snaps on your bag don't fret. That's what you have a platinum card for! – *Chardonnay* xxx☻xxx

Wondering what to do with all those left over chocolate bars when you've used the silver foil? Me too! – *Tanya*

Want to know how to get hold of seven dwarves for an on again/off again wedding at short notice? Get six and I'll stump up Jason for Dopey! – Jackie

Need to pay £10,000 to a blackmailer? Save money by tearing down curtains to make a dress?! – *Donna*

You can fool some of the people all of the time, and all of the people some of the time, and the press most of the time as long as you've got a good enough publicist! – *Tanya*

Don't show more skin than manners! – *Donna*

Tired of seeing your man in scandal after scandal in the tabloids? Make sure the next time he wants some column inches it's in the obituary section! – *Tanya*

Cupboard full of last season's dresses? Wear the long ones around the house so you don't have to polish your floors and Jackie can't tell you off for not doing enough housework! – Chardonnay xxx☻xxx

If you want to liven things up by telling a joke, make sure you explain it with pictures and talk slowly to ensure Chardonnay isn't left out! – Jackie

Tired from your work out at the gym? Haven't eaten enough to walk upstairs? Live with an old person (a mother-in-law in her forties should do) buy a stairlift! – *Chardonnay* xxx☻xxx

If at first you don't succeed, redefine success. Or keep your cheque book handy! – *Tanya*

Don't hate me because I'm beautiful! – *Chardonnay* xxx☻xxx

No job is so simple that it can't be cocked up by Jason! – *Tanya*

Everything is possible except skiing through revolving doors! – *Chardonnay* xxx☻xxx

Your husband won't notice – dress to impress someone else's! – Tanya

I find if I need to go in denial – dusting helps! – *Donna*

tipple$

From the never knowingly underused bar of The Turners…
To be a footballer's wife, drink like a footballer's wife.
But in moderation please. You need to keep your looks.

CHARDONNAY
Kir Royale

- 2 dashes crème de cassis
- chilled champagne
- umbrella
- cherry
- crazy straws

Put crème de cassis in extravagantly elaborate glass and top with champagne, umbrella, cherry and crazy straws. Sip demurely in small quantities and look fabulous.

TANYA
Cocaine Lady

- ½ oz. White Rum
- ½ oz. Vodka
- ½ oz. Kahlua
- 1 oz. Irish Cream
- 1 oz. Light Cream
- 1 oz. Cola

Shake with ice and strain over ice. Float 1 ounce of cola on top. Sit in darkened room, sipping bitterly until errant husband returns.

HAZEL
Ruby Shy

- 1 part Malibu
- 1 part blackcurrant cordial
- ice cubes
- lemonade
- slice of coconut
- grated coconut

Blow that. Just buy in a couple of crates of something fizzy with a price tag.

MARIE
Virgin Marie

- 4 parts tomato juice
- 1/2 part lemon juice
- 2 dashes Worcestershire Sauce
- 1 dash Tabasco Sauce
- Stick of cucumber
- Celery salt and lemon wedge for frosting

This drink doesn't actually exist and even if it did would be foolhardy effort when Marie would make do with sucking the lager off an old beer mat.

SALVATORE

Fancy Free

- **1½ oz rye**
- **2 dashes of maraschino**
- **dash of orange bitters**
- **dash of angostura bitters**
- **and a whole dollop of love**

Sensuously dip your rim into lemon juice and powdered sugar. Passionately shake the mix with ice cubes and sensitively pour with love and understanding.

JASON

The Whore

- **1½ oz tequila**
- **1 oz kahlua**
- **3 oz chilled pineapple juice**
- **soda**

Wait for Tanya to make it. Tire of waiting. Put in glass yourself but don't stir. Suck through a straw before picking up glass and smashing it against a wall in a hissy fit.

DONNA

Tea Surprise

- **1 tea bag (previously used once for savings)**
- **Hot water**
- **mug**
- **cow milk**
- **slippers**

Boil water. Do this in advance at night time to take advantage of energy savings. Dunk previously used but still perfectly acceptable teabag in mug with hot water to taste. Not too long – don't go crazy, you caffeine junkie. Add milk before or after as this is highly controversial and Donna does not want to be seen taking sides. Apply slippers to feet and mooch around house with duster.

FRANK

Corpse Reviver

- **30ml Brandy**
- **20ml sweet vermouth**
- **20ml Calvados**
- **Orange Zest**

Fill a mixing glass/bed pan with ice and pop all the ingredients in. Quickly now, before you lose a pulse. Stir gently using a spoon or a thermometer or something. Transfer ingredients to plastic bag and consume intravenously.

Chardonnay's guide to being a working girl

Pocket money, how to get it – and yourself – taken seriously

One of the many things I've learned from the Spice Girls is that at least in the twenty-first century women have been emaciated. And the good news is you don't have to go to polyversity to get ahead! So I've asked some genuine professional professionals to give you the same sort of good advice that got me what I wanted what I really, really wanted.

Glamour model
(from Herb 'Knockers' Mullon, photojournalist – **Mugs and Jugs*)***

If you're a Footballer's Wife it's possible your bosom has already contributed to your success. If you have a front like an inflated airbag then I'd say you might as well whip them out for hard cash in airbrush controlled conditions. If you don't, someone less reputable than myself with a zoom lens the size of the Channel Tunnel will snap them anyway, probably when you're flat out on a sun-lounger with them lolling under your arms like water wings.

There's nothing more feminist than knockers

How to: Get agent, approach tabloid, yell 'timber'.

Pitfalls: It's a short career and I can't say gravity won't impose early retirement. Gravity or a freak Hawaiian Lei flambéing accident – sorry Chardonnay.

Positives: Sod the Feminists – there's nothing more feminist than knockers, that's what I always say.

Television presenter
(from Anna Pert – Good Early Morning with Anna; Merry Mid-Morning with Anna, Doing Lunch with Anna and Sit Down with a Biscuit at Teatime with Anna)

Probably think *GMTV* rather than *Newsnight*. The smart presenter dresses like an air-hostess and nests in a pastel studio chatting about babies. Everyone likes watching people chat about babies. Whereas *Newsnight* correspondents often have to wear safari jerkins. Combat clothing is all very well if it's 1998 and you're an All Saint but if you're not careful you could find yourself squatting under a tank and dodging bullets before you can say Kate Adie. No, think daytime, think quiz show concepts and think sofas. Why not interview some of your celebrity friends about their babies? I also think it helps if you have a name that ends with an 'a' for example Michaela, Anneka, Anthea and Ulrika. If you need more proof look no further than Margaret Thatcher whose career in light entertainment never really took off.

Watch your back for the ambitious weathergirl

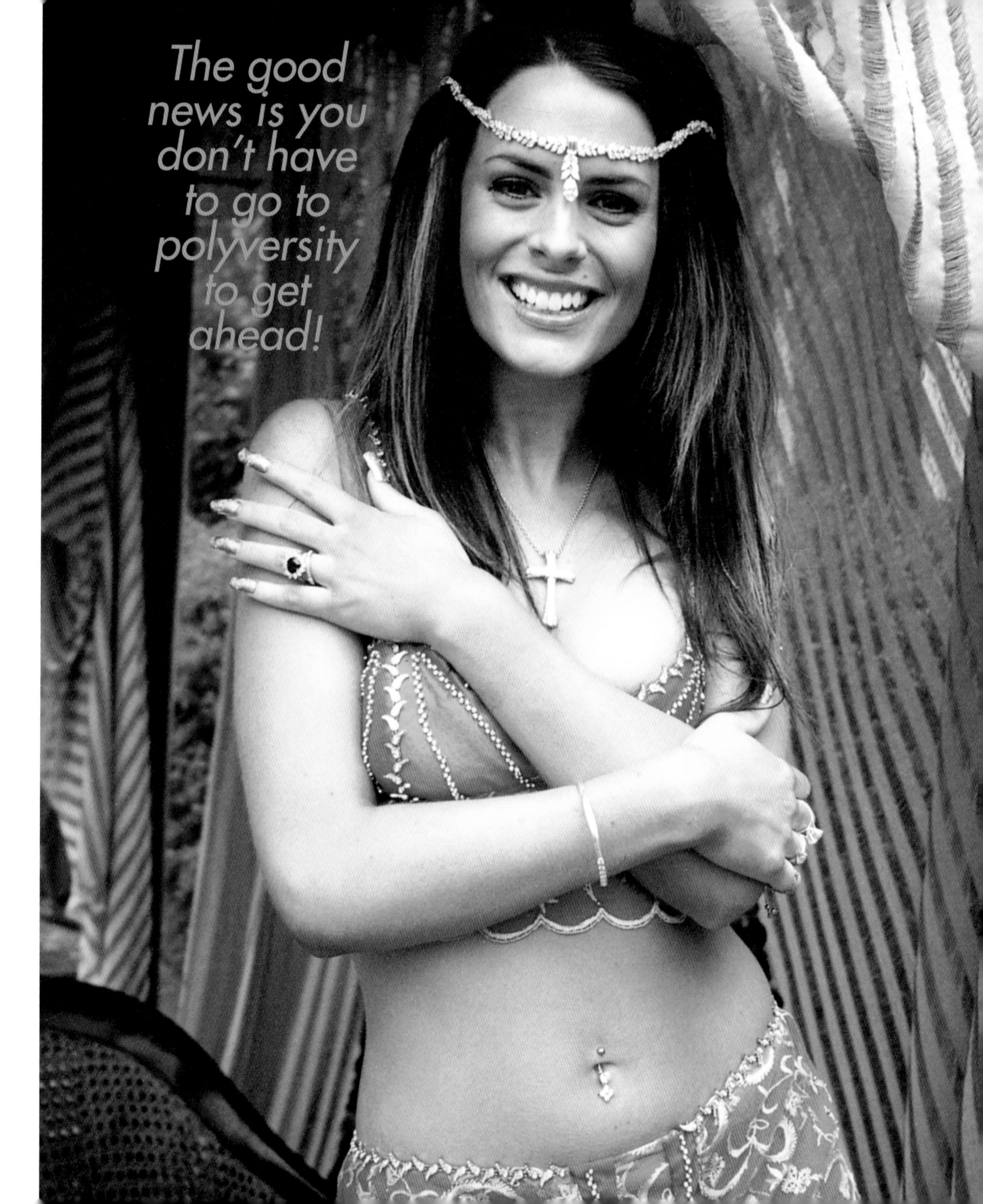
The good news is you don't have to go to polyversity to get ahead!

If you were a proper housewife rather than a Page Three girl Kyle might just get on Through the Keyhole

How to: Get agent, chose sofas. I always think peach is very flattering.

Pitfalls: It can be dog eat dog in daytime television. Always watch your back for the ambitious weathergirl.

Positives: You get to wake the nation with a smile. And Chardonnay sounds like it ends with an 'a'! Well done!

Homemaker

(from Jackie Pascoe – live-in mother and glamorous granny)

I don't know why you even ask Chardonnay, you know my opinion. Kyle already earns a good living. Most girls would be grateful for the roof over their heads and the rocks on their fingers. How do you think Kyle feels knowing all his mates are ogling his missus? If I wasn't here nothing would get done. If you spent as much time jogging round our lounge with a Hoover as you do at that fancy gym of yours I might get to live a little myself if that's not too much to ask! What Kyle needs is some support, not to come home and find you looking like a lesbian mechanic. Anyway you'll have to be at home today – someone's got to be here to let the pool man in.

How to: Well, you could start by picking up your own dirty laundry – I'm not your maid!

Pitfalls: Well, you wouldn't know Chardonnay, would you? You don't even get up until midday.

Positives: If you were a proper housewife rather than a Page Three girl Kyle might just get on *Through the Keyhole.*

Mel DD

(pop star, one-fifth of Nuclear Mitten/fiancée of Earl's Park winger)

These days with all the manufactured pop acts it seems all you need is to hum a few bars on *Pop Idol* and you're in *Smash Hits* modelling kitten heels. I believe in doing an apprenticeship the old-fashioned way – touring the holiday camps and learning how to actually dance in kitten heels. It's one career your husband cannot compete with as it's statistically proven that footballers only sing Frank Sinatra covers on a karaoke machine. Be aware your sportsman may not feel sporting about you eclipsing his success though. On the plus side, you might not care, having traded him in for one of your buff acolytes. I know I'm planning to…

All you need is to hum a few bars on *Pop Idol* and you're in *Smash Hits* modelling kitten heels

How to: Sing, dance, have good hair.

Pitfalls: At some point the public may demand talent of its pop stars.

Positive: It's unlikely the public will demand talent of its pop stars.

Charity Figurehead

(from Finellia Valentyne-Dykes, It Girl/Clothes Horse)

Whether it's save the squatter or kittens with no mittens there's always a good cause that needs a celebrity auction. There are positively entire pages of society magazines that need filling – sometimes weekly – so one must do what one can. Remember you don't actually have to meet people with diseases – just have your photo taken with Lady Double-Barrelled or Miss Children's Television at a £600 a seat banquet. Alternatively you could just get community service for snorting 3 lbs of talcum powder and spend seven months rinsing someone's false teeth.

You could just get community service for snorting 3 lbs of talcum powder

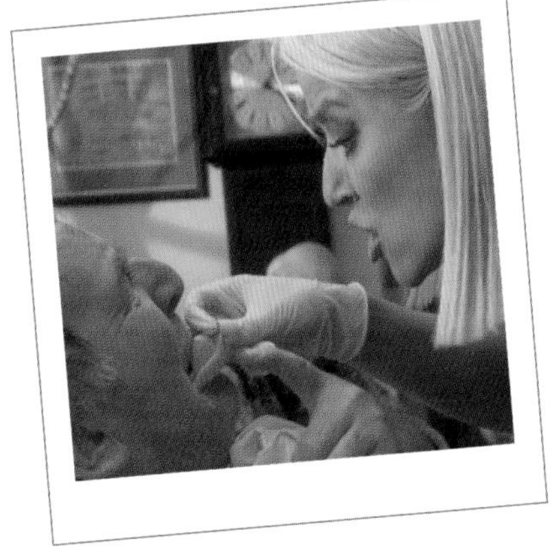

Getting community service is very much the new detox – I convinced Daddy to let me do it rather than Swiss Finishing School.

How to: Get a cause, get added to headed notepaper, learn that patron doesn't just mean restaurant regular darling.

Pitfalls: A photo call may require you to ladle out soup to squatters.

Positive: That warm fuzzy feeling you will get from orbiting the worlds of galas and soup ladling.

captain's wife's log

Monday
Ah the fickle tides of fate. A few months ago I was kept up at night by the thought that my short, but glorious career in being glamorous was about to be ended by my premature ejaculation into jail. Now I can't sleep because I've been trying to put someone else in the clink, in my place. Still it's survival of the fittest now. It's me or Frank. It's hardly like my sacrifice is virginal in the guilt stakes I keep reminding myself.

Tuesday
Did a performance worthy of someone from EastEnders today. He says I assaulted him, I say he tried to rape me. Hazel says let's call the whole thing off.

Thankfully Frank agrees to change his plea to guilty with mitigating circumstances, namely that he was barmy at the time.

Thank God really. We've been having to live like born again Christians over the last few months to protect the case. Jason's back has gone out more times than we have. Now everyone's a winner. Frank gets his 'Get Out Of Jail Free Card' with it decided that there's already been enough cells lost since his head injury without the prison service losing another one and I get out of court in time to have my legs waxed.

Wednesday
Nope, the nightmares continue. Cruelty thy name is Laslett.

Thursday
Had own problems put in perspective. Jason

said Ian is ruining his own career because he is in despair. Apparently his kid Holly is still missing.

Jason home late. For once his story checked out. Stefan had asked him to take Ian out for a drink and break the news that he's at risk of being dropped from the side. Sometimes it's easy to dismiss Stefan as a cold-hearted bastard when he goes and surprises you by doing something soft and fluffy like telling a broken man whose eight-year-old daughter is missing to pull himself together. He's a real diamond. You know something's morally reprehensible when even Jason is aghast.

To do: see if the Ivy's got a table for a celebration slap up 'I got off with attempted murder' tea. May drag Char along. Will have to tell her I'm celebrating my new haircut or something.

Friday
Went over to the Pascoes for a barbecue. Kyle must be really secure in his sexuality – he drives a real pussy wagon. Or maybe I'm just used to Jason's tank.

Really touched when they asked us to be godparents for little Paddy. Touched and appalled. For two such doting parents they really couldn't have made a worse choice in whom to entrust their offspring. I've got all the maternal instincts of a spider. I can't even keep a plant alive. No flower ever died from over-watering at Turner Towers. And Jason. To know him is not to trust him even if you like him (or love him as I'm fool enough to). If his lips are moving he's lying. Either that or he's suctioned onto a beer or a barely legal girl.

Jason seemed preoccupied and out of sorts for the rest of the night – weird. Perhaps he's coming down with something.

Saturday

Well, one in the eye for Kaiser Stefan. Ian's daughter Holly turned up safe and well. There's a happy reunion for the Walmsleys when Ian arrives home with Holly. I'm pleased that every so often something nice happens to someone associated with the club – even if, alas, it's never me.

Sunday

I think I preferred Jason when he was a misogynist pigman who should have been drowned at birth – repeatedly – just to make sure. Nearly choked on my vodka when he asked if I ever felt broody and if I wondered what our 'kid' would look like. Now there's a vision of hell. If it didn't come out as a snake then you know that yours truly would end up holding the baby, awkwardly and at arms' reach. He thinks all birds get clucky. I told him very clearly that there's already two kids in this house without giving up the gift wrapping room for another one.

To do: subtly take Jason's temperature and check house for toxic gas leak.

Monday

Baby Paddy is now officially the youngest creature to have his own six figure glossy magazine deal. Apparently, his people got together with their people and hashed out an exclusive contract. They were allowed unlimited access to his nursery, home and paddling pool, but were legally obligated to provide five different types of on-set fruit basket and his choice of hairstylist. Lord. That's entertainment,

Jesus. More disturbing news from Happy Valley. Chardonnay just called in floods of tears to say that the photoshoot was interrupted by the discovery of a woman's body in the Pascoes' swimming pool. The police just want to take a statement from Kyle. I didn't know he had it in him. I've broken the law often enough in the last year to know that statement is a clear and undeniable sign of guilt. Apparently she was a blonde thing called Sheena. Maybe I should actually be checking on Jason's whereabouts between the hours of 3 am and 10 am this morning. He certainly has been acting oddly lately. 'Blonde thing' certainly has the ring of Jason's work stamped all over it.

Tuesday

Frank is like an ugly, old, drooling mutt who just won't let go of the bone. Namely, my neckbone. Frank's determined to prove that he and I had an affair. God, in his dreams. But he

keeps threatening to tell Jason about our one real night of – I hesitate to use the word passion, I really do. I keep thinking – who in their right mind would believe I would willingly dance the horizontal tango with Frank? Then I remember that Jason is anything but in his real mind. He's been walking around the house for days with the sort of expression that you see psychopaths sporting when they dose them up on the sort of happy pills that make them want to sit tidily with some macramé rather than stove in someone's head.

Wednesday

And in breaking news... I'm now officially the Earl's Park bike. Jason stood me up at another charity do. Like I go to them out of the goodness of my heart rather than trying to make the ungrateful bastard look good... Hazel rescued me from the social death of being entirely on my own. She's actually very good company. I see myself fifteen years and a bad dye job down the line in her.

Talking of lines, we did too many which may well explain why I woke up to Jason's key in the door with Hazel naked as the day she must have been born all that time ago next to me. I have a vague recollection of her encouraging me to try a different flavour and I'm almost 100% certain she wasn't talking about ice cream - and then nothing till the key. That completes the trilogy. I've had the rottweiller Jason, an old mongrel Frank and in the latest interesting development Hazel the glorious bitch. Don't think it will be a permanent arrangement though.

Thursday

Yes, the world has truly gone mad. Jason has made me fake throwing away my birth control pills. As if one Jason Turner is not enough in this world. May yet take Hazel's advice and only deal with the sort of male members I can stow in my hand luggage in future.

The Tanya Turner Cup Winners Celebration Necklet

A stunning work of jewellery art partially hand-crafted in radiant tin alloys with a silver coloured finish

Tanya Turner brings exclusively to you the exclusive limited edition exclusive Tanya Turner Cup Winners Celebration Necklet™ (2,500,000 units) celebrating football and exclusive jewellery.

Do you want to be a winner rather than a pitiable dirty loser? Are you currently physically repellent? Are you fed up with keeping that shelf warm worrying that you'll never know the fulfilment of marriage? Are you wanting answers to the ecclesiastical infighting that is giving the devil a foothold in our secular society? If the answer to all or even one of the above is YES, YES, YES – you need the Tanya Turner Cup Winners Celebration Necklet™.

Expertly crafted in tin alloys with a silver-like finish, the Tanya Turner Cup Winners Celebration Necklet™ will literally change your life with its completely non-refundable splendour.

Used by nuns to heal the sick, the Tanya Turner Cup Winners Celebration Necklet™ holds power previously unbeknownst to man and can help you – YES YOU! – get a husband. Our friendly operators are standing by to ramraid your credit card so call them and say 'YES, YES, YES, I want some happiness in my terminally drab existence.'

Not quite actual size

24 Hour Express Order Line

08000 8000 0000

Our Pledge of Limited Satisfaction

Tanya Turner Inc. takes pride in offering works of compromisingly high standards of quality, created by semi-skilled craftsmen working out of a sweat shop in Wolverhampton. Each issue comes with our assurance that it will meet your expectations as long as they are not misguidedly high. If you are not satisfied with your purchase, simply return it within 24 hours by hand and we'll see what we can do but you'll have to find us first. This probably affects your statutory rights.

Exclusive Reservation Form for backward people who can't use phones

Please take the last of my redundancy money at the remarkable issue price of £399 payable in easy monthly instalments of £3.50 a month (89% APR). I need send no money now but understand my house and first born are at risk if I don't keep up payments.

Name: ____________________

Address: ____________________

____

aunt jackie's angst answer$

Cruel to be Kind Truisms from the Mother of Straight Talking

Dear Jackie
I need advice to deal with my interfering mother-in-law. Honestly she's a mentalist. I know she gave me Paddy her baby to bring up because she's too old but she should keep her milk to herself. And she talks about me not getting my breasts out – at least I get paid for it! I just want a happy family and I think we'd get on if she'd shut up a bit. What should I do?
From Lambrusco xxx ☻ xxx

Dear 'Lambrusco'
Grow up Chardonnay. And another thing... that haemorrhage in a cotton wool factory wedding of yours wouldn't have got organized without your mother-in-law interfering. Honestly...bloody dwarves!
Hang in there, Aunt Jackie

Dear Jackie
I feel a bit of a silly-billy for writing – as it's a rather embarrassing problem. I fell for the most charming man in the world. We never quarrelled, spent all of our time together and our intimate moments – well, Jackie – they were truly fantastic. The only problem was that he was in a coma at the time and now he never calls and I'm worried we've grown apart.
Concerned and Blackmailed Nurse 'Bunkley'.

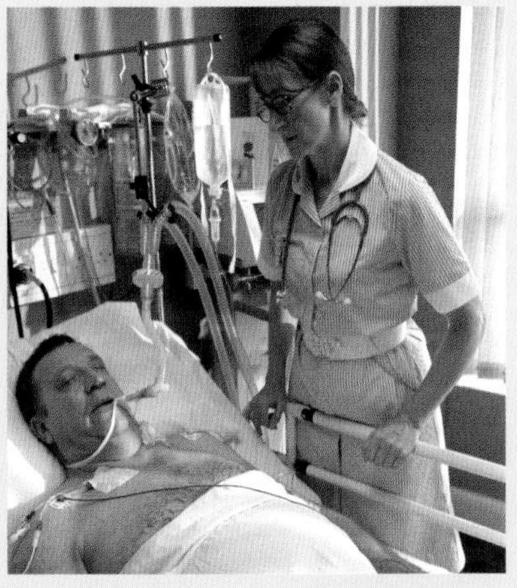

Three words ... 'get help sicko'.

Dear Nurse Freaky
Three words ... 'get help sicko'. Unless ... is that you having a laugh, Jase?
Hang in there, Jackie

Dear Jackie
I'm in love with a married footballer. I know we are meant to be together and he's not happy with that vicious old cow. I'd been stalking him for ages so I've put a lot of work into the relationship. We finally had our first shag in a cubicle. Honestly Jackie it was beautiful. We now do it whenever he has time and no one else lined up. My sister tells me he's just using me. But he does love me doesn't he Jackie?
From Gagging for it, of Earl's Park

ALL LETTERS ARE GENUINE

Although I would die for my rose I need advice because he's the size of a gorilla and could knock me into next season. Do you know anyone who does low-to-medium level violence work and can be discreet? I get my first pay cheque at the end of the month – so any time from then on would be ideal.

From Romeo

Jason dunks more bags than Tetley … he's like a battery love, ever ready.

Dear Tart
Jason dunks more bags than Tetley … he's like a battery love, ever ready. And I wouldn't let Tanya catch you calling her that. She's got a temper and talons so long her hand looks like a rake.

Don't hang in there, Jackie

Dear Jackie
I am being bullied at work. It all started when I fell head over heels for a beautiful mature woman who took my boyhood and made me a man. Our candlelit nights of romance have shown me we are two hearts destined to beat as one. Her husband is not worthy of her love and I can but try to defend her honour when he insults and berates her. I feel that while he does not suspect our ardour he senses my disgust at his behaviour.

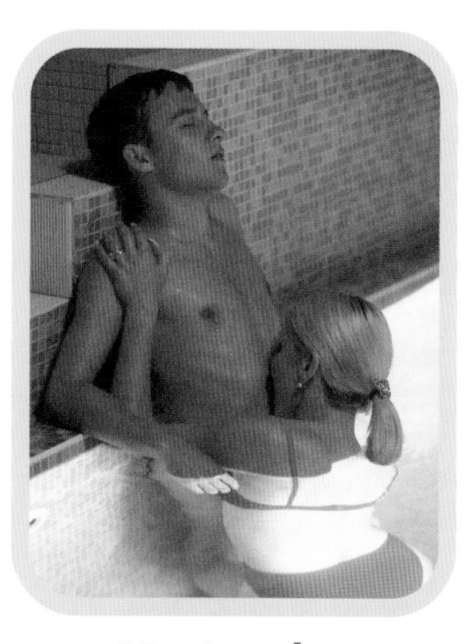

Dear Jackie
The total for repairs to your snooker table is £340. I confess the boys here have been scratching their heads vis-à-vis the damage. We've never seen anything like it. Normally when people 'break' they don't mean the table. You're right – he must have been a strong lad! Anyway hopefully it's now all fixed and you're fully satisfied.

Best regards
Tom, Snooker World

Dear Tom
Please find cheque enclosed. Yes he was a strong lad. Re: satisfaction – you haven't met Jason Turner have you…

Yours Sincerely, Jackie

You're about two million quid and three more years of puberty away from being Tanya's dream date

Dear Misguided
Get off your white horse, Saturday boy. You're about two million quid and three more years of puberty away from being Tanya's dream date. But thanks for your letter – it's good to know Jason has had a taste of his own medicine. Next time I see him I'll make sure he takes it. Cheers.

Get a life, Jackie

$prechen zie football?

Parlez vous offside trap?

To be part of a tribe one must learn the vibe. Study these bon mots from trained professionals. Study them, feel them, live them. If you get stuck try adding 'ist' to the ends of words (mentalist, racialist, dirty rotten sexualist) and throwing them casually into conversation. In time you'll forget words with unnecessary syllables. What are syllables you ask? Exactly!

Happy chatting!

'Here's some advice for free – slap her head under the shower and her arse in a taxi … and if you want my opinion on top : damaged goods!'

'Get it up you while you're young, girl.'

'How do you know what your favourite flavour is, until you've had a taste of everything that's on offer?'

'Come on, I like a good fairy story before bed.'

Jackie: 'Jason, I haven't slept with anyone else.'
Jason: 'The speed you get your knickers off? Come off it!'

'Even if you gave both of your kidneys to dying babies you'd still smell like a septic tank.'

Tanya: 'The minute they stop fiddling with his tubes he's going to tell someone.'
Jason: 'How? Morse bloody code?'

Frank: 'I had some short-term memory loss.'
Hazel: 'Wanna know what I think? The more you "remember" the more you do sound like a loony. Wormwood Scrubs, babe. Fancy it?'

'Screwing your best mate's mum is the eighth deadly sin, Jase … or don't they teach you nothing at shag school these days?'

Jason: 'I know what I need to take my mind off this crap … a nice pair of thighs to get busy with.'
Big Ron: 'Your missus has got a nice pair.'
Jason: 'Yeah, but her gob comes with 'em.'

'Going out with a Page Three model is one thing but getting married to one is embarrassing.'

'He's not a bleedin' Gucci bag, Chardonnay! You can't just use him like a fashion accessory.'

'Are you deliberately trying to humiliate Kyle? You look like you've gone lesbian!'

'Oh grow up Chardonnay, you look like Friar Tuck for God's sake!'

Frank: 'I'm not crossing that bitch again till I've got some real, hard evidence in my hands.'

Stefan: 'Christ! Even Jason Turner with fifteen pints inside him and his cock on red-alert manages to stay off the front pages!'

'I should have divorced you when I had the chance Jason! Commitment? The only way to keep your dick under control is to cut it off! But sadly, I don't have my nail scissors with me!'

'Nothing serious, just a little therapy shag … make you feel special.'

'That's it. I'm going to hell.'

'Don't touch him, you crazy bitch!'

'You're not going anywhere till I'm finished with you darling, so you may as well lie back and enjoy.'

Janette: 'I've only just had my roots done.'
Tanya: 'By who? Helen Keller?'

'Unless I'm wrong, shagging your patients wasn't part of your job description.'

'What's the point of kicking a football if you can't kick a bit of arse?'

'I'm not a bloody addict. I just got caught!'

'You are Mr Spilly tonight, aren't you?'

'I've got a cool bath and a hot dress to get into.'

'All the same though aren't they, blokes? No point swapping one wanker for another.'

'Just a friendly warning for the future, you go anywhere near my husband again and it'll take more than Botox to sort your face out!'

'Who'd have thought it eh? Little Donna and the Italian stallion … and there's me thinking that her idea of passion was microwave chips.'

'Just how gay are you exactly?'

'It's not the psychos you should be worried about. It's the women.'

'The only vows you'll ever make will be with your right hand!'

'I don't blame you … first the tits and then the hair, must be like shagging a boy.'

Tanya: 'From now on there's only one bloke for me…Charlie! Who needs the rest?'
Hazel: 'Come on darlin', let's be fair to dicks … they're great bits of tackle.'
Tanya: 'Yeah, it's just what's on the end of them right?'
Hazel: 'That's why I keep mine in my handbag.'

'Tell you, when you hammered that last one home, I could've shagged you right there on the penalty spot.'

'Darling, trust me – no way is *this* shooting blanks.'

how to be an author

by Chardonnay Lane-Pascoe (Author)

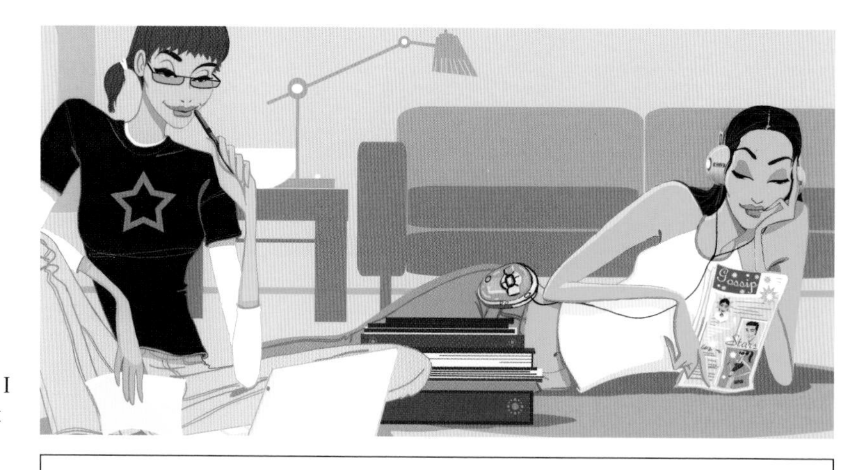

When my agent approached me with the idea of writing a book I laboured long and hard as to whether I could accept a six-figure advance. But as a glamour model I've often been asked to share my insights on romance and with a small team of thirty-two ghostwriters my first novel (which I've since discovered is publishing speak for a book without pictures) is complete.

Here is an exclusive extract, unabridged and edited of my debut work, *A Tale of Two Titties – A Novel by Chardonnay Lane-Pascoe* by Chardonnay Lane-Pascoe.

Here we find our two heroes finally ready to embrace their burgeoning love in this tale of passion, fashion and intercontinental diplomacy. Hopefully it will inspire all you budding soccer scribes out there. Unfortunately due to the terms of my serialization contract with the *Croydon and Leatherhead Messenger* I have stopped just before the juicy action. So if you want the full smutty version you'll have to buy it at the recommended retail price of £1.89 like everyone else. Note the subtle and seamless use I made of a dictionary to find longer and more intellectual words.

A Tale of Two Titties – A Novel by Chardonnay Lane-Pascoe
by Chardonnay Lane-Pascoe

The moonlight filtered through the shutters as Clint stole a glance at the glacial beauty of the one true love at his side. Montana demurely cast her gaze back to the protuberance in his Pringle slacks. She had yet to experience carnal abandon but was in no doubt their union would result in simultaneously blissful release. Catching her shy inquisitiveness at his manhood he smiled brutishly and compassionately.

'Do you want fries with that?' he exhaled seductively.

'No need to super size it,' she rejoined bashfully.

They threw back their heads and expressed amusement freely yet chastely at their passionate intimateness. Reclining in their matching Gucci sunglasses they shared several more minutes of contented silence as the sun basked their supple bronzed figures. Montana allowed her memories to flood over her like a lush masseuse. Since she had first met Clint at a transnational celebrity party her life seemed to have changed so very much. At first she had wondered how their relationship would ever survive Clint's occupation as a test pilot and international chiropractor. But here they were enjoying the sunset at his exclusive Caribbean hideaway and with her barely giving a thought to her previous life as a swimwear model and cultural ambassador. Could Clint really be the one to make her hang up her honorary doctorate once and for all?

AS A GLAMOUR MODEL I'VE OFTEN BEEN ASKED TO SHARE MY INSIGHTS ON ROMANCE
A Tale of Two Titties
A Novel by Chardonnay Lane-Pascoe
by Chardonnay Lane- Pascoe

Her reveries were disrupted when Clint brushed askance a stray strand of her magnificent mahogany mane.

'You've got truly great knockers,' he gasped adoringly.

'Well, I do work out,' she retorted coyly.

'No really – you've got a rack like two colossal beach balls,' he reassured reassuringly.

She flashed a ready gleam of her superlative smile. Beach balls reminded her of their perfect day frolicking along the perfect pink sands of the perfect Leonardo Da Vinci Bay. Surely as the fifteenth daughter of gypsy coalminers her life could not have foreseen such contentment. Forced to work as a chimney sweep's pole from the tender age of four she had been salvaged by her ravishing beauty. She thanked again the twists of fate that ensured her slender waist, enhanced by years of being too poor to eat anything apart from what she could forage on the wild unkempt highlands of Bradford. She had come so far. She could finally buy her father the new lungs he needed to counteract the mine dust that had devoured his unfailingly robust spirit.

She took another bite of her healthy low-cal muesli and readjusted her yoga position effortlessly.

'Will you be my wife?' he pleaded caringly, the stars reflecting in the glistening pools of his raven eyes.

'But what about my commitments at the UN?' she despondently countered magnanimously. 'Who will take the New Millennium's message of peace to the war zones of the world?'

Clint cupped her porcelain cheek in soft but manly hands.

'Communism must find a new enemy,' he comforted benignly.

'My answer is unconditionally yes my love. But I obviously cannot accept if we must share our life with your beloved mother,' she reacted probingly.

Clint's chiselled jaw set strappingly.

'No fear. I've arranged her custody at a twilight sanatorium for the imminently menopausal,' he comforted sweetly. 'Besides, she would not have it any other way and I could not jeopardize our incomparable love by asking you to compete for me.'

Montana blushed through her copper splendour and seized his throbbing tool. She was finally ready to become a woman.

Critical acclaim for *A Tale of Two Titties – A Novel by Chardonnay Lane-Pascoe* by Chardonnay Lane-Pascoe:

'A tour-de-force of raunchy rocks-off and political satire' – *Croydon and Leatherhead Messenger*

'A rollercoaster ride of rags to riches with a fairytale ending to warm the coldest heart' – *Croydon and Leatherhead Messenger*

'Lane-Pascoe storms into the canon of English Literature to sit comfortably astride Shakespeare' – *Croydon and Leatherhead Messenger*

Critical indifference to *A Tale of Two Titties – A Novel by Chardonnay Lane-Pascoe* by Chardonnay Lane-Pascoe:

'One is left to question whether English is the first language of Mrs Lane-Pascoe or indeed whether any language is' – *Croydon and Leatherhead Examiner*

'Someone's been reading too many Jackie photo stories. Unfortunately' – *The Times*

'Whole minutes of my life which I will never get back have been squandered on reading this pile of unadulterated…' *Everyone Else*

…Well, anyway … Good luck to those who would like to try and emulate my literary accomplishments. Remember to write about what you know and to change the names of who you know! *Char* xxx☻xxx

being a cunning
footballing nation lingui$t

Olé!

We now live in a multi-transfer society which means we all have to adapt and learn about foreign cultures. You will hear new and strange names that will confuse spellcheckers and won't fit on the back of their football shirts. Try eating out at a pizzeria to learn about Italians or eating sausages to understand Europeans. Welcome foreign transfers to our shores and homes. Remember to look them in the eye and don't show fear.

Bonjour Monsieur – vous are soooo *mal – Voulez-vous coucher avec moi ce soir? Hallo Holland boy, want to see my Netherlands?*

Even though British people obviously do things the normal way, foreigners with their strange and peculiar customs may feel a bit nervous and confused. Some of them are not bright enough to speak English but are nevertheless attractive in a swarthy way so it's definitely worth learning how to speak a few words of continent speak. We've included the most important phrase you will need below in all sorts of different tongues. If you are unsure which tongue will best suit him, pick one and just say it loudly and repeatedly.

!No! Mi sujetador se abra por delante.

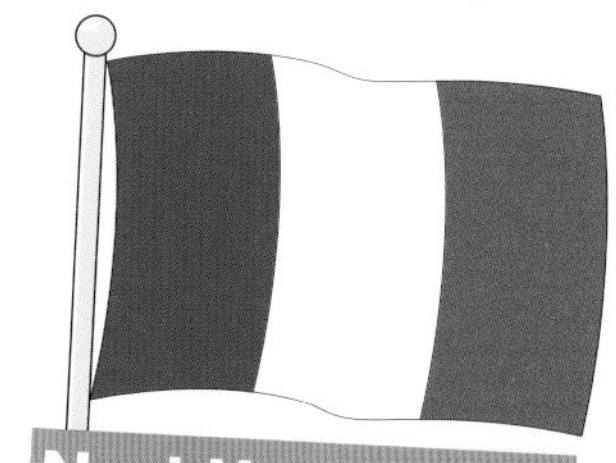

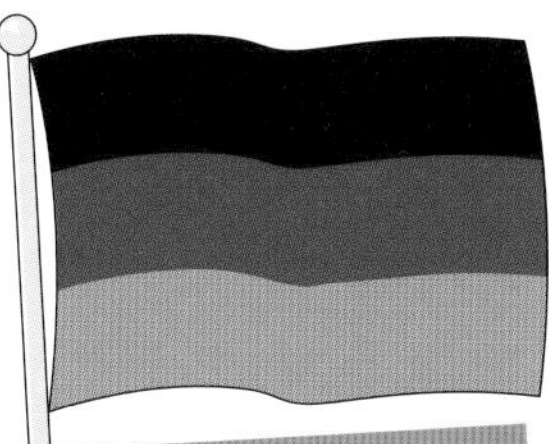

keeping your po$ition

Or 'Footballers are from Mars and Wives are from Bolton'

We asked Kyle, Jason and Ian to tell us what they thought every wife (that's YOU if you play your cards right!) should know. Here are the top tips you need for ball control ... Remember even men have important things to say if you listen long enough.

Reflections as a Footballing Husband

Q: Boys, what should every wife know? And thank you for being here.

K: Thank you for having me.

J: So that's where you got to when I was getting the drinks in.

K: Shut it, Jase.

I: Is this the time to say I'm not sure the photographer got my best side?

J: Why – weren't you bending over at the time?

K: Anyway – thank you for having us. Well, first and foremost there are no hard and fast rules.

J: Speak for yourself Pascoe – I can think of a few hard and…

K: … we know that every wife is different.

I: There are ash, strawberry and golden ones for a start.

K: It's important that every wife is herself.

J: Yeah – I can get the other flavours elsewhere.

I: But for any wife wanting to keep her husband happy it's important she knows the strain he's under.

J: But not who he's under.

(At this point the interview was temporarily suspended while Kyle told Jason that if he intended to proceed in this manner he would have to field the rest of the interview on his own. Jason happily agreed.)

J: I've given this some thought – in fact I've written down a few tips on the back of this fag packet…

'Stay at home and play with your pills'
Jason 'New Man' Turner

(At this point the interviewer upon seeing that Jason had just written down his phone number permanently suspended the interview in favour of a written questionnaire that could be done by proxy. Here, with only the basic grammatical and spelling errors removed are Jason Turner's tips on marital servitude. We leave it uncensored as well – it's important you know now than find out the hard way.)

Foreplay is not an alternative to sex as there is no alternative to sex.

- Kissing is not a substitute, it is showboating plus it usually costs extra.
- Try apologizing even if you are in the wrong – that's when it really means something.
- I'm not shitting Harrods. Anything that does not fall into my outstretched arms is unreasonable effort so don't call me at training and ask me to pick up milk on my way home.

They are not
man breasts –
it's pronounced
muscle tone

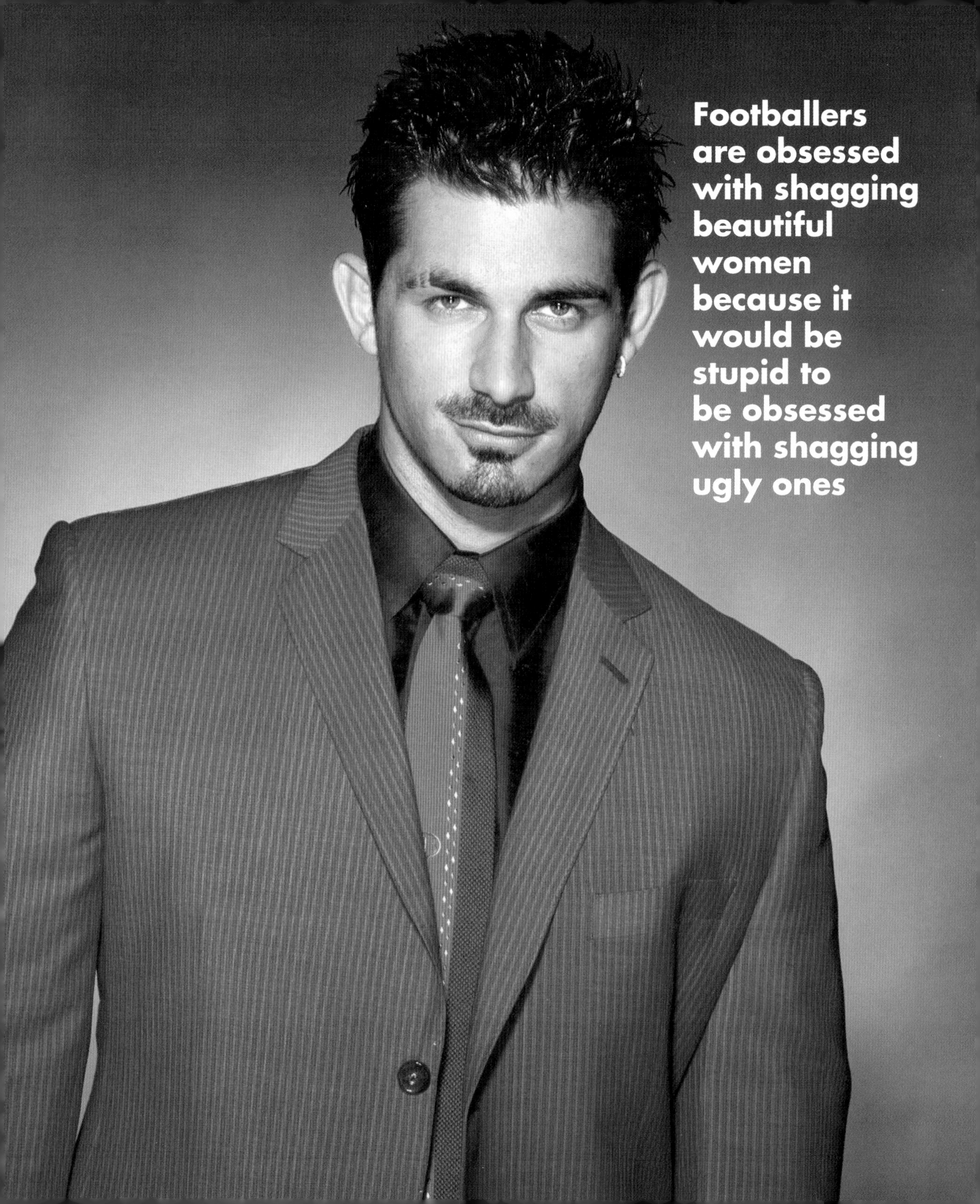
Footballers are obsessed with shagging beautiful women because it would be stupid to be obsessed with shagging ugly ones

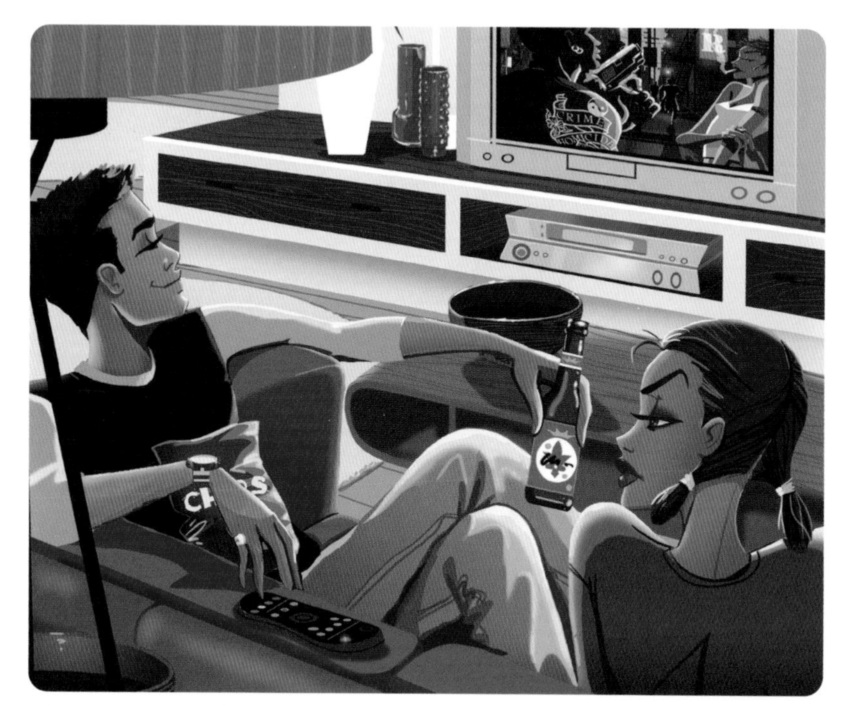

When you bring me a beer – how much effort would it be to actually open it first?

- If I meet a younger woman who's more attractive than you any bloke would say it's reasonable for me to sleep with her. Don't take it so personally.
- I won't be hostage to your hormones. If you're on the rag – go out into the garden like they would have done in the old days.
- Men die first statistically so you can wait and enjoy yourself after I've gone can't you.
- Nothing says 'I love you' like keeping your roots under control.
- If you've got a problem finding out about all my affairs – don't call me all the time. Why shine a light on it?
- Honesty is the quick way to knacker any good relationship as are the words 'Jason – we need to talk'.

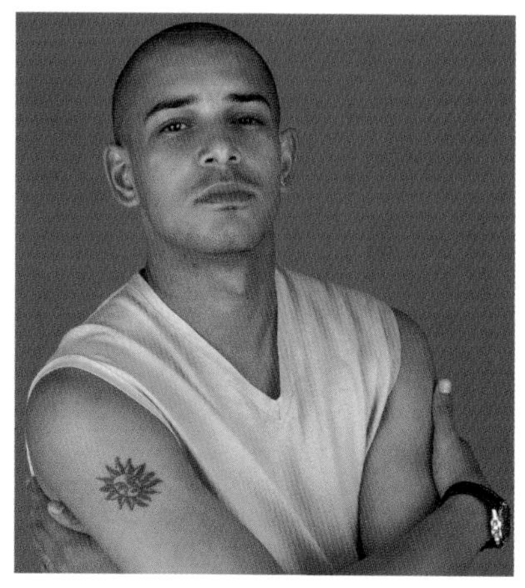

- If I have an affair with someone who is not you – it is actually a compliment. I wouldn't have done it when we first met so it just shows how secure and comfortable I am with you.
- I can't be expected to answer every time you ask a question – it takes time to think of convincing lies and you don't want me to take the piss do you?

- Tying a cardigan around your waist to hide buttocks like swaying bongos isn't fooling anyone.

'It's done . . . he's a cabbage and we're sorry, right?'
Jason 'New Man' Turner

- Footballers are obsessed with shagging beautiful women because it would be stupid to be obsessed with shagging ugly ones. And even if we did beautiful women would then be up in arms. I am but one man – I can't keep everyone happy.

If I say I love you, anyone would know that is actually code for I'm sorry I wasn't listening.

- Footballers often publicly rearrange themselves on the pitch because, like zoo animals, the larger the beast the bigger paddock they need to roam in. Being in public is just an added bonus.
- If I look blank and unforthcoming it's because I don't want to confess to an indiscretion you don't actually know about yet.

captain's wife's log

Monday
Haven't had a moment's peace since pretending to agree to incubate the devil child in my belly. Jason is now exercising his conjugal rights with alarming frequency. Not that I'm complaining. Normally he has no stamina left after servicing Surrey – I always remained rarely troubled. It never ceased to amaze me – you'd think for convenience sake as much as anything else it would have been worth him staying home a few nights every so often. No wonder he had no energy left to waddle about the pitch like an old woman.

Anyway – love's young dream is a house of cards. If he finds out I've been popping the pill down my throat like a kid at a slot machine they'll probably find me – days later embedded deep into one of the goal posts.

Tuesday
Starting to feel like a car that Jason is determined to keep filled up. Amazed by the enigma that is J. Turner. Sometimes I swear that man is almost human. An insane human – but a human nonetheless. He told me today that his christening present for little Paddy was a hundred thousand quid, insisting that while Ken and Barbie are a two income family, Ken won't have his longevity of career and he wants to safeguard his godson's education. Honestly, he's lost the plot. Who does he think he is – the patron saint of failed footballers? Normally the only time he does a good

turn is when he wants more of the duvet.

Wednesday
Jason has banned me from smoking – now that I could be an expectant mother and all. Have taken his health warnings on board and upped my cocaine intake instead. His persistence is nothing if not total. I'm even starting to feel a little empathy for his girlfriends. May have to start experiencing flash headaches.

Thursday
Was thinking earlier that I should have got an ISA rather than Jason – at least they mature and they are certainly less voracious in scattering their seed.

Friday
Paddy's christening. Proved to be one of those days when I should have stayed at home with a litre of brandy and a copy of Playgirl. I'll omit to tarry on the service itself. Suffice to say that about twenty major ethnic groups should sue for copyright infringement and a share of the magazine rights and it was about the most

hallucinogenic experience one could get without licking a Bolivian toad. Luckily Jason's typically odd behaviour convinced me there weren't toxic fumes in the font.

Anyway not long after the service I was powdering my nose – unfortunately literally – when the drug squad descended like an episode of Starsky and Hutch and hauled me off to the cop shop. Typical. I've kept my dirty little secret all these years, even from my own husband to be uncovered to the world at a function that must have been born of drugs stronger than any I have snorted up my delicate little nose. I'm out on bail. Jason – loyal as ever – has filed me with my marching papers and changed the locks. Apparently the man whose idea of safe sex is making sure I'm out of earshot feels quite within his rights to judge me and cast me aside like a used pole dancer. He seemed less upset about me wrecking my body with illegal narcotics than seeing all my still in use contraceptive tablets – courtesy of the rozzers. The cat – or should I say the cap was out of the bag.

It's now 3 am. I won't lie. I'm terrified. The thought of sharing a cell with a chamber pot and an arsonist called Madge the Match fills me with unbridled terror. I just want to go home. I'll call Hazel in the morning.

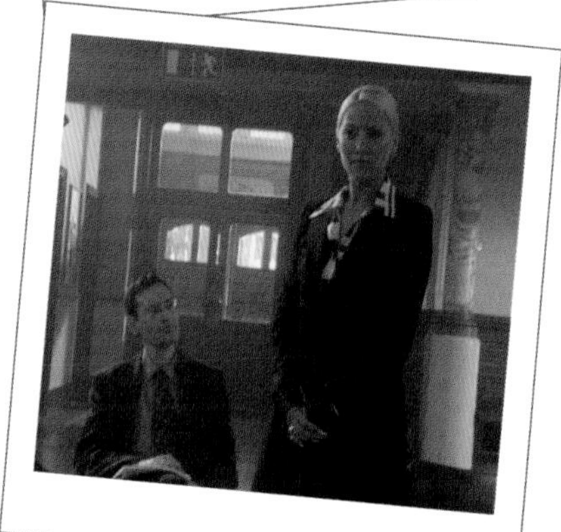

Saturday
Feel slightly more positive. I have a plan forming with Hazel. Lord knows she's better than bloody Houdini at getting out of tight spots.

Sunday
Feel like Kathy Come Home.

Monday
Got hair done.

Tuesday
Made a conspicuous visit to Narcotics Anonymous. Arranged for a few 'photo journalists' to candidly capture my tearful exit. Even took a bit of my make-up off to help the effect. Thank God I had my hair done to balance it out a bit.

Wednesday
Swam a few laps, checked out the papers. Pleased to see my having my hair done paid off. For someone ravaged by addiction I thought I looked pretty good.

Thursday
Who'd have thought it eh? Little Donna and the Italian stallion … and there was me thinking that her idea of passion was microwave chips. It would seem her husband Ian wasn't just under-performing on the pitch. I have it on good authority (Chardonnay) that she's been providing

more foreign exchange than Thomas Cooks. Of course Chardonnay didn't put it like that. She just looked flushed and kept chanting 'poor Ian' in some sort of mantra.

Friday

Did a 'revealing' TV interview on Chardonnay's pastel fest. My performance was so good – I almost made myself cry for real. I'll have to keep a check on my emotions.

Saturday

Jason's on the warpath. Apparently he didn't take kindly to the press questioning him about his impotence and seedless grapes. He was in a right hissy fit and said that it was all my fault, that I had ovaries like concrete bunkers and that he'd already fathered a kid of his own, sans me. He finished by telling me that me and my eggs could go and get scrambled!

Sunday

Am still inconsolable. What child?

Monday

Decide to get a 'child' of my own. Teen wonder Darius arrived at Earl's Park and has been tipped as the next big thing. He's legal and willing so invited him to dinner a deux at the posh hotel I'm staying at. Well you know what they say – a new lover a day keeps the sliding, all consuming dark depression away. He wasn't Jason but not having trotters is really a plus when you stop to think about it.

Tuesday

Need to concentrate on getting Jason back. Unfortunately it's one thing that Hazel can't or won't help me with on account of the fact she'd prefer to keep me out of Jason's bed and in her own, bless her. We have reached a code red though. Even me threatening to remove every last penny from his airtight wallet has made no impact thus far. The only thing he seems interested in is cooing after Jason Junior, which for the first time in his life is not the tiny beast he keeps in his trousers. I'm starting to worry that I may have lost him for good.

FOOTBALLERS' PAST WIVES:

THE 1950S – MEN IN LONG SHORTS

SHORT OF TAKING AN AXE ON TO PLAY, PLAYERS WERE ENCOURAGED TO FIND NEW AND NOVEL WAYS TO BREAK EACH OTHERS' LIMBS. FOOTBALLERS VIED WITH EACH OTHER TO BEAT THE CRAP OUT OF THEIR OPPONENTS.

LEAGUE TABLES AWARDED POINTS FOR HOSPITAL-IZATION, DECAP-ITATION AND EXSANGUINATION. IT OFTEN DECIDED THE CHAMPIONSHIP.

JEALOUSY ABOUT THE BREADTH OF ONE'S SHORTS WAS RIFE AND OFTEN RESULTED IN AGGRAVATED THEFTS WHEN THE REF WAS ON A PIE BREAK.

SUBS SNACKED ON PIES AND BEER TO KEEP THEIR STRENGTH UP ON THE BENCH.

HOWEVER PLAYERS WERE NOT ALLOWED TO LEAVE THE PITCH UNLESS THEY HAD A MISS UNIVERSE CONTEST TO JUDGE OR A BEVERLEY SISTER TO MARRY.

PENALTIES WERE AWARDED FOR EFFEMINATE BEHAVIOUR.

OH… AND THE 1950S FOOTBALLER'S WIFE? WELL WE KNOW THERE WERE SOME, BUT AS WOMEN WERE BANNED BY LAW FROM ATTENDING GAMES UNTIL 1978, SHE DID NOT ATTEND MATCHES, FUNCTIONS OR EVEN LEAVE THE HOUSE EXCEPT TO WORK IN A PIE FACTORY. SHE WAS PROBABLY A LITTLE DUMPY AND HAD CHILD-BEARING HIPS. DARK TIMES, DARK TIMES… SENSIBLE SHOES, DISH-PAN HANDS. SHE PROBABLY WASN'T EVEN BLONDE!!

$pin it so you win it

With Soccer Spinner Supremo – Straight Speaking, Sassy Siren – Hazel Bailey

Roll up, roll up! Come marvel at soccer's grandest, most spectacular Big Top. Watch Messrs Turner and Walmsley perform dazzling feats of mindless daring on the trapeze of taste. Gasp at boy wonder Darius as he attempts the mighty stilts so he can finally look his teammates in the eye. Revel in the eye cotton candy and savour spectacles in scandalous stupidity in the most sensational, inspirational, providential, manipulational Dog and Pony show in town!

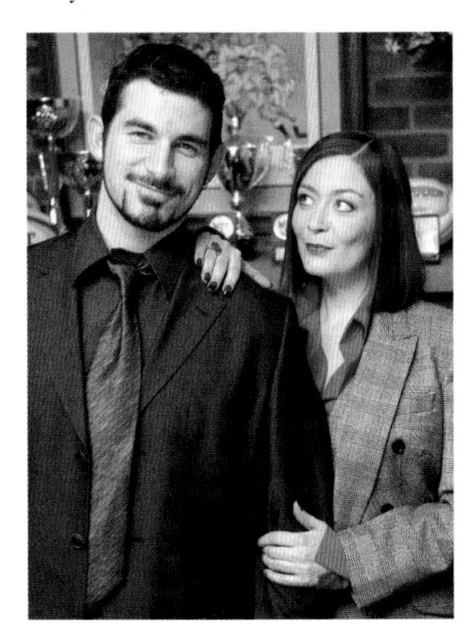

If you've got the IQ of a breath mint it pays to pay me

Right – enough of all that pony. How many Footballers' Wives does it take to change a light bulb? None – they're used to being in the shadows. How many footballers does it take to change a light bulb? One to hold it in the air and wait for the rest of the world to revolve around him. Hazel Bailey at your highly paid service, football agent and your worst nightmare so don't screw with me. My boys kick the balls and I break them. Every star needs 'people' and I'm the only 'people' you'll ever need.

So how do you micro-manage a primate like Turner? When he first came to me I asked him how many months along he was. He'd let himself go and so had Earl's Park. A couple of weeks of eating hamster food and getting jiggy to Tracey Shaw's 'Salsasize' and he was back pulling on a blue shirt and making me 20% gross. If you've got the IQ of a breath mint it pays to pay me.

When it comes to dealing with the press it's all about spin. Spin and lying your ass off.

'Bollocks! Nothing the soccer world loves more than a comeback kid. We package this right and you'll have the league wedged so far up your arse you'll be shitting studs!' © Hazel Bailey

Case Study 1

Chardonnay hadn't been in the papers for four days and on the Celebdaq portfolio her shares were plummeting. Now she's a nice bit but a supermarket trolley's got more of a mind of its own. I told her to pack her suitcase, fly somewhere toasty and show a bit of thigh. Now Chardonnay doesn't really have cellulite. She doesn't have enough surplus on her flesh to get through a nippy day in November. But a bit of photo manipulation with Tippex and we've got a 'Look at the thighs on that' spread in *Heat*.

You might be thinking – I don't want to be notorious for bum dimples – I'm

not appearing in panto for God's sake (note to me – there's a thought). But if your ascendancy is in the descendency any news is good news for you. As Nelson said to the uppity pigeon, it's column inches that count. Besides, three months later you cash in with a best-selling exercise video showing how you trimmed and slimmed.

'Eyes, teeth and tits, Ladies – leave the rest to me.'
© Hazel Bailey

Case Study 2

How do you solve a problem like Marie, eh?

Marie had had more bounces than a trampoline. The only difference was you'd have the courtesy to take off your shoes before climbing on the latter. She wanted me to get her a mag spread and a few quid. I said to her, 'Doll you ain't a glossy – the only thing that would look good on you is a rottweiler – so we'll get you a Page Three tie-in and one of those bleeding heart rags that print on tissue paper.' Two hundred and fifty quid – which is the most she'll make standing up...

So what can we learn here?

1. Sod subtlety.
2. Get in first and claim you're the victim.
3. If you can't be good, sell your story.
4. Sod subtlety.

When it comes to dealing with the press it's all about spin. Spin and lying your ass off.

Case Study 3

Tanya Turner, Wife, Saint, Stunner

Tanya Turner ... my favourite client. She's got it all, including a few things she could have done without thanks to the missing link husband. Shapely media savvy, firm but soft intelligence and taut, luscious resourcefulness. When you look like Tanya every time you get your downstairs loo redecorated you can have a photoshoot that pays enough to get it decorated again. In titanium. Welcome to the effusive adjective school of journalism...

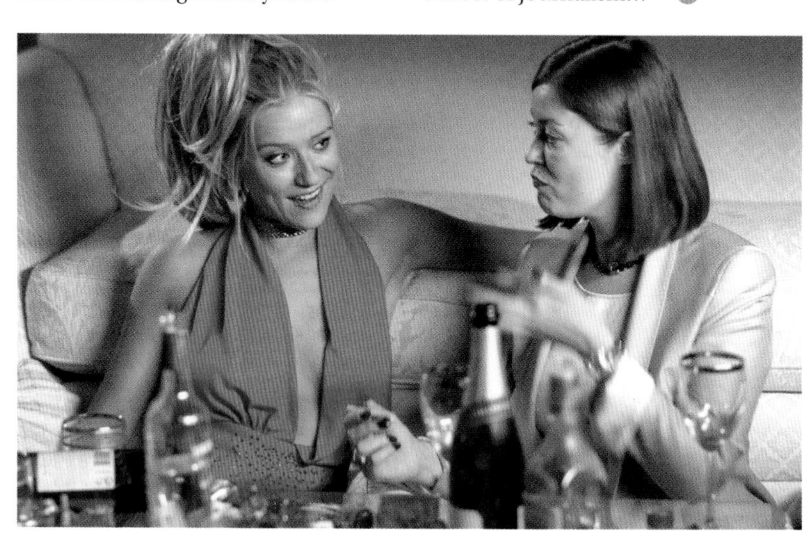

SOCCER STUD STA

Marie was glad to have a new friend in her life. What she didn't know was her heart was about to be broken by a cold hearted love cheat in this totally true, impossible to disprove tale of deceit. Marie Minshall, 19, explains...

I naturally assumed that this meant we were unofficially engaged

He smiled and removed his designer sunglasses. I could tell he fancied me right off. 'Are you wearing knickers?' he grinned. In hindsight I think it was then I fell in love with the tall, stately Jason Turner.

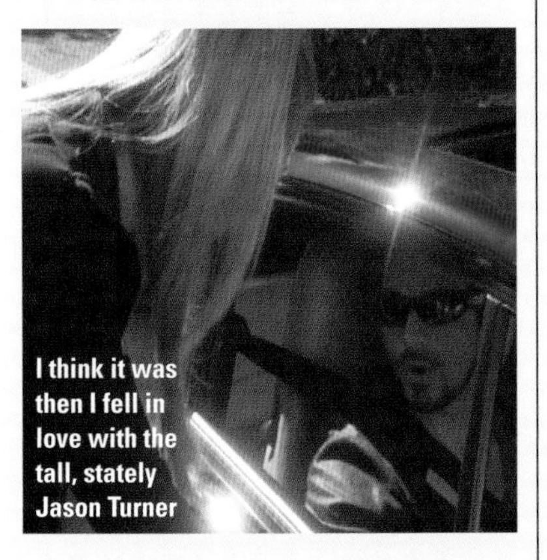

I think it was then I fell in love with the tall, stately Jason Turner

A friend told me he was an Earl's Park footballer and actually quite famous. I hadn't known this and was surprised to discover that his initials exactly matched those I had tattooed on my thigh. Call it serendipity if you will but Lady Luck was not to know she had matched me with Mr Misfortune. I had only been at the training ground that day because I was lost and needed directions to the meals on wheels voluntary group I'd joined. All I knew was just being in his presence made me want to listen to classical music. It was that serious.

'Knickers?'

It was a few days before I got to talk to him properly when we met quite by chance in a local nightspot. I've always been rather shy and didn't think he'd recognize me in my wimple but he told the bouncer I was his sister so I wouldn't get ejected. The gentle way he confirmed my little white lie was intoxicating. I felt as giddy as a schoolgirl when he told the lap-dancer to remove her tongue from his ear. I knew then that he loved me too.

'Classical music'

We clinked glasses and I naturally assumed that this meant we were unofficially engaged. He certainly didn't tell me otherwise.

In retrospect I probably should have asked whether the ring on his left hand was a wedding band but as a born again St John's Ambulance volunteer I didn't even suspect he could be a love rat. I'd always been rather innocent. I was saving myself for my wedding night and I'd never even heard of alcohol before that night. When I asked the waiter for a mineral water I think Jason spiked it with Panda Shandy. It was my first encounter with the rollercoaster world of the celebrity lifestyle.

'Tongue from his ear'

We talked about everything that night, our hopes for the future and my dreams to adopt a child of every hair colour. Jason put his tongue in my ear and confessed that he shared these goals.

'Spiked it with Panda Shandy'

For the next few weeks we spent a couple of hours with each other here and there. I felt like I was floating. We would take long walks quite

Would he really choose that Margot Leadbetter, housecoated throwback over me?

MPEDED MY HEART

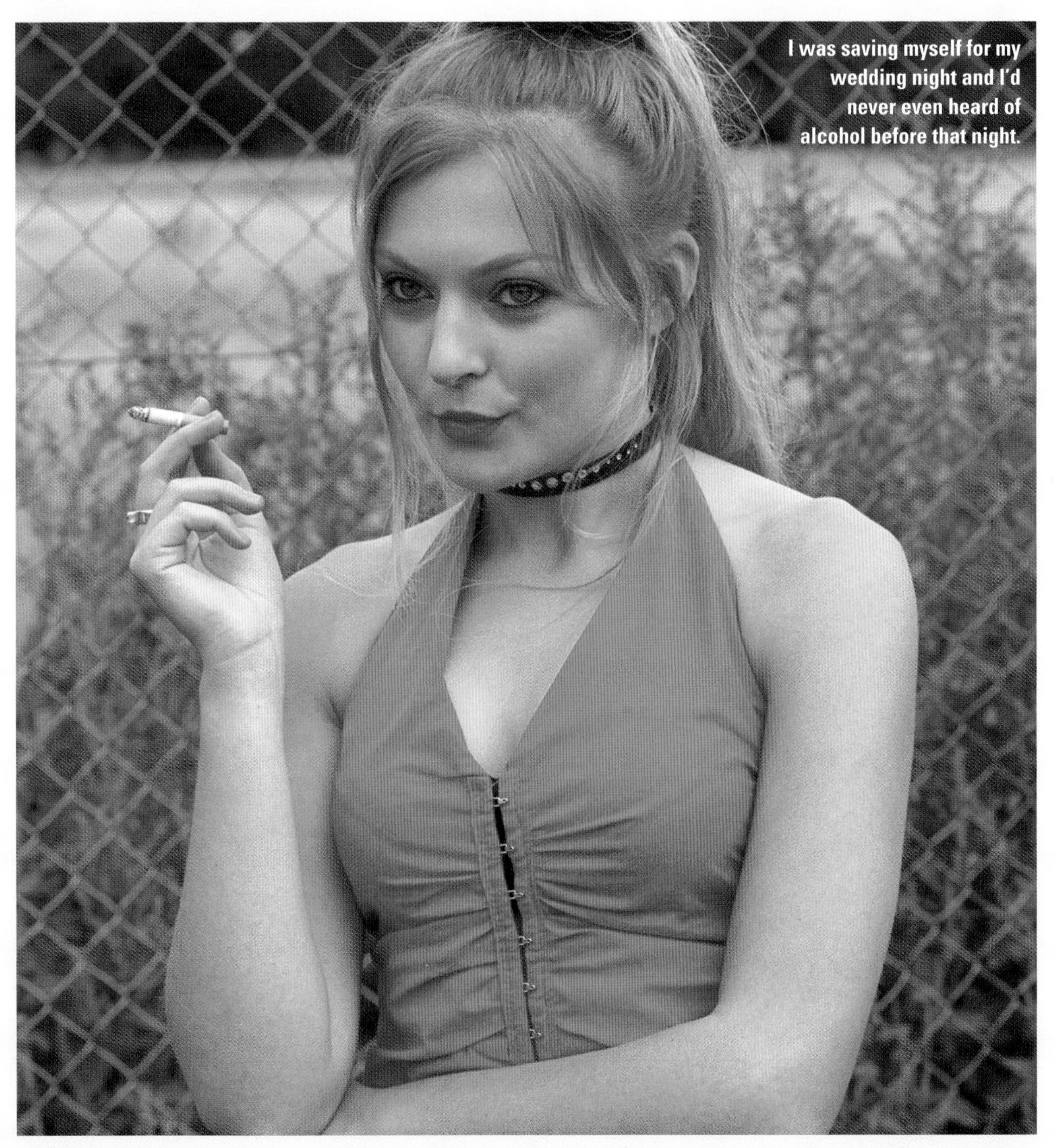

I was saving myself for my wedding night and I'd never even heard of alcohol before that night.

A very dowdy older woman grabbed me by my hair and dragged me to the pavement.

'Guarded about revealing too much about my plans to become a heart surgeon. Little did I know how soon I'd need those skills to mend my own broken heart. One day he bought me an ice cream.'

near beaches when his team played away at a cup tie in Brighton. 'Even a ginger kid?' he had asked me. I nodded shyly. I believed that all children were beautiful. I wrote to my mother and told her I'd found the man I wanted to spend the rest of my life with. The whole family were delighted – they'd been worried my studious nature would condemn me to a lonely life of reading books and stuff. They'd always been rather old-fashioned and I'd been guarded about revealing too much about my plans to become a heart surgeon. Little did I know how soon I'd need those skills to mend my own broken heart.

One day he bought me an ice cream. We were sitting eating it in his car when I lost control of my Flake. As I innocently bent down to remove it from his lap with my teeth the car door flung open. A very dowdy older woman grabbed me by my hair and dragged me to the pavement. She called me horrible names that made my soft milky skin blush. I tried to explain that I needed to get my Flake back out of Jason's flies before it melted. She screamed that I should keep my mouth away from his Flake and that knowing him it would have already melted. My eyes pleaded for him to tell me she was just his mother or his old, ugly spinster sister but he couldn't face me. Then the heady truth sank in. The man who I'd thought was my soulmate was a football flirt and potential sex pest. Worse – he was married!

At first I couldn't believe his innocent smile could have hidden anything but sweet little lies. Were those tales about his ball control just subtle, seductive strategies? Would he really choose that Margot Leadbetter, housecoated throwback over me? I felt sure from looking at her she wasn't the type to have any GCSEs but then as I look back he didn't seem interested in having a woman of substance. On the occasions that I'd tried to talk about intellectual subjects like politics he'd look down my top. He told me the only caucus he was interested in discussing was a naked one.

I've since returned to my family home to recover. I'm currently considering a career in the cloth as there is a ladieswear factory near me that is hiring.

On the occasions that I'd tried to talk about politics he'd look down my top.

'Milky'

We contacted Jason Turner who declined to comment on the basis that he didn't have a leg to stand on and that his wife was in the next room.

We also contacted Tanya Turner who said she would happily tear the little tart's eyes out if she ever caught up with her and confirmed she would be imminently entering the next room to terminate her husband's manhood – such that it is.

IN HER REALLY LOVELY HOME

TANYA TURNER

GIVES AN EXCLUSIVE INTERVIEW TO *A MAGAZINE WITH AN EXCLAMATION MARK IN THE TITLE!*

Committed to good works, Tanya sometimes stands in the road to warn cars of tight corners by wearing this year's fashion hit, chevrons.

Tanya Turner has made more impact upon British society than any woman since Bucks Fizz did the skirt thing. But being the most marvellous creature on the planet is not all plain sailing for football's first lady as our exclusive interview reveals.*

Tanya you are literally the most fantastic woman on the planet. Is it hard work staying so indefatigably superlative?
She laughs modestly before gliding a graceful hand through her flawless, silky blonde hair. 'I wouldn't say I was "superlative" because that sounds like a cure for constipation. I'm a survivor. And I've been blessed with lovely famous people around me who keep my feet firmly on the ground.'

'Geri and I have had lunch a few times. She's a lovely girl!'

Tanya, speaking of your lovely feet, do you pumice?
She pats my arm playfully. 'Well, obviously as someone in the public eye I don't need to. We're all just born perfect. Don't think for one minute though that I take this position of privilege for granted. Once a week I go to the local shops to show normal women how lovely I am. I think it gives them inspiration and quite possibly is the highlight of their week.'

Some members of the press have suggested that in the event of a revolution against the current monarchy, you might like to step up to the role as Queen of the Britons. How do you respond to that obvious attempt to get into your knickers?
She laughs touchingly and delightfully. 'Well, obviously I'm touched and delighted. It's a lovely thing to say. But possibly our current Queen might have a thing or two to say about it. I think the corgis would have to go. Living with Jason all these years – I've had enough of old dogs sniffing around!'

'NOT TO NAME DROP BUT NATURALLY I'M FRIENDS WITH ELTON JOHN. HE'S A LOVELY MAN!'

You're almost too sophisticated to be British. Are you a goddess sent to Earth?
'Sometimes it seems that way doesn't it! No, I think that if not heavenly I'm certainly quite continental and chic. I often feel like I've got a bit of European in me. But only one at a time, I'm not gauche.'

'Fern Britton is a lovely girl!'

A reformed character. Since her rehab Tanya has realised she's not a chicken.

*Through her agent and a copywriter. We thought no one would actually bother reading the text – because, well, you don't really do you. You just skim through the pictures and cling on to the rare moments when someone's shoes don't match. We've actually never spoken directly to a famous person because it's just me and Tatiana in the office.

'PRETTY MUCH
EVERY CELEBRITY
IS A LOVELY
PERSON!'

'CHARDONNAY IS THE ABSOLUTE MOST LOVELY GIRL'

On a serious note, how do you respond to your recent, well publicised problems with drugs which have left some people questioning your right to be part of normal, civilised society?
'Drugs are wrong. Very wrong. They came close to wrecking my life, marriage and looks. But as you can see – not quite. I've learnt a lot from my experience and have tried to channel those lessons into thoroughly commendable community service. I'm pleased to report I've beaten my problems and my life, my marriage and my looks are better than ever. Have you got a powder room by the way?'

'Pretty much every celebrity is a lovely person!'

We know there are a lot of charities that are close to your heart and that you donate some of your time to thinking about doing something for one of them one day. One such cause is world poverty. There is considerable debate currently raging about whether we should cancel Third World debt and the role of the economic community in helping these developing countries without imposing Westernized notions of quality of life upon them. Do you think that a purple palette will really provide the hot colours this season?
Tanya pauses to consider the question, her blue eyes glittering. 'Yes.

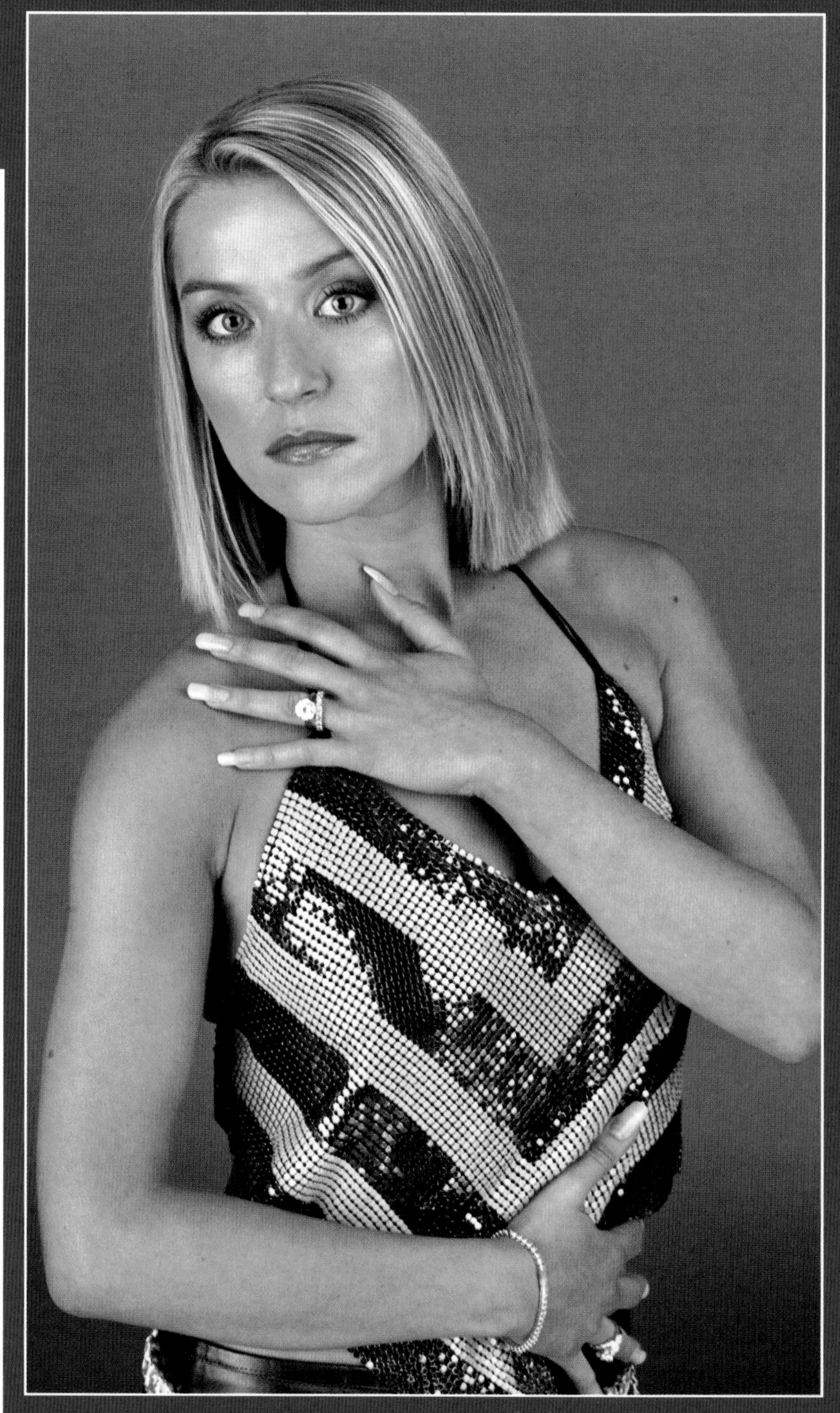

'Tanya Scissorhands.' (Wedding ring model's own so keep your hands off and find your own husband.)

Yes I do but I have mixed opinions about it being a positive development.'

It was clear when you stepped into the media spotlight that the world had a new definition of the word fabulous.
'I believe that will be formalized in the latest edition of the dictionary, yes. But I don't think it's changed me.'

Now we know you are busy so one last question so we can fit another advert for a Swiss watch on this page. Our readers want to get to know the real Tanya Turner, the woman behind the legend. Tell us, favourite celebrity chef?
'I just couldn't choose – they're all lovely!'

'Yes I have met Donna Walmsley. I suppose she's a lovely girl.'

Tanya demonstrates her svelte figure by effortlessly wearing a stocking.

away game$

The top ten for potentially straying spouses

We have compiled the major do's and don'ts for a successful extra-marital life. They are the product of often hard earned experience and Chardonnay had to cancel a colonic to put these together so make sure you heed them. Remember – 'marry in haste, cuckold at leisure'…

1 Thou shalt not recognize any other player right under your husband's nose. If thou dost then try to be discreet and always recognize the international FIFA ruling on keeping to the barest minimum intra club transferring with his teammates. However for a footballer to stop recognizing other female images would involve invasive sex change surgery and must be accepted with good grace as him just being a bloke and playing the field.

2 Thou shalt not worship any photographic images as this puts you firmly in the stalking fan category rather than that of serious wife material. You may get a shag but your arse will skim so fleetingly over his leather interior you'll break some sort of land speed record. If you are going to prostrate yourself try to learn from the cautionary tale of stalker Sheena of swimming pool infamy and wait till you've got a ring on your finger.

3 Thou shalt not take his/her name in vain by plastering a kiss and tell all over the tabloids. Your marriage will be a passionate one – just not necessarily with each other. This is how it has been and shall always be so. Besides, emotional attachment is not only tiresome but could cost you extra. However do be protected. Safe sex is not just making sure your husband's out of earshot.

4 Remember the Day of the Match and sanctify it. Footballers are like fires and will go out if unattended. Unlike fires, footballers do require that

matching underwear is sported at all times and that you flirt but not sleep with their management.

5 Honour your teammate's mother. Try not to have a tug of love child with her (with you doing most of the pulling). It is written that whosoever should get jiggy with a mate's mum shall be given a bloody good hiding condoned by all. If that makes us wrong – we don't want to be right.

6 You shall not murder but you may limit yourself to attempting it if it binds your husband to you in a web of deceit and tragic lies. Remember that throughout the ages violence has achieved many means. Armed prophets were victorious whereas those that turned the other cheek and let their spouse carry on perished or at least ended up with a player in the second division wondering how they got there.

7 Thou shalt not commit adultery too often. But if he does then a pair of blunt scissors is an excellent antidote. Most men find it easy to be monogamous. No sorry that's our typo. That's monotonous in a relationship. As a wife, better behaviour is expected of you. For you – wife – strong and silent men who draw you into temptation away from your husband may simply be so because they have nothing to say. If all else fails and sometimes it is hard to be a woman – giving all your love to just one man – the simple answer is: don't.

8 Thou shalt not steal a good friend's husband unless she is a bitch who never deserved you or him in the first place. Or unless alcoholic consumption such as ten tequila slammers makes it an inevitability. Or unless it seems like a good idea at the time and she won't be back from the gym for an hour. But generally it's really up there with spanked bottom offences. Thou shalt also bear in mind if you chase someone – you may catch them and other things that you may not really want.

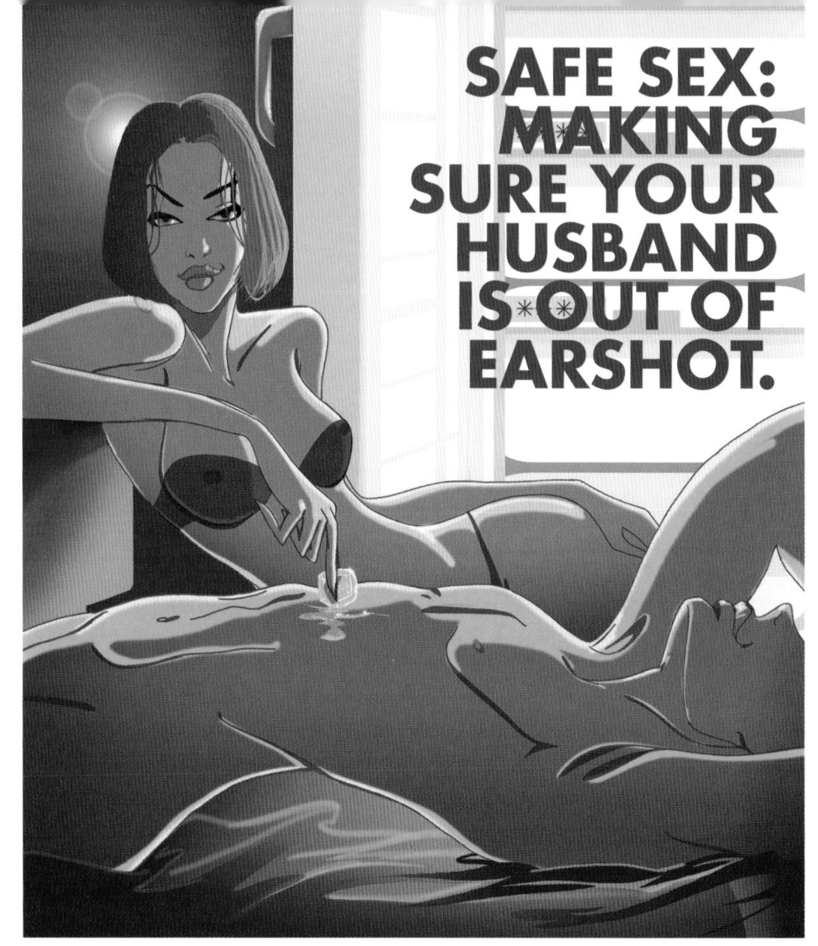

9 Thou shalt not bear false witness against a friend who did manage to keep their legs together unless they are agreeable, well paid for their contribution and it's part of a well concocted plan to frighten your husband out of some tart's bed – at least for one sodding night. Other exclusions include bearing false witness in a trial against the club's chairman who you only had an affair with to convince him you were having an affair with him and didn't try number six on him. Then it's not only okay but advised.

10 Thou shalt not covet his teammate's ass. Or his manservant or his Tony Adams. However footballers are rather like computers and no one would blame you for keeping a backup from the reserves. And if the teammate in question has a problem with that, he shouldn't bend over in tight shorts, should he? Recycling, after all, is ecologically responsible. You may also covet his teammate's ass and anything else he has which may be alluring if your ignorant husband brings him to live in the marital home and he transpires to be infinitely more sensitive, understanding and more knowledgeable about dishwashers than said husband. Then covet to your heart's content.

captain's wife's log

Monday
Hit the treacherous bastard where it will eventually hurt – his wallet. Funnily enough, Jason has decided that keeping me in the style to which I'm fast becoming accustomed is proving too expensive and as a policy may have to be reviewed.
To do: book facial.

Tuesday
Back in the marital home which Jason has decided is financially less crippling – ah – the memories. Through rainy rain and shiny shine – all those memories. I have at least three which are happy.
To do: book more facials. Remembered that Jason's paying.

Wednesday
Scrofulous tosser is telling all and sundry about his new Munster's arrangement. It's war. Luckily I can immerse myself in the boyish arms of Darius, wonder boy and enthusiastic if inexperienced lover. It's like dating Westlife – without the aural punishment though on occasion it feels as if I am doing some sort of social work – which are two words

I've hither to tried to exclude from my vocab. By allowing Darius to train with a master – or I guess mistress – I'm setting him up for a lifetime of fantastic sexual prowess with women that will never match me. For my part – I need the distraction – I've got the drugs bust hearing tomorrow. It would be just my luck to get away with attempted murder, false rape charges and God knows what else to get sent down for an ounce of Charlie and Tate and Lyle.
To do: three facials today – two more planned for tomorrow. My beautician has threatened that any more will leave my face peeled back as if it had been sandblasted. Have decided after tomorrow to have something lifted instead. I don't even need it. I might get them to put it back afterwards.

Thursday
Bastard magistrate.

Friday
OK – I've had a good night's sleep and the picture doesn't look any rosier. I was annoyed of course about the fine – until I realized that Jason would end up coughing and spluttering that up. But community service? Will I ever get the festering rot of human decay from under my fingernails?
Honestly – did the magistrate not catch my tribute to weeping on Chardonnay's programme? My husband's run off with a woman old enough to be Solomon's mother, having made her great with child and taboot – as far

as they know I was probably violated by Laslett earlier this year. Talk about kicking a girl when she's down! Are they certifiably insane? If you're married to Jason Turner drugs should be a right not a privilege. And here I am destined to have my arm up old people. I don't even – retch – clean my own toilet let alone have it in me to get up close and personal with a pensioner's bottom.

To do: book Turkish baths. Will need scouring with a wire brush to get the stench of old flesh off my hands.

Saturday

Two more days of untainted youth before I must face my own mortality, which I think at the sight of a bed sore – may be sooner reached than expected.

Sunday

Cometh the hour cometh the woman with the dishpan hands. I swear I can hear the death knell toll ...

Monday

Too tired to talk. Have had three showers and I still can't remember the lemony glow of clean.

Tuesday

It's my – retch – 'day off'. God – I never thought I'd have to spit out those words.

I've had to come back for a second entry. I've heard on the jungle drums that Ken and Barbie's progeny has one ball in the Albert Hall.

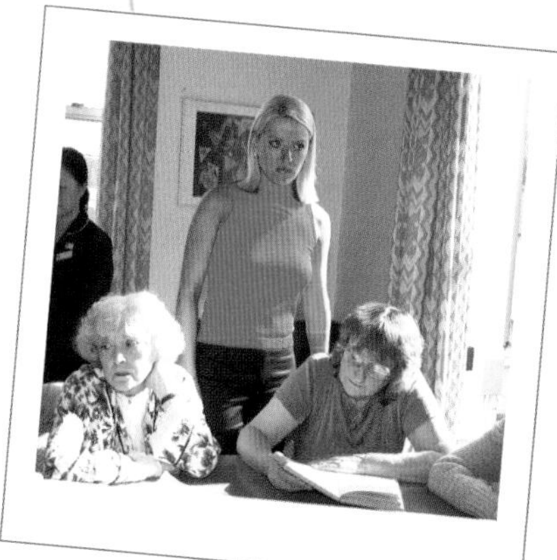

Wednesday

Feel bad about my kneejerk comments regarding Ken Junior yesterday. The fact I got through another day without sporting a lightning bolt through my head amazes me. Still – I can't wallow too much in empathy – I'm back with my head halfway down a commode at Sunset Towers for the Imminently Dead. I don't know what the place is really called. I don't want to know. Maybe 'knackers yard'? My – retch – 'boss' is a matron who makes the Bride of Chucky look gentle. I swear she was too ugly to get a footballer husband for herself so is revelling in her revenge now.

Thursday

Had sauna to sweat it out of me. Will start campaigning for euthanasia, the rest of the day I had to sit down with a bottle of something stronger than Anthrax. I couldn't even reach up to the remote control. At 9 pm I had a worrying interlude when for about twenty seconds I fantasized about – retch – buying a pair of slippers. Just for a couple of mad, bad minutes something in my head said they would be comfortable. Something's got to be done.

Friday

Rosa Klebb, Sunset Towers' matron has ordered me to cut back on the number of surgical gloves I use. It's me or her. That nursing home ain't big enough for the both of us.

Saturday

Was having a friendly bout of water sports with Darius in the pool when Jason tipped up unexpectedly. Bundled a startled Darius into the sauna to find Jason reeling. He launched into the sort of story that would make Jerry Springer shake his head at the humanity.

Apparently Jason was playing happy families with the wizened hag Pascoe and THEIR, yes THEIR spawn. As much as I hate his guts right now I have to give him credit. He's not even shown that much responsibility for his own life before – let alone someone else's. Almost regret not breeding with him – but he was obviously waiting for Jackie the Jackal to come along to fulfil the prophesy. Anyway, now he thinks in his infinitely limited wisdom that his spawn is defective – he's decided to put it back in the box and return with the receipt for a refund.

Don't even know how to get my head round this one. Decide that if I take him back – at least I'm in a strong position. He'd die (or I remind myself – he'd make sure I'd die) rather than let word get out about him having fathered an intersex baby. I may not be able to work the dishwasher but I can work salacious secrets almost as well as the spiritual leader of such things – Hazel.

Remember Darius some time later and rescue him surreptitiously from the sauna. Threw him back like the guppy he is, naked and about two stone lighter than I'd remembered into the night.

Sunday

Apparently Jackie is spitting glass. I hear she was watching our reunification television conference like he was her worst enemy. Not while I'm still alive she's not.

Monday

The reign of terror at Sunset Towers is drawing to a close. After gauging Rosa Klebb's love of the almighty dollar I came up with a plan and a stack of fifty pound notes which seemed to encourage her to my way of thinking. Within two hours we'd installed one of Jason's old cast-offs who can pass as an uglier version of me to anyone with no concept of seasonal trends and can act as my permanent stand-in. Big Ron and Lara Bateman's old nanny – Mel – is no stranger to wiping bottoms and cleaning up sick so should be right at home. Harrods here I come! Vive la English Judicial system!

dre$$ me like...Tanya

Here is a little exercise in dressing. Contrary to popular opinion, dressing is not all about making sure you put the right limbs through the right holes so that you aren't arrested. No, inadvertent flashing is the least of your many worries. You must also resist the temptations to buy within your budget. No woman will find love until they've found couture. So just say no to outlet centres. It's not worth it.

We have also been informed by various charities that the world's poor when asked have stated that their preference would be towards food rather than last season's cast-offs illustrating that you are never too poor to have taste. Practise having 'taste' with our handy mix and match guide to mixing and matching.

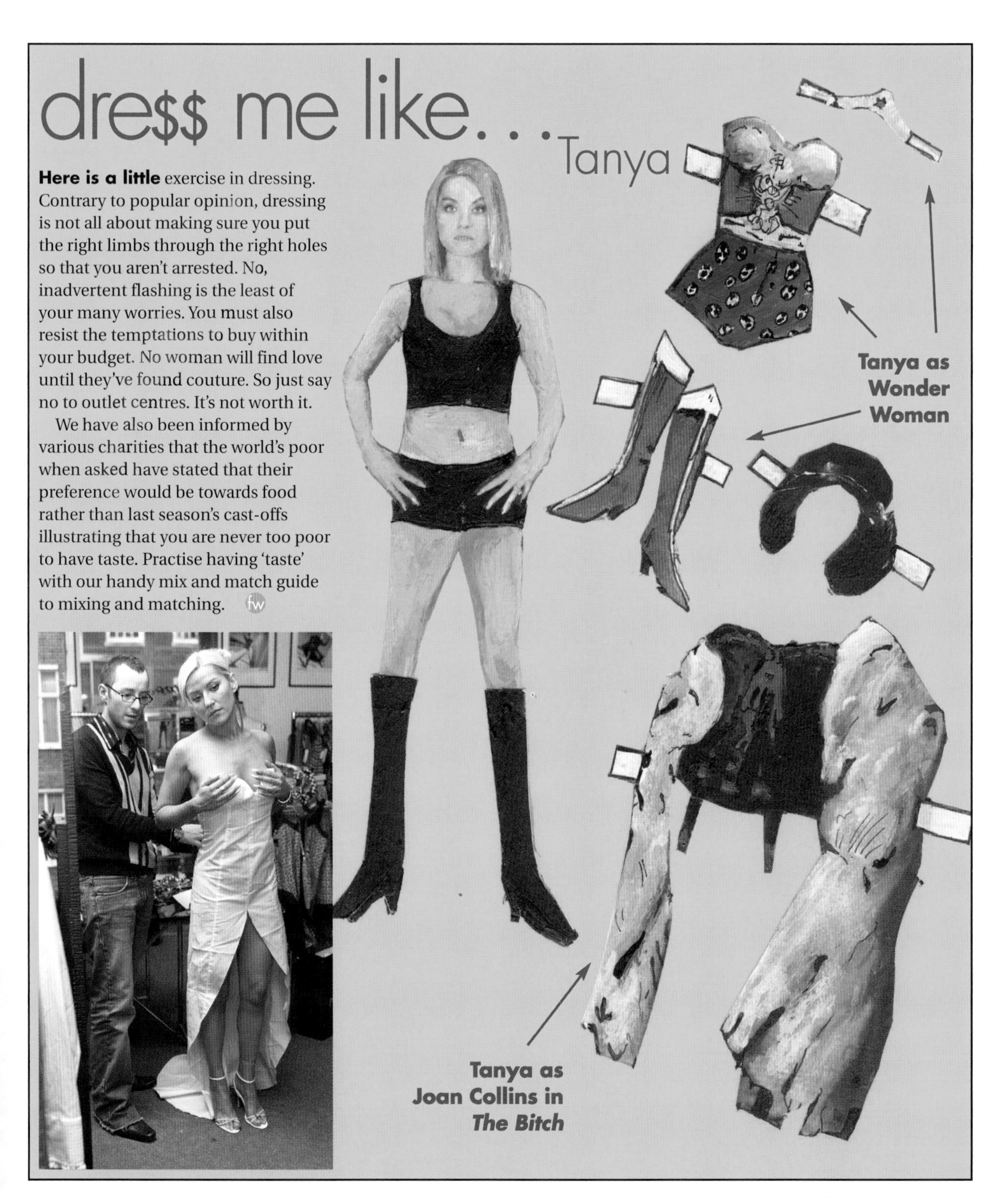

Tanya as Wonder Woman

Tanya as Joan Collins in *The Bitch*

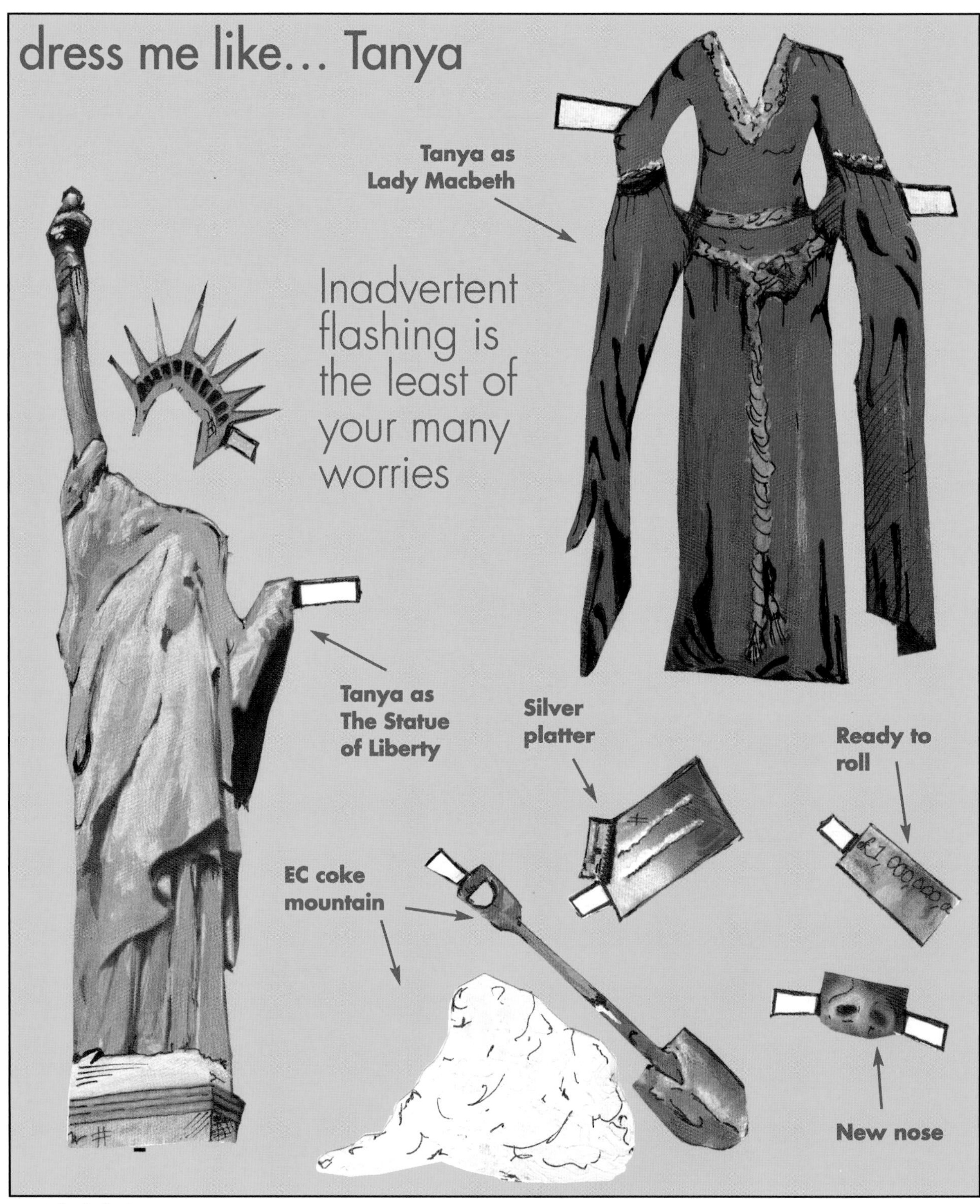
dress me like... Tanya
Tanya as
Lady Macbeth
Inadvertent
flashing is
the least of
your many
worries
Tanya as
The Statue
of Liberty
Silver
platter
Ready to
roll
EC coke
mountain
New nose

dress me like... Chardonnay
Breakdown matt-brown hair
Fake baby and milk
Breakdown pyjamas
Nail scissors for hacking breakdown matt-brown hair
Vaguely ethnic christening wear to accompany *Tales of the Unexpected*-style dancing
Just say no to outlet centres. It's not worth it

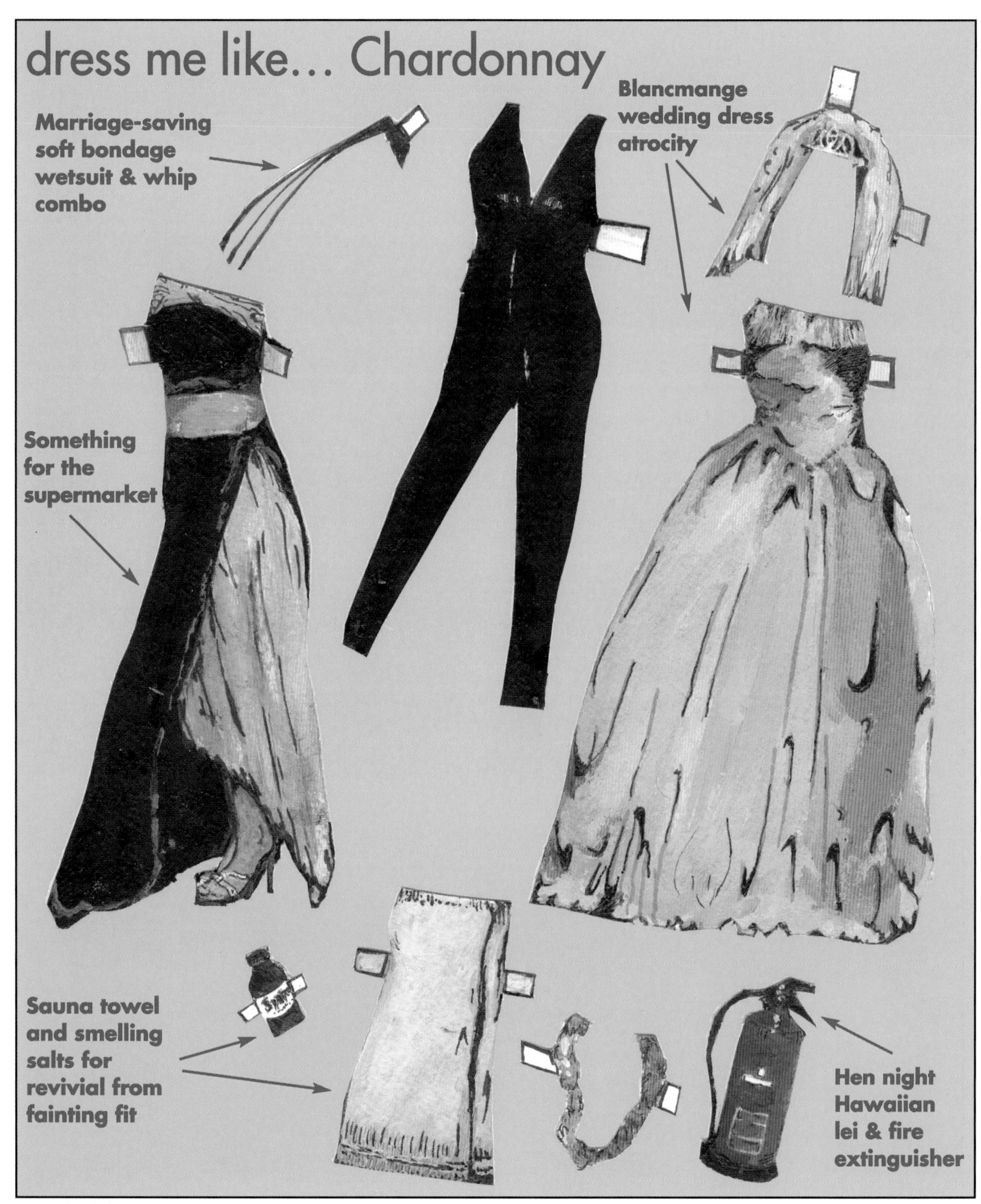
dress me like... Chardonnay
Marriage-saving soft bondage wetsuit & whip combo
Blancmange wedding dress atrocity
Something for the supermarket
Sauna towel and smelling salts for revivial from fainting fit
Hen night Hawaiian lei & fire extinguisher

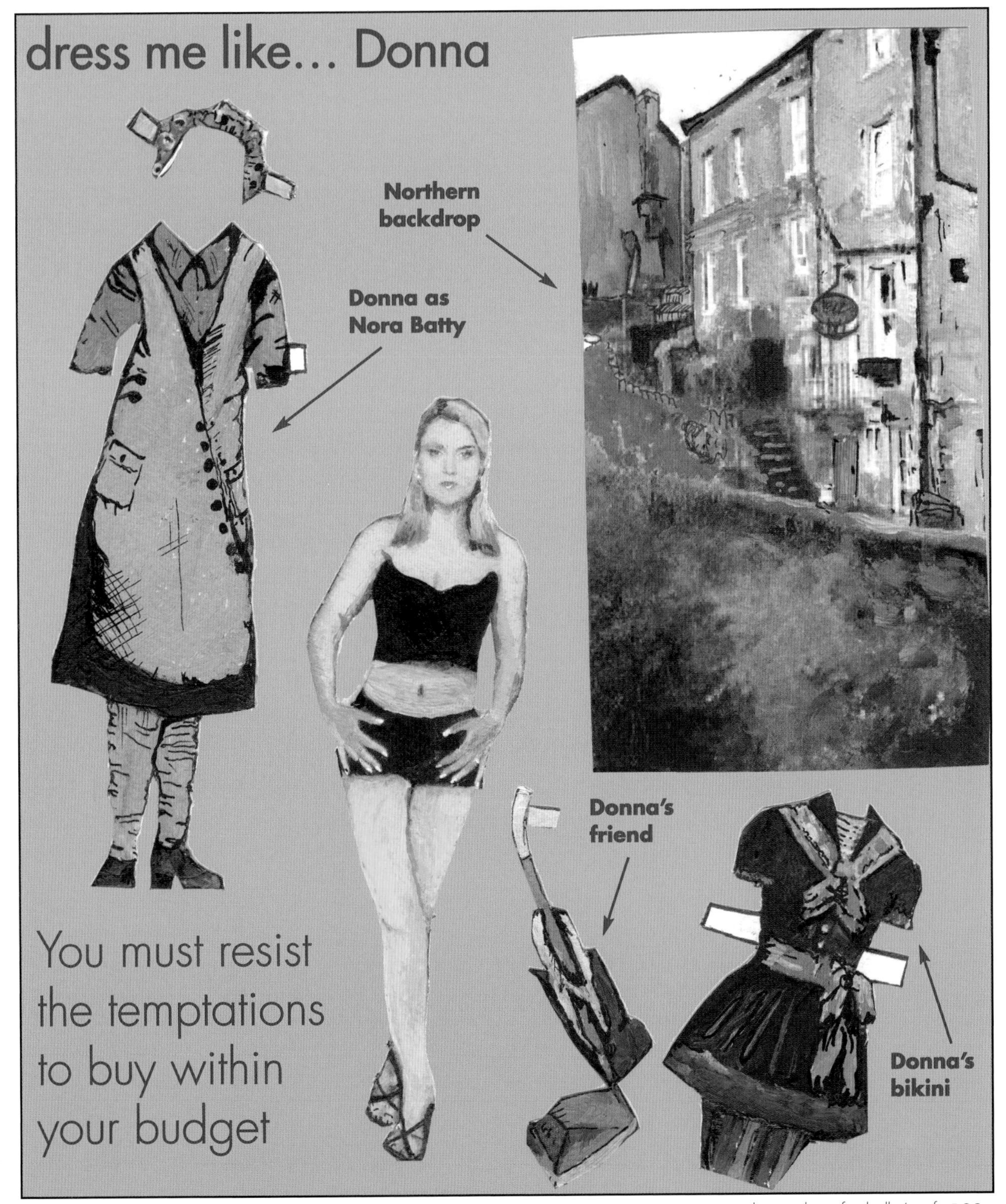
dress me like… Donna
Northern backdrop
Donna as Nora Batty
Donna's friend
Donna's bikini
You must resist the temptations to buy within your budget

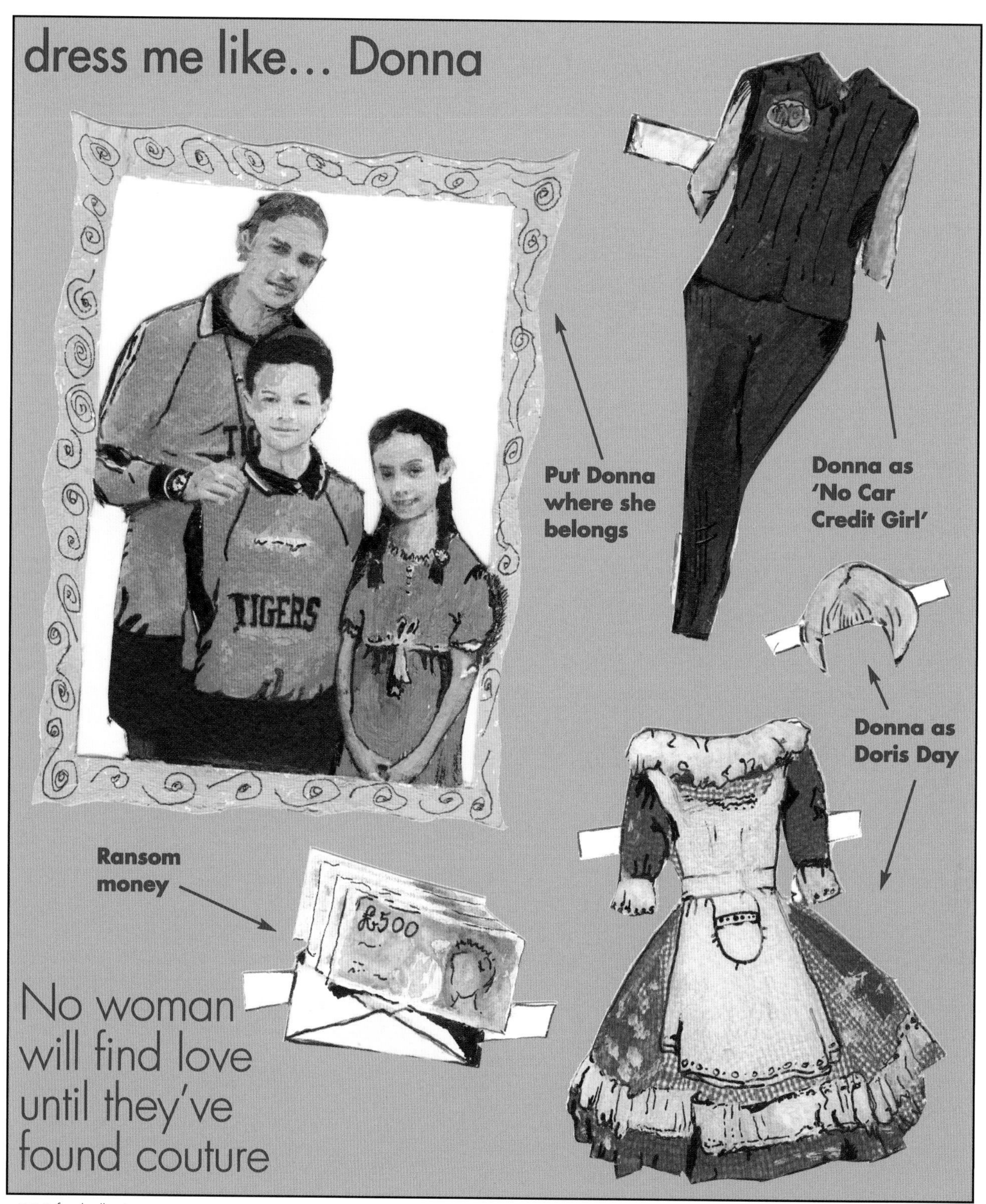
dress me like... Donna
TIGERS
Put Donna where she belongs
Donna as 'No Car Credit Girl'
Donna as Doris Day
Ransom money
£500
No woman will find love until they've found couture

Welcome to Issue 1 of 'Visible Ribs', my tri-weekly magazine dedicated to thinness, being thin and not being fat!

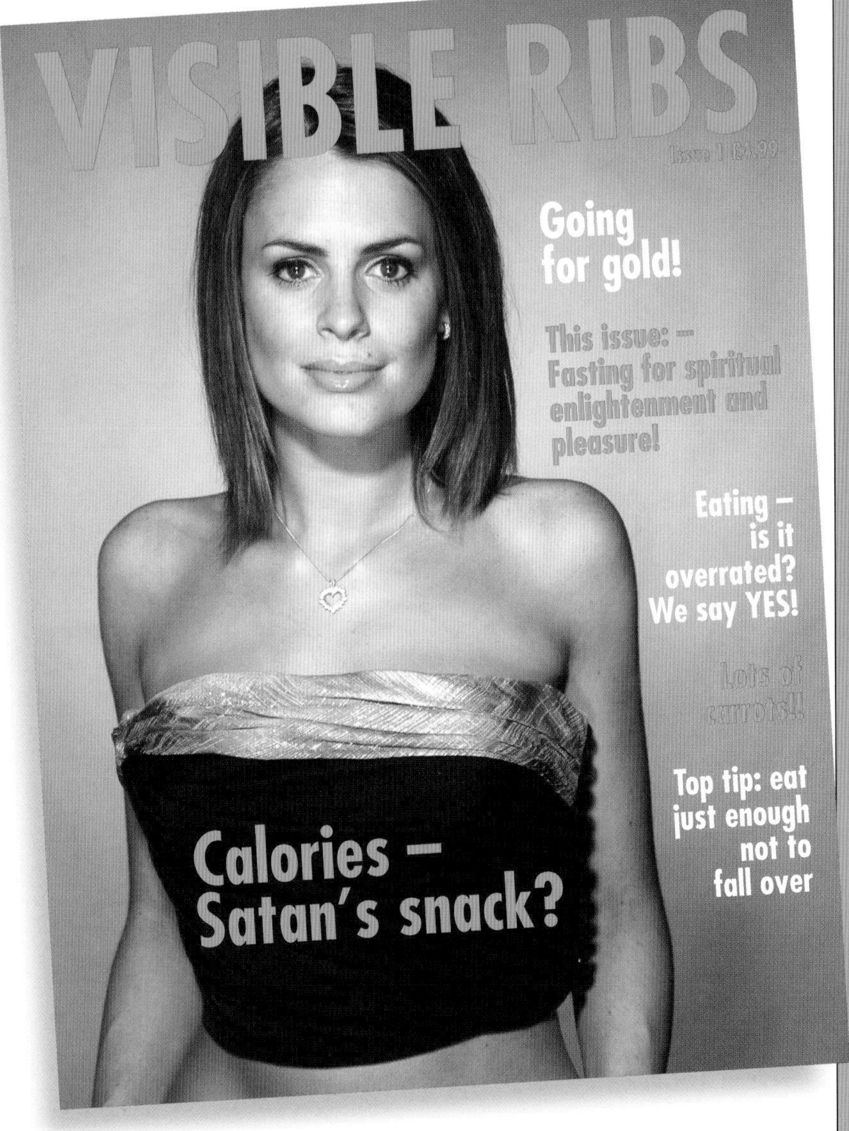

In Issue 1:

Gold is said to be a natural boost to weight loss. So if you are planning a divorce – plan to eat your old wedding ring! If you trim down you might even nab a new footballer and not live out your life as a sad and lonely old crone!

There is a reason rabbits get laid a lot – they all share the habit of eating **lots of carrots**. We must all try to get a healthy balance and that translates as a thirty a day carrot habit. The balance must be between eating enough not to fall over and not getting piggy. And remember the more jewellery you wear the more you'll work those muscles.

Top topic inside this issue – **Eating** – is it overrated as a life-giving force? We assume in our medical inexperience – YES!

Work out while you're working

Just because you're a busy working mum – there's no reason to pile on the pounds while you're earning them. **Try to become a light grazer**. When your photographer is reloading his film, eat some celery. Try to find a quiet corner to masticate properly and you'll find yourself actually burning calories and probably having fun.

Instead of drinking a sugary drink, try **sucking air through a straw**. It will fill your stomach and pleasantly bloat you. You can keep active too – there are many muscles you can clench without being seen.

Ways to stop being a porky pig!

1. Dinner **don'ts** – don't do dinner.
2. Understand your relationship with **food**. Is your body telling you that you need it? Time to retrain it through rigorous exercise and monklike self-denial.
3. If you find it hard to beat the temptation of **chocolate**, don't go into shops. Order in a healthy food parcel from Harrods instead.
4. Beating **food** addiction is a lifetime and therefore a fairly long-term commitment. You're just going to have to find other ways to have **fun**.
5. Just stop cramming **food** into your **mouth** – it's not that hard is it?

The Footie's Wife's Prayer

(to the Patron Saint of FWs – Queen Beckham)

Our Mama, who was at time of writing still in Beckingham Palace, Manchester but just before going to press moved to Real Madrid (not the false one), and by the time you're reading this who knows – could be orbiting the Earth like Mir, as the first FW in space,
Hallowed be thy Married Name
Thy Spice World come,
A footballer's legally binding Will be done and dusted,
Forgive us this day our daily bread and numerous other too much dietary trespasses,
As we forgive those who report these illicit feeding frenzies in the press and generally cling on to every word or style statement you make you classy Queen of the Victorias.
Lead us not into premature autobiography/ill-advised comeback album/ + 5 calorie individual meal temptations,
Say you'll be there to spice up my life,
As two becomes one in a football/pop dream team
As I get Girl Power,
While he gets the Glory,
Viva forever.
Amen.

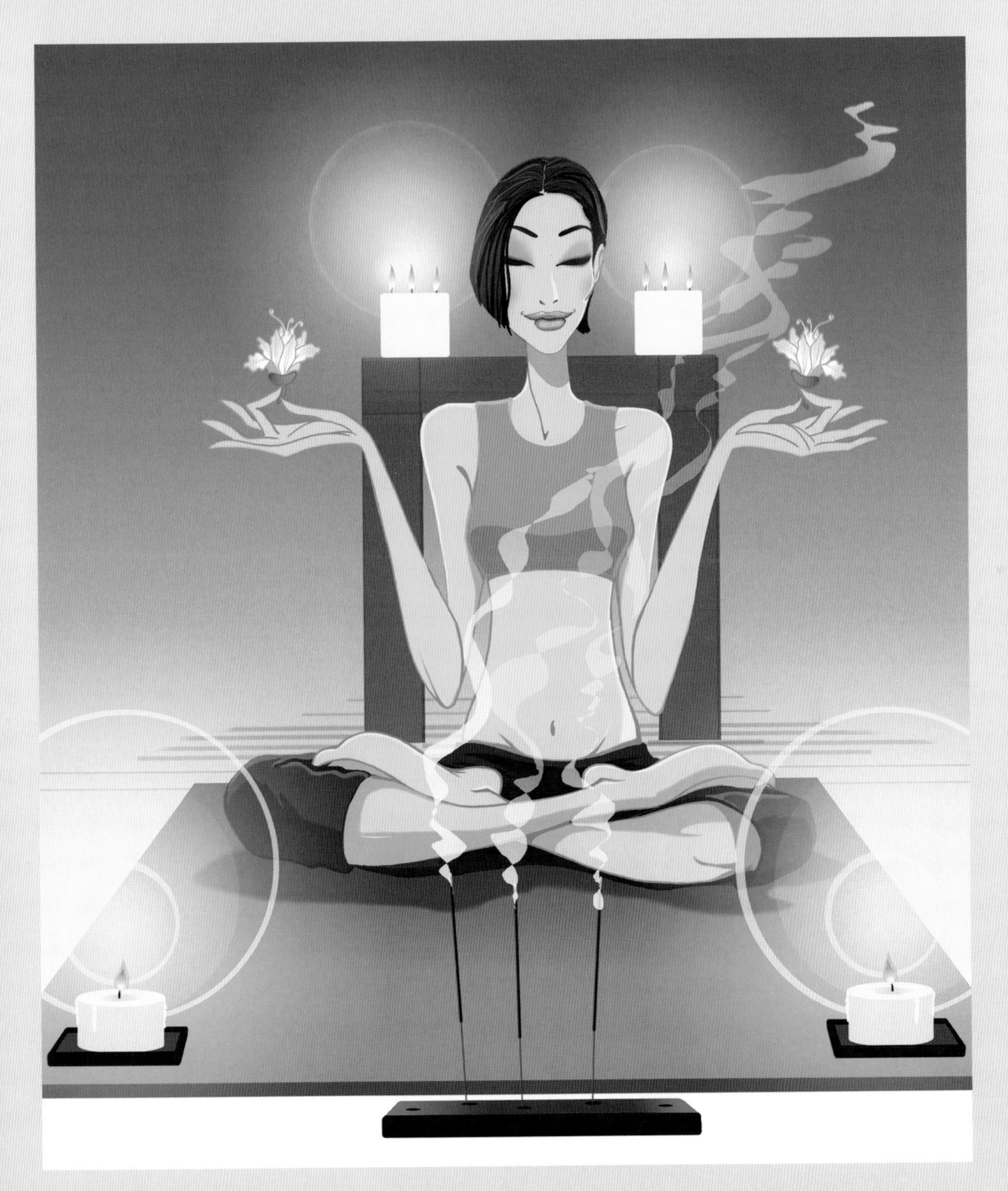

the beautiful game for men

It's not beautiful, it's sweaty all-man action

Football is a beautiful game, particularly if one compares it to darts which is notably short on loveliness and smells of beer. In a world without football we would be overrun with YTS mechanics loitering around shopping precincts on a Saturday afternoon. These fine adolescents could not hope to earn more than the prime minister for the singular ability to run on grass. Heaven forefend, they might turn to violence and play rugby.

To start your career in ball kicky-bouty there are a few important things you – yes YOU – need to know and they so follow:

- Don't study at school. If you do you might end up earning minimum wage as a prime minister or

Practice endorsing product placements to your friends

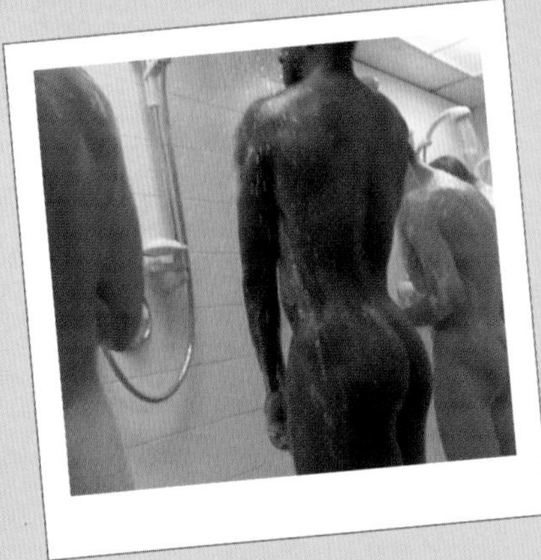

something. Hey teacher. Leave those kids alone.

- Practice kicking a ball.
- If you like catching a ball you are either misunderstanding the rules of football or playing netball.
- Practice kicking a ball.
- To really look like a pro run ten yards and spit.
- Have a go at putting your hand up while looking shocked and aggrieved. Real footballers do this when they want to be given a throw in/free kick/avoid paparazzi.
- Don't be a cry-baby, wet hankie. Sobbing has no place in football unless it can be incorporated into a montage scene to 'Nessun Dorma'.
- Practice endorsing product placements to your friends. Make sure you're not caught behind the bike sheds with a rival brand. You will lose all credibility and possibly your retirement nest egg.
- Practice kicking a ball.
- Do get all homoerotic on the pitch. However, sticking your tongue in a team member's ear when he hasn't just scored is frowned upon.

There is a fine and noble tradition of post-match interviews where players get to state the glaringly obvious. A little known insider secret is that these are all recorded at the beginning of a season and constitute three categories, 'we won', 'we lost' and 'we were made to look like schoolgirls'. To keep it applicable for any situation non-committal phrases were developed by pundits in 1902 and no one has seen any reason to change them now.

(EC Council Directive: Changing these phrases for something more intelligent will get you accused of being a foreign sort who writes poetry.)

A load of old balls – platitudes you must learn to say while looking sweaty and distracted (and what they really mean):

- **All credit to the lads:** You scored the goal and put in a couple of important tackles but must share the glory with ten other bastards who were pretending to tie their shoelaces or having groin strain every time you could have done with a hand.
- **Funny old game:** Come on – this is a Third Division club. Their sub bench is made up of people they press-ganged from the crowd.
- **It's a game of two halves:** And there was you worrying you'd have to wait until after the game to get beaten with a wet towel by the manager.
- **I'm flattered by their interest:** You were caught with 3 oz of nose candy and you're about to get a discreet transfer to a pub team in Wigan but you have to appear nothing short of delighted about it.

To really look like a pro run ten yards and spit

- **Home draw:** A quiet night for lap-dancers and in silent revenge, probably for your wife too.
- **Sleeping giant:** A large club with increasingly desperate but geographically obligated supporters that hasn't won anything apart from a flu epidemic mid season.

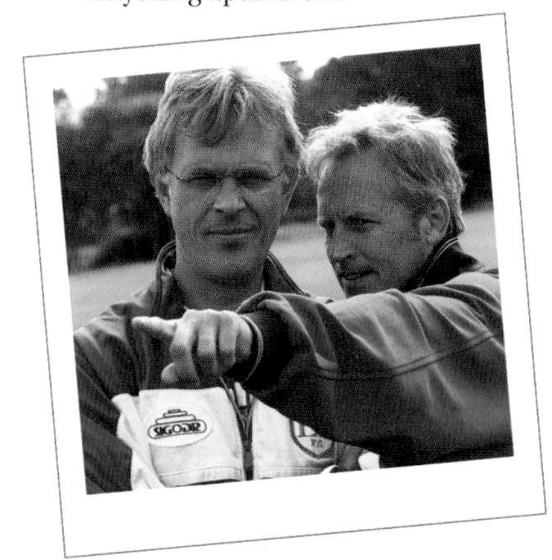

- **Onion bag:** Another word for the net which no one has used since footballers played in black and white but best know it just in case Des Lynam has a moment.
- **Have a pop:** Wearing headphones and sing/shouting on the World Cup song. You are legally and contractually bound to have a mullet unless you are of ethnic origin in which case you will be required to rap.
- **Very much so/As I say/ Obviously/To be honest:** The interviewer asked an inane question but he's got a microphone stuffed so far up your nose he can hear your brainwaves so you'd better stall while you think of something to say.

Kept it tight: You picked up the wrong jockstrap in the dressing room.

- **It's a young side:** We couldn't afford to buy anyone new and had to field the teaboy.
- **You know...:** The interviewer is still looking at you and you have run out of words.
- **You need a bit of luck if you are going to get the rub of the green:** No one knows the meaning of this phrase and you're not meant to ask.
- **The game isn't over till the final whistle blows:** So you have to wait for that pint.

the beautiful game for women

Men may play the game but women know the score

Football is a beautiful game, especially from a distance when you can't pick up the aromas of lint oil and socks that smell like road kill. If you are a woman don't be seduced by the subtle arts of the flat back four and be tempted to actually play football yourself. Beating men at their own game has all the aphrodisiacal qualities of Ann Widdecombe and you get mud in your hair. No, football is a beautiful game because unlike rugby which requires inbreeding the qualities of a pitbull and a public school education over generations, it can be played by anyone with limbs. And for beautiful women it's their ticket out because if they attach themselves to someone with said limbs they'll be sitting pretty in shag pile splendour come Micklemas.

The minute you grasp ball control you have his attention so memorize these facts. Football…What YOU need to know:

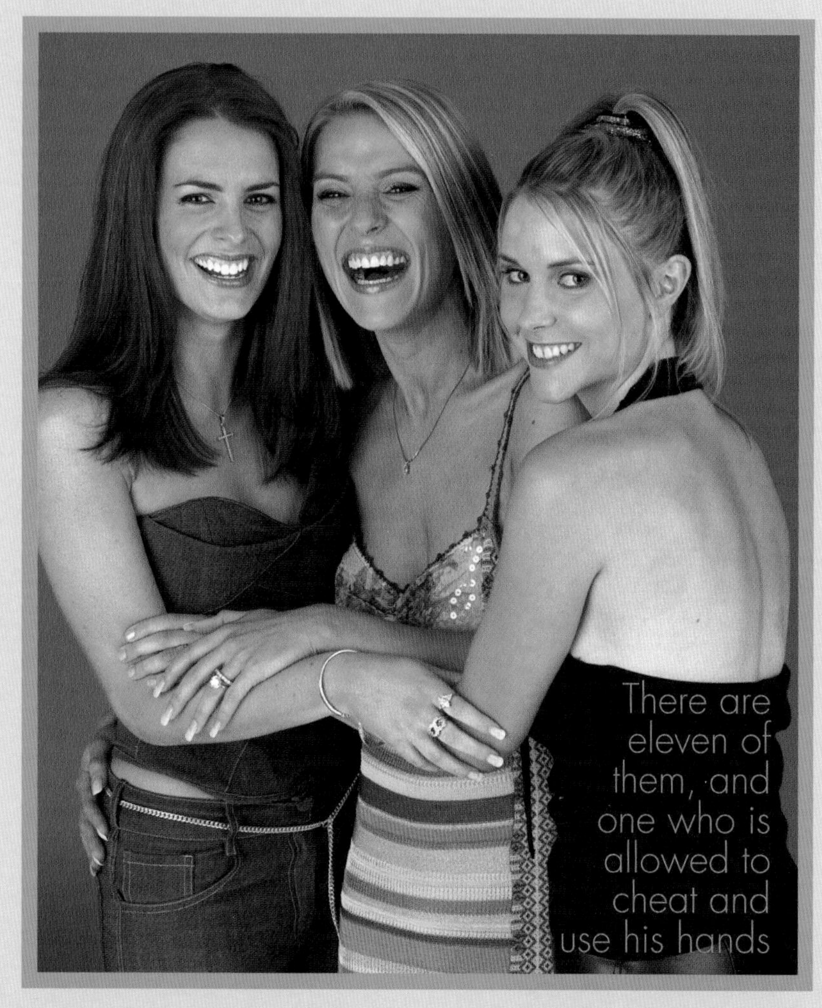

There are eleven of them, and one who is allowed to cheat and use his hands

- Footballers must use their *'feet'* to kick the *'ball'*.
- They are not expected to do this alone. There are ten more of them and one who is allowed to cheat and use his hands.
- The object is to *'score'* more *'goals'* than the other men who wear different colour shirts.
- You score goals by tidying up the *'pitch'* (or lawn) of balls and storing them in the *'nets'* at either end.
- Apparently it matters which net you get it in – though confusingly this changes at one stage in the match so check first.
- You are allowed to hit the ball with your head as this is considered the least valuable part of a footballer's body.
- You are not allowed to use a tissue to pick up the ball even if it's muddy.
- You can't pull an opponent's hair at least while anyone is watching.
- Football has never been a celebrated cavalcade of colours – red and yellow seem to be the palette – regardless of seasonal trends. Add interest with an Alice band. Not on you obviously, on your long haired hubby at Liverpool.
- Even if they run at you really fast you aren't allowed to run away squealing like a stack pig.
- A referee's official name is not 'you mother-f*&^ing c%£t' when addressing him directly.

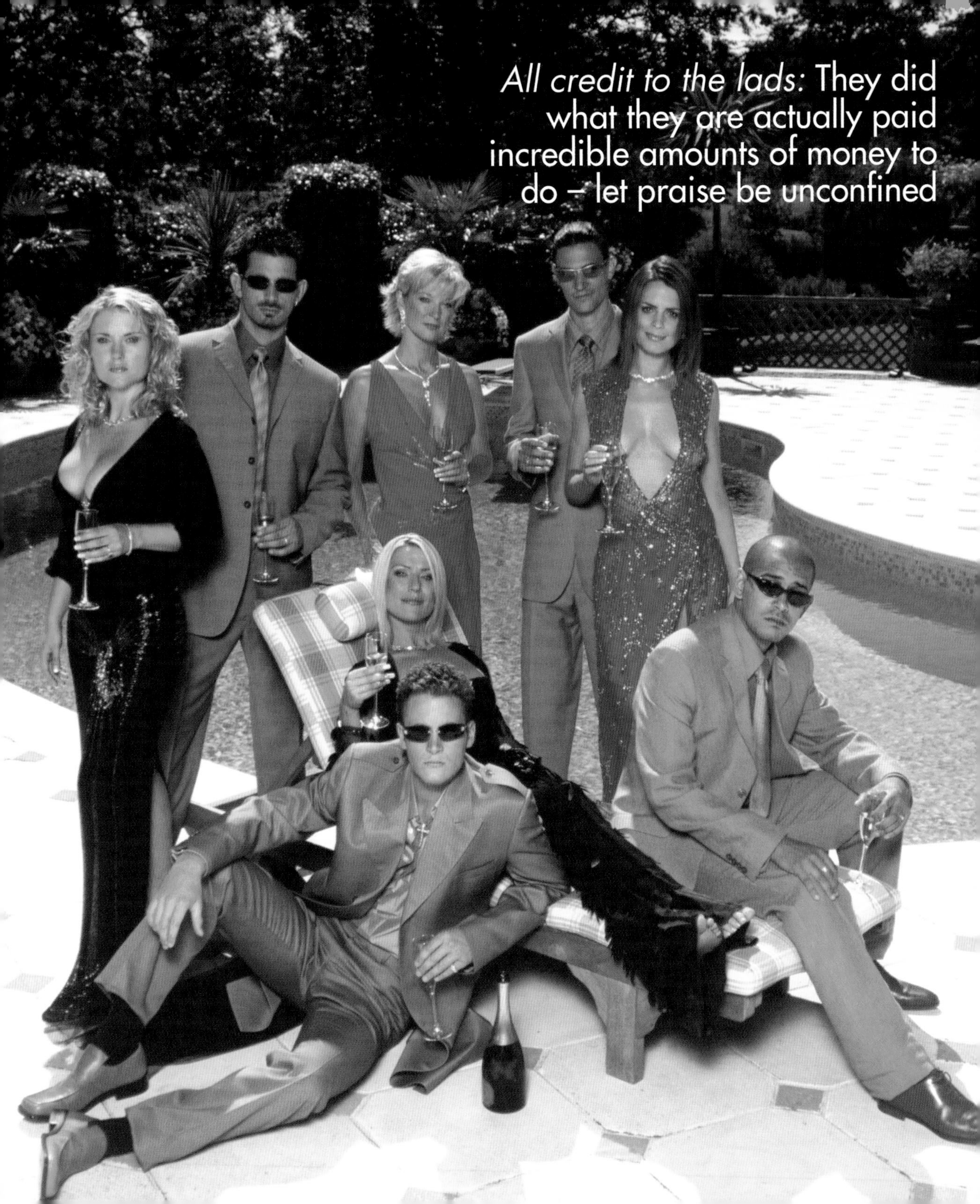

All credit to the lads: They did what they are actually paid incredible amounts of money to do – let praise be unconfined

A load of old balls – football sayings you should learn:

(Note, women should be seen making tea and not heard with regards to football, so consider the fact you understand your dirty little secret.)

- **All credit to the lads:** They did what they are actually paid incredible amounts of money to do – let praise be unconfined.
- **Funny old game:** But not as good as *Friends* or *Sabrina the Teenage Witch*.
- **Game of two halves:** Apparently you are given a toilet break to redo your hair.
- **Home draw:** One less chance for him to take the three tarts he picked up in Stringfellows to a hotel with him.
- **He kept it tight:** His shorts shrunk in the wash.
- **Onion bag:** Euro wife.
- **Have a pop:** Hoddle and Waddle's 'Diamond Lights'.
- **Quality player:** Designed a hand-made wedding ring for you rather than bought one on the high street that looks like a hula hoop dipped in cubic zirconia and possibly is.
- **Squad player:** He'll be under your feet more but you have a wider pool to choose from if you want to trade him in.
- **Unfashionable club:** Ugly team in an ugly kit from an ugly town.
- **Going to the wire:** You can't nick off early on holiday this year.
- **At the end of the day:** It's time for a vodka.
- **Over the full 90 minutes:** There's time to nip out for a couple of impulse buys.
- **It was all there to play for:** But your idiot husband threw away a sitter.
- **Where it counts – on the pitch:** He's a notorious arse off it but the little bugger is most adept when it comes to playing with balls.
- **The lads have given it 110%:** He won't have the energy to mow the lawn again tomorrow.
- **You make your own luck in this game:** Or his poor wife has to make it with the boss.
- **It's the referees' decision that counts:** So it may be necessary to make it with him too.
- **You can't question the players' commitment:** But you could almost certainly question their haircuts.

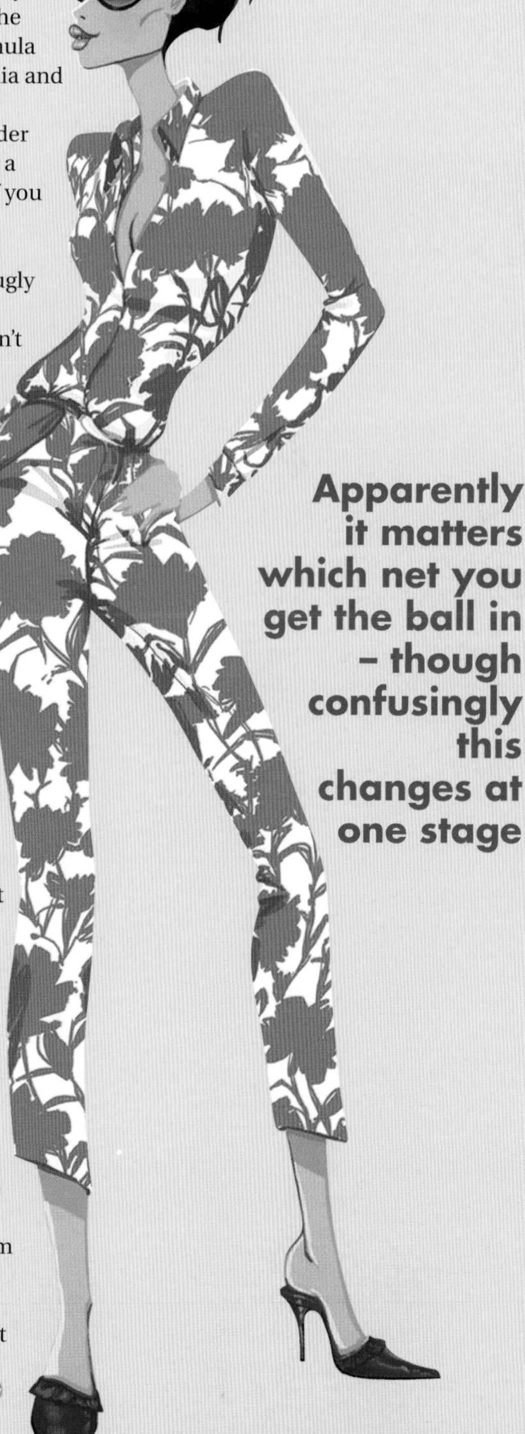

Apparently it matters which net you get the ball in – though confusingly this changes at one stage

the fourth divi$ion: down but not out

So all of our best and most contrived advice has failed… Possibly it isn't our fault. Possibly it isn't even your fault. Perhaps you weren't cut out to be a Footballer's Wife and there's no shame in that. And in saying that we're obviously just being kind because it is the zenith of any woman's life reducing all else to abject failure. Being a Footballer's Wife (and we use the capitalization advisedly) is for the chosen few and you have found yourself when tested to be inadequate. Pat your plump and dowdy little shoulder and say, 'Best put the kettle on and see if there's a manual tradesman out there who'll have me.'

We could dwell at this point on painful post mortems but it's probably best to just concede you're either too fat, too brunette or a lesbian feminist. Let's just skip to the contingency plan section and find you some sort of a future with a non-footballing husband before it's too late. But you'd better hurry because if you pause until the menopause (which starts at thirty to the best of our understanding) then you'll find yourself living until you die with your sister and an increasingly bitter scowl.

Warm fronts

If you are not a total minger then you may still have a career in the media. Perhaps you didn't get a footballer because you just weren't wearing enough lipgloss that day. Show them what they missed by becoming a weather girl or by presenting the National Lottery Show. Remember you don't need talent to get ahead (see Russian tennis players and *Pop Idol*). This may not directly help you with a last-ditch effort to marry a footballer but could net you a children's television presenter. He'll have a reasonable salary, a long-term career as long as you keep his greying temples in check and no limit to any amount of potential drug taking you wish to engage in.

Winning the Lottery

Well, maybe, just maybe. God loves a tryer and you've been really trying. If you win lots of money there'll be no shortage of men willing to marry you, or for that matter women. In fact, we'll marry you.

Celebrity hanger-on

A fine and noble tradition. It's not just about ripping off someone who presents the National Lottery Show; it's about finding your spiritual tribe. This will include people who are famous for no particular reason like all those people in the party pages of *Hello!* Mention famous friends but discourage them from popping over and trying to get in shot if you manage to get some press space, the grasping bastards can get their own photoshoot.

IT girl

Being an IT girl – and please don't confuse this with information technology – is normally something you have to be bred for – preferably inbred for but you could always fly in from Switzerland and call yourself a Marquee.

I'm blonde therefore I am

'Let's get metaphysical' sang Olivia Newton-John, almost. Either way – we do know she lived in a leotard for most of the early Eighties and therefore has much to teach us. To be blonde and bland you could just shake your hips and hope for the best. Or you could take to watching GMTV for tips – which is like public access broadcasting for inane grinners everywhere.

Fantasy football

Just pretend you are married to a footballer. No one can take the mock Tudor from your mind though some may try with electrodes and counselling.

Inheritance

The increase in daytime television concerning antiques has taught us much. First, even men who look like they smell of mothballs can have a media career and secondly it's worth staying in favour with your elderly relatives who also look like they smell of mothballs. There could well be gold in them hills.

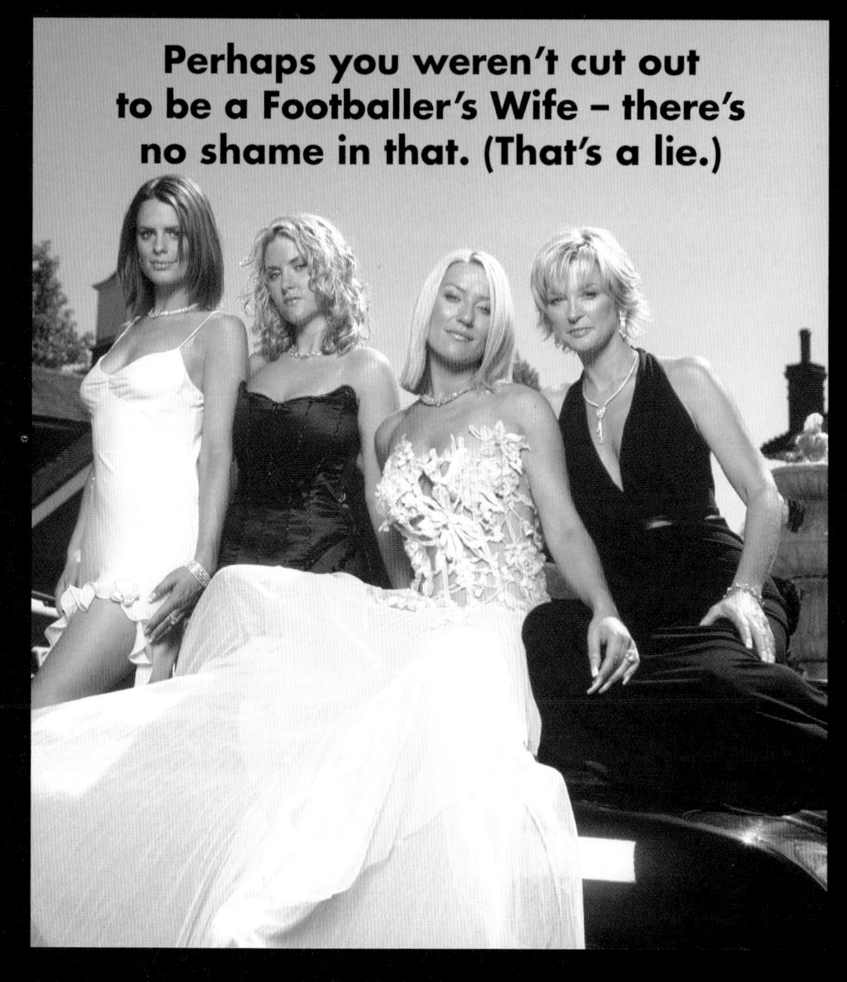

Marry a non-footballing sportsman

Let us objectively and mercenarily review our options.

- Cricket – better get the coffee in. Cricket is like taking the slow train to nap-nap land.
- Rugby – for the connoisseur of the bulky thigh and violently posh.
- Darts – here's hoping you like the smell of beer and the dulcet tones of grunting.
- Swimmer – moving on…
- Tennis player – nice legs, humourless. You only have to watch Wimbledon for five minutes to see how desperate people are to laugh at just about anything. If a player even drops his racket – there's mass guffawing. If he drops his shorts, St John's ambulancemen are called in to cope with the hysteria.
- Racing driver – not rally car: they all listen to Pink Floyd and wear Def Leppard T-shirts. Formula One is acceptable but there is a high turnover and you may be expected to walk around the pits in a swimsuit holding a flag.
- Boxing – possibly a little intellectual. Speech defects are commonplace and you may be expected to walk around the ring in a swimsuit holding a round number.

Marry a non-footballing, non-sportsman, man

There are other wives in the public eye. If you don't mind wearing menopause clothes and a geriatric on your arm you could be a politician's wife. This is the only career that attracts more sexual voracity in its major players than football. Or you could just marry that bricklayer. We're sure you'll be very happy together. And frankly you'd better be because you won't have any plasma TVs to take the sting off misery.

Don't marry a man at all

Well it's AN option. No you're right. It's not.

Reality TV

The modern equivalent of public hanging. Please bear in mind that with most reality television you will have no script. That means we're just watching you and your sparkling personality.

How to cope with the public shame of spinsterhood

If smug people with husbands ask you – 'hey, mother superior – no footballer would have you eh?' – come back with these sharp ripostes that can be made sharper still with the swift application of a kick to the lean marrow of a shin.

1. I was hoping to do something meaningful with my life and the Miss World organization likes their candidates to be untainted by the carnal attentions of a man.
2. White is so last season.
3. I'm waiting until I'm a little older. I want to get my GCSEs under my belt.
4. Maybe not – but I'm thinner than you.
5. I'm a dirty feminist. 

captain's wife's log

Monday
Well, just when you thought it was safe to get back in the water ... Get home to find there's been more attempted murders. I sometimes feel like I live in a one-woman snuff movie. Hazel arrived to find Jason taking Kyle for a gentle dip in our pool to test his lung capacity. Jason insisted it was Kyle's fault but I don't care who started it. Kyle's now threatening to walk from Earl's Park which is great because I'd just been thinking to myself that it had been a bit quiet in the life-destroying scandal stakes. Jason should be glad I wasn't in the pool with them. I suspect I would have been hard pressed to remove my foot from his head.

Typically in the life of T. Turner, this wasn't even the most dramatic event of the day. Something nasty crawled out of the woodwork namely Janette 'Dr Crippen' Dunkley who asked me to meet her in the railway station car park. I should have driven on a couple of yards and dumped her unceremoniously on the track. Was feeling fairly confident until the witch told me she's onto my Sunset Towers scam and wants cash. Don't know why I don't just put a keypad on my cheek and turn my mouth into a cash point. Give her what I can but she's not going to be satisfied until she's got her pound of my flesh. Lost it when she wanted to meet tomorrow for payoff – what is it now – 36? Countries' defence secrets have been sold for less. Then she whips out a copy/100 copies of my one off (there's a laugh) initial payment with some convoluted plan about this proving I'd bribed her. She told me there's a copy with her lawyer so I don't kill her. I've taken on a football chairman so I can easily stretch to the attempted murder of a kinky nurse and her high street solicitor. Frankly with the amount of emotional stress just seeing her sow's ear in those earrings I had to buy her – what jury would convict me?

Anyway the thin little smile was knocked off that ferret face when I told her that if I had to take any more of her nonsense I'd go straight to Chairmeister Frank and tell him about her playing horsy with him.

Tuesday
Saw a programme about executive stress. Like they could even begin to imagine.

To do: try to book in massage this week. TV programme suggested it was a good stress buster – though in my opinion they'd have to pummel me with the strength of an industrial drill to make an impact.

Wednesday
More angst chez Adams family. Am too upset to write – I'll have to come back to it tomorrow.

Thursday
OK, Kyle and Char held a press conference about Paddy's intersexuality once and for all showing all is not as it seems at Happy Valley. I'm sure Paddy will look back and thank them for that. His will make Tom Brown's schooldays look decidedly Enid Blyton. Of course Jason with the usual sensitivity of a rhino immediately

remembered that in Jason land he's the only one who counts. He's worried the world will believe the product of his loins to be not 100% masculine. I think – well if the cap fits ... Jackie should have worn it shouldn't she ...

Of course his prehistoric attitude only gives further argument to Ken and Barbie's theory that it's the world that needs educating – not Paddy – but no one's even stopped to give me a thought. I'd just been thinking that all I wanted for Christmas this year was the public humiliation of everyone knowing that my husband was rumbling in Grandma Pascoe's jungle.

Leave a friendly warning with said pensioner. If she goes near my husband again it will take more than Botox to sort her face out. If Jason goes near her again he might be interested to know it won't just be Paddy unusually configured in the pant department.

Friday

Sunbathe. I might as well fry my body to match my brain.

Saturday

Ha, ha – Jason was flambéed like Chardonnay. Sadly he had less scarring. It would appear – and clearly Jason wasn't being entirely forthcoming on the subject – that he'd been drooling all over Sal's girlfriend like a St Bernard and Sal inadvertently held his arm over a naked flame. Whoops...

Sunday

The Lord's Day.

Monday

Just got back from meeting Janette for dinner. Jesus – they say insanity runs in some people. With her it gallops. She gets me talking about Frank then I notice her doing this shifty thing with her collar when I mention her 'hands on' approach. Even by her standards pouring a glass of water down herself is odd. Then I clicked – the bitch was only wearing a wire! I think I've been a bad influence on her I really do. Had to think quickly. Decided that Janette had to go into hiding from Frank for the sake of both of our skins before we end up as roommates in Holloway.

Tuesday

Chardonnay popped around to 'encourage' me to prompt Jason to track down his birth parents. I'd love to have helped Paddy while simultaneously sharing a drink and a gossip with a friend but unfortunately I had Nurse Necrophilia upstairs slowly turning grey with a home hair dye kit. She had the cheek to complain that she'd just had her roots done. If that was true Helen Keller must be alive and well and running a salon in Surrey. However – particularly inspired idea of mine and, frankly, in the cause of staying out of jail – I've had my fair share. I'm going to hide her in Sunset Towers where hopefully she'll meet a grisly end in a freak false teeth accident.

Wednesday

All's quiet in the State of Surrey. Can't help but think it's the calm before the storm. The old adage of never trust a dog to watch your food probably applies to never trust a nutter nurse currently holed up in a bedjacket to keep you out of jail. And to think – a year ago I didn't even know what a metaphor was. I've certainly had to grow as a person.

Thursday
Hazel in her infinite wisdom decided that what Paddy and the Pascoes needed most was good publicity. Actually, it's Hazel's answer to everything. Chardonnay was easily convinced as publicity to her is like a religion – something she can cling to and believe in during times of crisis. Anyway, Jason went through the roof when he saw the photo spread Hazel had planned. It was like watching a particularly manic firework being let off indoors. The idiot promptly sacked her – smooth move spanner man – rebel without a clue. He really is a charmer.

Friday
Spent whole day smiling at Jason until my face felt like a tautly stretched elastic band. All of this acting should mean I either get wrinkles or an Oscar or both.

Saturday
More smiling, face starting to crack like an old pot left outside in the rain too long. I'm too young to look weathered.

Sunday
Met Fuhrer Frank to discuss the tape he'd got from my dinner date with the Night Nurse. He was wearing smugness like a new suit. Luckily no one outdoes Tanya Turner in the fashion stakes. I told him he'd have to find Janette first. 40–Love.

Monday
Chardonnay filled in more details about Jason's attempted philandering with Sal's girlfriend – he was planning to do more than salivate all over freaky Freddie. That truly is the rice cake that broke the diet. Nothing to report apart from that – and of course – more smiling. Jason the idiot doesn't suspect a thing... Oh revenge will be as sweet as my smile...

Tuesday
I've just taken a few minutes out of the celebrations to come and record lest in my planned alcohol consumption later – I forget any details – my triumphant last stand. If I may say so – I think I look even more radiant than on my first wedding day to Jason Turner. I stood before our friends, acquaintances and Tara Palmer-Tomkinson and dumped Jason once and for all. It was beautiful. Who'd have thought that a diamond ring could travel so far when thrown across the room at your soon to be ex-husband? My piece-de-resistance – 'I should have divorced you when I had the chance Jason! Commitment? The only way to keep your dick under control is to cut it off! But sadly, I don't have my nail scissors with me!' It was even worth the punch in the face. I've told everyone to stay and enjoy the reception – I certainly intend to. Hold on – someone's shouting at me to hurry up – apparently Jason's had a little accident ... Could this day get any better?

Welcome to issue 2 of 'Visible Ribs', my tri-weekly magazine dedicated to moderate thinness, being sensibly thin and not being too fat.

Thanks to some well-publicized cases of celebrities being carried off by light breezes and snapping in two when wearing belts – we think it's time to say no to crash diets and no to media pressure on women. In addition, we are currently under investigation from the Medical Council who have ordered us to distribute emergency mars bar rations to our readership. We grudgingly hope you enjoy them and don't choke on them, much.

TRY ... our new meat on a plate regime! Animal fat used to look best on animals but our new fad diet you can now press the flesh (with a fork). Stick to our new Meat and Gummy Bears programme and see your body lose 10 ounces a year and gain circulatory problems that will last a lifetime!

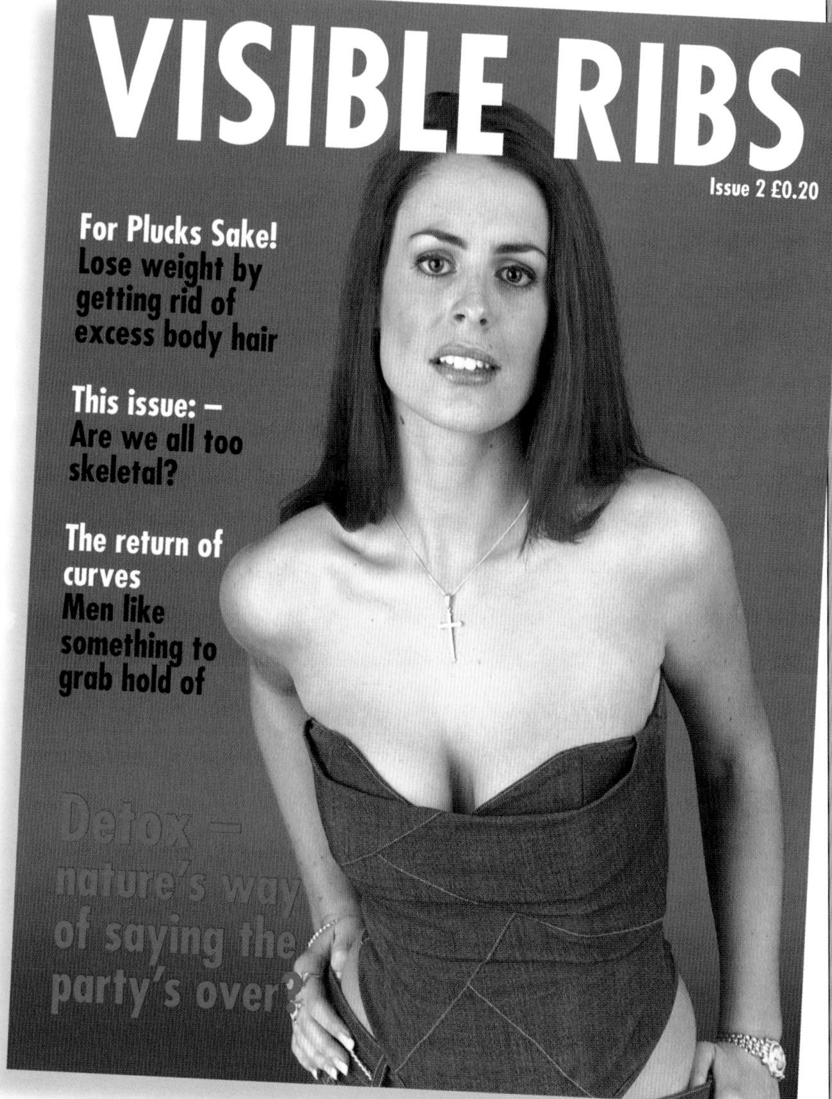

Detox – Nature's way of saying the party's over?

Detox is a marvellous and slightly mystically scientific thing. Complicated words like 'tincture' are used with abandon so we know it works.

We have long known that **organic foods are better** because they cost more but there are other steps you can take to rid your body of nasty little Pacman-like ants that are literally to the best of our medical knowledge eating you alive. Only drink **bottled water** sourced by nuns. Instead of drinking caffeine which increases your desire for food, drink only alcohol.*

** Detox does not apply to alcohol. It is important to keep your liquid intake up.*

3 ways to be luscious and rounded

1. Is your **bottom** concave? Try placing some cyclist's kneepads in your jeans pockets and taping chicken fillets onto your thighs!
2. Do most men have bigger **knockers** than you? Try taping some more of those **chicken fillets** into your bra. They should protrude enough so that your **breasts** act as little envoys – entering a room before you but not so much they end up steering the wheel of your car.
3. Does your **belly** have problems providing the scaffolding you need for hipsters? Not a problem – thongs are *meant* to be visible these days.

footballers' ex-wive$

Or 'Options for the recently matrimonially disadvantaged'

So the snivelling Lothario's gone and done it. You've given him the firmest years of your life and now you're left warming a shelf. You tamed the beast, took him out of rayon/polyester mixes and hurtling into male skirts. You made a man out of a boy and now he thinks he's too good for you. Be not afraid or screwed over, here's where he starts paying.

Important divorce facts:

1. It may surprise you to know that statistically almost 100% of all football divorces start with a football marriage.

2. **You will survive. Remember you could spend thousands on therapy but there is none as effective as ripping a picture of him out of the album and scribbling a clown face or nose hair on it.**

3. Wedlock – is so called because the fun room is locked and the key thrown away. You are not in the room at the time. Now you are moneyed and free and free to spend that money to be free.

For your convenience the following fully legally binding document has been prepared for your use, simply delete as inappropriate.

Contract
of Full-Time Whistle to Marriage

I ______________________________ have been dumped/have done the dumping /have mutually agreed to a permanent transfer to another club. I hereby desire for the sexually depraved pervert /closet homosexual/Mr 'More Dorsal Droop than Free Willy' to take his tart/tarts/performance anxieties out of my house and go drown himself/make like a rocket and piss off to the moon/tell another sucker it's never happened to him before. He is hereby entitled to take nothing/his tart/faded memories of his dear departed career and can have partial/full/no access to the children/bank account/Steps albums. May he rot in a cesspool of his own making/tart's making/soccer punditry's making for I will no longer make any attempt to salvage his career through murder/flirting with the chairman/flirting with the chairman I attempted to murder. I simply throw my arms to the heavens and question how we dragged this sham out as long as we did but would like to thank the gardener who could rut like a stag/chauffeur who could rut like a stag/Helga the au pair who could rut like a stag. Let's not be friends. If you were another woman I wouldn't even do lunch with you. You have all the sensitivity of forceps and throughout the course of our marriage have distributed yourself with all the restraint and selectivity of a garden sprinkler. For future reference why not try using those unnaturally large ears for listening as they are not simply decorative. If I see you in ten years I'll say cod and chips please/thanks for introducing me to your teammate/if you dance and bark like a dog I might give you 50p to buy some turps. I am happy to impart as I depart that he has singularly disproved the old wives' tale about large noses/that I completely understand why he felt the need to have a large car/the younger model he traded me in for has been encouraged by an 'unknown' source to kiss and tell and intends to dump him for *his* younger model which is divine justice and order has thus been restored in the world. Lastly, he can sort out his own hairstyles in future and let's see how long it is before he starts wearing sheepskin coats. So shall it be.

Signature ____________________ Date ______________

final thought$

...So what have we learned?

Well, first that we've already had quite a lot of thoughts. But good to the last drop – here's a few more.

- Remember, the majority of Footballers' Wives are just normal folk who happen to have fallen in love with a footballer and are leading productive and satisfying lives. There are no stereotypes with these women. They are mothers, they have careers and they are pillars of the community. Unfortunately they're so busy doing all this they haven't concentrated on having a media career and they haven't written a book like we have so they really cocked that one up. You'll just have to guess at what their advice would be though it's safe to say it would be sensible, have no hazardous or morally dubious shortcuts and ergo – would be as boring as an oil rig.
- Anyone who says brains pay obviously hasn't watched a quiz show. If you spin a wheel or get gunked you get a motorboat and a holiday. If you win ten concurrent victories seeing off all-comers and remember the names of politicians like Tony Blair you get a cut-glass vase and a dictionary. You don't need brains to be a wife. You need patience. Patience and staff.
- Beauty is the natural bed partner of wealth. Intelligence is the natural bed partner of a good book. A little lesson for us all there.
- At the end of the day man can achieve many things like *Shiny Cups of Cups* and *Sports' Answer for a Personality of the Year* shiny cups, but they are not infallible. Man can put a man on the moon but has not yet put all of them there so hold your head up high, you are a footballer's wife and your head would rebound off your breasts like a space hopper if you looked down anyway.
- Wives must also humbly accept the limitations of their own minds. You can control Fleet Street but not your husband and you will never be able to spell the word ~~yought~~ ~~yaughet~~ yacht first time even when you have one. Call it a ship.
- Be resolute and determined in your goals. Remember where there's a will you want to be in it.
- Behind every soccer legend there should be a wife keeping him in a lower tax bracket.
- Thinness is not just a size – it's a state of mind.
- What separates the gonnabes from the wannabes is being yourself. Obviously you bought this book because we're just a little bit like role models for all ladies but remember you are unique – just like everyone else and if you copy us then you'll be like us but younger and that makes you dangerous...
- ...so get your own husband.
- All the money in the world does not equate to love. Love just isn't that valuable.
- Further, love is not recognized as legal tender in Knightsbridge.
- Never laugh if he says he has a groin strain.

That's all Folks... 

Happy Hubby Hunting!